SWITCH

Scott Norton

First published in the United States of America in 2010
by Yellow Horse Publishing

ISBN 978-0-9828364-0-8

Yellow Horse Publishing
LANDISVILLE, NJ 08326-0227
CAMBRIDGE, UK

Contents

PART ONE — Off

PART TWO — On

PART THREE — Automatic

PART ONE
OFF

CHAPTER 1
CUL-DE-SUCK

Barbara Ducharme coughed her eyes full of stars as she dumped another tray of smoking cookies into the garbage bin. The charred contents safely deposited, she shut the lid and threw the tray into the sink. Not bothering to remove the oven mitt from her hand, she scuffed to the breakfast nook and slid onto the bench. It was useless, she confessed to herself, her choking fit subsiding into the occasional sniff, and she didn't just mean the cookies.

Her husband would be home from his ball game in two hours, and the coconut macaroons were supposed to be a pleasant distraction in case she hadn't yet returned from church. Now it looked like she wouldn't be able to get there at all, and the fact weighed heavily on her soul—but not for the same reasons it would for most church-going folks. More than the promise of salvation within, what she really needed was the WiFi connection without.

For her, logging onto the Internet was a way of exploring society's seedier underbelly without catching anything, and it was positively exhilarating. She could click link after link after link, allowing her unbridled curiosities to dictate her path, traipsing blithely through alleyways and unmarked doors as if jaunting in a foreign dreamland. Whenever she wanted to wake up and go home, she simply logged off and gave the soles of her mind a good scrape on the welcome mat. And if she wished, she could sneak a few things inside under her coat. One of those things just happened to be a not entirely accidental friendship with a man by the name of Jasper Dix.

She found www.pennedpal.gov while searching for a Halloween costume for her son. That part was total happenstance. Some links look exactly like others, and if you were in a hurry, there was no telling where your eyes would end up. Once she'd found the site where ordinary citizens could reach out to those who had chosen less lawful paths of survival, it was as if her hands were moving entirely of their own accord. Like her one and only foray into the world of cuckold pornography, she simply couldn't help herself, and before long she was volleying encouraging sympathies with the one man on the site she felt needed them most.

Unfortunately, she hadn't been able to communicate with J.D. in two days, and she was concerned he might think she'd forgotten about him. J.D. was important to her. He was the only man in her life that listened to her without shoving his opinion down her throat like an unwelcome tongue. If she was forced to keep their friendship in the back of the cupboard, she couldn't allow herself to become so absorbed in her own minor dilemmas that he was inadvertently left to suffer. The poor thing was in prison, after all—a real one, not just some imaginary lockdown that lazily described the interpersonal dysfunctions of the modern family.

Despite a long list of violent offenses, Barbara found J.D. to be extremely sensitive, with an artist's demeanor that drenched their correspondence with a sublime, if unrefined, ennui. After emails that went on and on about his self-taught soap sculpting techniques and the dilemma of the prison's changing from solid soap to powder, she was convinced a victim lived deep inside the victimizer. When she sent him a few unused decorative soaps that had been collecting dust in her home's two and a half bathrooms, it was as much her gift to society as it was a simple way to make a confused man happy. The fact that he didn't understand women any better than any other man she'd ever met really didn't matter; he was willing to learn, and believed in the power of focused thought—something she had also begun to explore. Still, he was only an "emotional friend". That they would never meet face to face afforded a wider opening for their friendship to blossom and breathe.

The last time they exchanged emails, she told him about the decaying old fixer-upper she had inherited from her grandmother on her mother's side, and attached a photo of the hideous beast from the real estate listing. In retrospect, it was inconsiderate of her to do so. She was complaining about a second home that had been handed to her for doing exactly nothing and J.D. was struggling every day trying to make his first one within the system. Not since she applied sixteen credits of an incomplete fashion degree towards organizing a group opposed to "prominent nipples" on department store mannequins had she been so driven to make a difference. If rehabilitating inmate #7734206 were her crowning achievement along with raising a healthy and happy family, she would be proud as punch to say so.

She closed her eyes and soaked in the silence that would be rudely interrupted once the kids returned. Silence was all she had any more that she could really call her own. The one thing she genuinely liked about their little housing development was not that Heaving Meadows was the exact midpoint between Philadelphia and the Delaware Memorial Bridge—something their agent had pointed out at least two dozen times. She had even shown them a map with the precise math hastily scrawled over any helpful geographic indicators, conveniently rendering this statement of supposed fact irrefutable. But whether Heaving Meadows was exactly between the city and the bridge or slightly askew in one direction or the other didn't matter to her. They had also promised quiet, and save the few days when you could hear mowers going and children crying over scraped knees, they delivered.

An idea disturbed her like a curious mouse: maybe she could pick up a wireless Internet connection from someone in the development the same way she did in the church parking lot? Just because there was no sound didn't mean there wasn't a whole lot of other stuff happening up in those airwaves. All she would have to do was jump in the car and drive around a bit until she hit a rich vein of connectivity. Barbara could feel her breath shortening in anticipation of a soon-to-be answered prayer, and started working out where her car keys might be hiding.

But just as quickly as hope entered, true to form it fled. If she found a signal, she would still need a password. At the church it was simple: A-M-E-N-T-O-T-H-A-T. She had been given it several times by the church committee to scour eBay for used artificial candles, and now her computer magically logged on without her having to put it in. The laptop computer she used was her daughter's—something she had won in her divorce settlement but refused to touch for reasons Barbara still didn't understand—and without a wireless router somewhere in the house, only a phone line could connect her to the Internet. She would never use it, as she was afraid Ken Sr. would notice the charges and question her. He'd nearly had a stroke when Kenny ran up a $500 bill without realizing what he was doing, and she had no desire to incur his ire. Essentially, if she couldn't get to Broadway Methodist, she was helpless. She would never have enough time to figure out what sequence of nonsense some stranger was using to keep other strangers from piggybacking on their service, even if it wasn't very clever.

She looked to the cat clock above the refrigerator and watched the tail swing from side to side and focused on its shifting eyes, taunting her with suggestions of duplicity. She fought back the guilt with a thought: if she hurried, she might be able to get to church and back before Ken came home. It wouldn't give her much time for an exchange, but at least she could plant a seed of reassurance in J.D.'s fragile constitution. But as the ticking grew louder, it pulled from her another reason why she was balking at driving to church. On a subconscious level, it may have been the reason she burned the macaroons, a confection she mastered on no sleep with two children hanging off her hip.

She had never had an orgasm with her husband. She'd never thought it a big deal, as she had read that the inability to climax in the marital bed wasn't all that unusual. Lots of women had difficulty achieving the big "O" with their husbands, especially when they had agreed to marriage for reasons other than raw sex appeal. The sad truth was that she wasn't sure she had ever had an orgasm at all. She almost had one against the foot folded underneath her after a particularly emotional email from J.D., but the moment her pipes felt close to bursting, she clenched the valves in her vulva as tightly as she could. A vestige of purity somewhere in the back of her mind told her it wasn't right to feel that way in a church parking lot.

Then she got scared. Why had God touched her in this way? She never dressed in an overly sexy manner, and preferred to keep her dirty blonde, shoulder-length hair safely below her softly pronounced jaw line. She was reasonably proud of her sensible bust and she knew she had good legs, but not once had she ever recited a prayer with so much as a suggestive sparkle in her large, green eyes. Even now, her flour-covered apron made no other statement than "hapless homemaker", even if it did taper attractively along her narrow waistline. As far as she was concerned, there was no reason for a deity of any kind to give her a first look, let alone a long, lascivious second.

Still, ever since the incident in the church parking lot, she had become extremely uncomfortable every time she thought of Him. She tried to keep busy, but He was everywhere. When she brought her home to cleanliness, there He was flashing his Godliness. When she kissed her children, He kissed her back. When she watered the flowers, there He was, winking at her with His soft, glistening petals, inviting her to sit awhile. Oprah said the change in a middle-aged woman's body would make her think silly things and that there were home remedies for even the most persistent day-mares. The search for them had calmed her some.

Then one day, while watching a TV program about the homeless, she began talking to Satan. She didn't know if it was from J.D.'s frequent mentions of the necessity of evil, or her mild case of dyslexia kicking in as she watched a homeless Santa begging for food for his reindeer. Whatever the case, once she opened the line of communication, a red-faced man with a pointy black goatee popped into her mind and she immediately felt his powerful, dark presence chasing away God's filthy advances. And if she were completely honest with herself, the whole ordeal aroused her immensely.

Ah well, she thought, her chin resting comfortably in her oven mitt, at least she had the quiet.

BEEP-BEEP-BEEP...

The fire alarm pierced her respite, unfeelingly as they do. Barbara yanked off her mitt and threw it at the detector, missing by some distance.

⛤⛤⛤⛤

Kenny needed to get home. He'd made the mistake of riding his bike to school when the morning had proved seasonably cool and dry, but things had changed dramatically since then. It was close to three now, and the air was so thick and the heat so oppressive he was soaking through his brand new two-pocket Oxford. He hated to be sweaty unless he was naked, and even then he needed to not be touching anything or anyone—the "anyone" part never a problem. For a few months last year he'd thought he was starting to look like a young Matt Damon circa *The Talented Mr. Ripley*. Lately, however, he'd noticed an elongation of his face that began pushing him in the direction of Anthony Michael Hall circa *Sixteen Candles*. Girls and the procurement of their underwear was not something he had the luxury of even considering.

He pushed up his sleeves and pressed a little harder on the pedals, lowering his head into an aerodynamic position. He was thankful there wasn't anyone outside to see his dark pit stains and hoped it would stay that way. If someone did see him, *please, God, don't let it be a girl.*

He tried to take his mind off the suffocating conditions by imagining himself in his room, Ms. Langley from eighth period still vivid in his mind, his clothes off and in the hamper. Cooling off in front of the rotating fan, he could finally release his frustrations by yanking his penis for all it was worth. It would be the sixth time he masturbated today, with at least another three or four sessions to go before he drifted restlessly off to sleep. But before he could do that, he would have to hit the outside hose and wash off the rag he'd brought with him to school. It was so used up he couldn't bear letting his mother see it, and she usually followed him around for the day's laundry as soon as he walked through the door.

Pushing his mother from his mind, he thought about how some senior girl had almost caught him jerking off as she passed his homeroom on her way to the cafeteria. He'd been smart enough to keep a pencil sharpener in his free hand so that when she saw him, he was able to dump its shredded contents onto his desk. He didn't have a pencil, but he knew there was a good chance she would think she had seen one and forget all about it.

A loud CLACK interrupted his thoughts. He looked down to see the chain on his black, 3-Speed beach cruiser dragging along the pavement. This was the second time it had popped off since the school parking lot, and he cursed himself for having taken the gears apart the day before. Disaster loomed as he tried to finagle it back onto the teeth of the chainwheel without crashing. If he failed, he'd be walking it home in the awful heat and in mortal danger of losing the important details of Ms. Langley's wardrobe hidden in the top shelf of his imagination. Without the Internet to provide him with free wanking fodder—or at least he thought it was free up until last week—all he had was a crap short-term memory and the lame photos in one of his sister's fashion magazines.

He got the chain back on with his second try and resumed a cruising pace. Maybe he hadn't done as bad a job putting it back together as he thought. Maybe some good was actually coming from the hours he spent in his room taking things apart and tinkering with them. If it had been at his disposal, he had dissected and reassembled it: clock radios, TVs, DVD players, iPods, sex toys, his dad's "secret" gun, small animals—normal, everyday stuff one finds around the house. The good news was that most of his projects still worked once he finally managed to make them whole again. The bad news was that for a few of them, not so much.

He took a wide and easy turn onto Heaving Meadows Place, and saw his house waiting for him on the cul-de-sac at the end. To hell with the hose, he thought. It was too hot and he could barely picture the outline of Ms. Langley's size-D bra strap as she reached back to straighten it.

⛤⛤⛤⛤

Amanda dug the nail file under the middle finger of her final customer and scraped out the gelatinous gunk that was living there. She wiped it on a small rag and went back in for more.

"Breast milk soap," said the customer.

Amanda nearly shucked the woman's nail off like a

cherrystone clam. She sucked in a burst of air as if cooling her tongue. "Sorry!"

The woman rubbed out the sting and said, "That's okay, I don't think there's any damage." She continued rubbing, fine brow lines materializing on her adorable face.

Amanda waited until they disappeared and asked, "Did you say 'breast milk soap'?"

The woman carefully placed her hand next to the files, buffers and clippers that were lined up neatly and waiting. "Uh-huh, my husband makes it from what's left after feeding the baby. My breasts produce a lot of milk. I mean, a *lot*."

Amanda stole a glance at the woman's chest. They did appear slightly large for a woman her size. Her back had to be pretty strong to carry those puppies around all day, although it was fairly obvious she spent a good deal of her time lying on it.

Nausea hit. She didn't know if it was from the idea of her customer having sex or from the idea of conception in general. It wasn't that she didn't want a baby someday; of course she did. She wanted a family more than anything in the world. At one point in her life she had plenty of offers to take her up on the idea. Inheriting her mother's dark blonde hair and her father's large brown eyes assured her share of wolf whistles. And the generous hints of curve that gave her naturally thin figure a womanly finish had triggered more than their share of drool. But her prime breeding age had passed, and ever since her ex-fiancé, Eldren, had kicked her out, she was pretty positive she had missed her chance and would appreciate if the woman didn't mind changing the subject. She would appreciate it a *lot*.

"We use it on the baby," the woman continued, her head settling back on the headrest. Amanda watched her eyes look up through the ceiling to a piece of heaven where she probably owned a timeshare. "And you know what?" she giggled, her hand covering two rows of perfect teeth. "When I watch him scrub her, I get *sooo* hot."

The last part was said in a horrible, low pixie growl and Amanda wanted to stab her again—only this time somewhere more life-threatening. "Oh, wow," she said with the barest hint of enthusiasm, "that's *sooo* cool."

"Isn't it?" asked the woman, bouncing her knees apart into a full birthing—or screwing—position.

"Okay," said Amanda, reaching for her airbrush, "same thing today?"

"Same, but different. You know—shapes like before, but new ones. My husband's beginning to show signs of craving variety. A woman needs to pay attention to these things."

Amanda fought back a gag reflex and pulled a tray of stencils from a cluttered drawer. She laid them on the table and used her finger to search for something that suggested "variety". With a dainty precision, she plucked five shapes that looked like letters:

ᛒ ᛁ ᛏ ᚲ ᚺ

They were runes: Turkish or Germanic—she couldn't remember which. Nor did she care. What amazed her was how not one of her regular customers ever caught on to what she was doing. She did concede the letters may have looked even more unusual upside-down, but how no one ever pointed out what appeared glaringly obvious to her remained a matter she preferred to savor rather than address.

She sprayed all ten fingernails and applied a thin layer of gloss to each design with a soft brush. When she was finished, she instructed the new mother to wave them in the air until they were dry. The woman thanked her and pulled a five-dollar bill from her wallet with her teeth. Amanda took the bill and slid it into her pocket. She hadn't expected more than the minimum amount for a tip, and in a way she felt she deserved more. Her runic revenge may have been petty, pathetic and ultimately pointless, but at least she hadn't stabbed Ms. Chatty Chest in the throat.

⛤ ⛤ ⛤ ⛤

KRANGK!

The ball flew off the aluminum bat in an amateur impression of the Big Bang Theory, and as back-up right fielder for the Golden Grizzly Bear Cub Sluggers, it was Ken Sr.'s job to shift his frame towards the hurtling object and snatch it in mid-flight. Only, he couldn't help but be distracted by how similar it all was to the recent particle accelerator experiments in Geneva concerning the origins of the universe. The rawhide to aluminum collision had set in motion a contained chaos of sorts, in which a few bodies of energy attempted to gain control over others by manipulating the forces of gravitational pull. Forget about what was riding on these experiments being successful—evidence as to the likelihood of our survival as a species, among others—as a simple model it held considerable weight.

Of course, none of his teammates really wanted to hear a dissertation on one of engineering's most important potential triumphs after seeing the ball strike him in the fatty part of his upper arm and fall to the ground, thus allowing the winning run to cross the plate. And while he may have failed to do his part in supporting his supposition, it didn't make his observation any less astute.

In fact, Ken Sr. didn't see what the big deal was in light of it. Softball was an intellectually lazy recreational activity, and the Large Hadron Collider that had cost almost nine billion dollars to build held far more lasting implications than determining who had earned bragging rights in an over-the-hill time-burner. How he wished he had been a part of the collider's construction instead of kicking around loose theories in tight nylon knickers. He tried to imagine the amount of concrete they would need to make such an operation safe under any internal conditions. The total must have weighed as much as the earth itself.

Not surprisingly, Ken Sr. wouldn't learn of a seashore weekend golf trip his teammates were planning as they packed up the equipment and headed for drinks at a nearby watering hole—a gathering he also wouldn't hear about until it was too late.

Ken Sr. steered his certified, pre-owned Subaru Outback onto Heaving Meadows Place and caught his reflection in the rear view mirror. Not so long ago he could describe himself as a cross between The Professor from "Gilligan's Island" and a poor man's Kurt Russell, but that was before he started eating without tasting and stopped sleeping through the night. Somewhere between fathering children, building things out of cement, and dropping routine fly balls, he had gotten old. His father's jowls threatened him more and more with each passing month, and angry jowls, they were. His father may have loved him in a basic biological way, but it was clear he never liked him. He knew this for a fact, and there was never any need to discuss it with him or anyone. He was never good at the right things and always allowed himself to be bullied, or so his father said. Apparently the old man was right. He had gone from being a kid who got picked on to a man no one cared to understand—least of all, himself.

Ken Sr. took his foot off the gas and the car slowed to a crawl. On either side of him he saw homes that looked like his, with cars like his and grass that needed cutting like his grass did. After completing a master's degree in architectural engineering, he managed to make a decent living as an independent contractor. It was something he was proud of, along with three other things that together he referred to as his "soul square": the local post office building he had helped design, which included, at his insistence, emergency safety bunkers in the event of a violent employee outburst; the fact that his wife had never had to work outside the home a single day in her life; a set of Bob Hope signature golf clubs he'd won on the radio for being able to say all fifty states in alphabetical order; and his two children, Ken Jr. and Amanda Jean. Technically, that was five things, but he always considered one's children to be more alike than not, so they also counted as a set.

For the past few years he had begun to wonder if so much of his life had been spent collecting achievements to show for each mid-life milestone that, despite having plenty to show for the years, he had actually missed them happening. Perhaps his ferocious drive was a function of higher-than-normal testosterone levels and nothing more. His wife, bless her tireless attempts to act otherwise, had made it pretty clear what she thought it was. His marriage had slumped into that awkward phase where it seemed the more he wanted sex, the less she did. He wasn't about to blame either of them. The simple fact was that men and women didn't really fit. The institution of marriage was burdened by a poor design, all things considered. At the very least, it was one that, like a Quonset hut or ad hoc lean-to, was only meant to last long enough to serve a specific function of survival.

He wondered if everyone on his block felt the way he did, or if it was all in his imagination. He had to think he was the only nut on earth driving at three miles per hour with his house in plain sight, so maybe that was his answer right there.

He reached the driveway and pointed the nose of the car towards the break in the curb. A couple of taps on the gas and the car floated quietly forward until it was a comfortable foot away from the garage door. With a sigh, he threw the car in park and pulled open the center island caddie. After a quick check around, he retrieved the Smith and Wesson Model 64 SS .38 revolver he had purchased with his family's stimulus check and worked it inside the waistband of his uniform. Content that it was secure, he grabbed his fielder's mitt and pushed open the driver's side door.

Outside the car, he scanned the gentle slopes and amicable angles of his vinyl-sided home. He'd had zero say in its design outside of choosing from the few models available in his price range. He pushed the car door shut, causing it to rattle (entropy was everywhere) and realized a horrifying fact: he was no longer driving his life, and hadn't been for some time. Something beyond his comprehension was in control, and he was helpless to stop it. Checking the gun once more, he thought about tomorrow and how he and his family would be heading to a giant money pit his wife's loony grandmother had left to her in her will. From what he could tell, and more than the agent was willing to offer, the building and property were more of a burden than an asset in their present condition. While that thought held as many clues to his private condition as any he could think of, he knew he was only looking forward to seeing it because of the unlimited opportunities it presented to be distracted.

As he pattered on sore feet towards the front door, he thought about what his heart was really telling him and what he had to admit to himself at long last: he only wanted to go because it meant something new to help him while away the years until, true to the laws of the universe both proven and otherwise, everything fell apart.

Amanda was already in sweats and bunny slippers by the time her father walked through the door. She had beaten him home by about five minutes, and wasted no time getting into comfy clothes and jumping into his chair. The Lifetime Channel was showing a rerun of the TV movie *Extremities,* and she wanted to see if Farrah Fawcett's character was planning on setting the guy who tried to rape her on fire like she did the guy in *The Burning Bed*. Only, in that movie, the guy that got it was her husband, which made it an infinitely better movie in her opinion.

She spun a finger into her hair until the tip was cold and numb, and then let the whole thing unravel. It was very similar to how she treated the end of her marriage. Eldren had confronted her with the sex video and she had denied it on the spot. That was when things started to go irretrievably blue. The girl on the computer screen bobbing up and down on the lap of the guy with the Loony Tunes tie certainly looked like her, and when she talked, the voice was as familiar as her own. That's because it was her voice, only she had no idea such a lewd and lascivious event had ever occurred. She had gotten drunk and blacked out, just like women in their early twenties were wont to do all across the world. She couldn't say she was raped, because the girl in the video—the one that looked exactly like she did just over a year ago—was not only enjoying it, she was clearly the aggressor.

Eldren wouldn't hear a word in her defense, and that was because it didn't matter if she were sober, drunk, turning a trick for crack or in a hostage situation. Another man's penis had been in her mouth, and that was something his cast-iron morals could never forgive. She was tainted, which for a girl her age was the worst thing that could ever happen. It was even worse than going to jail or failing out of school. She might as well have three STDs and four kids, each a different color. As far as her social circle was concerned, she was off-limits forever to any man with above-the-poverty-line earning potential.

Several months after she moved out, she called Eldren to determine if there had been a change of heart. With each plea her self-respect waned until her sense of shame was so repulsively swollen there was no place left to store it. Her mind became so engorged with self-loathing that it appeared the only way clear was through a blown artery or a total nervous breakdown. Thankfully, neither was to be. The final month demonstrated a distinct loss of energy accompanied by a peep of self-preservation until finally, with nothing but the barest recollection of what had started the dreaded denouement in the first place, she completely gave up. It was all over but for the signing of a few papers and the settling of a few outstanding bills.

Ken gave a short wave as he passed the living room in case Amanda was looking. As he suspected, she wasn't. She was laid out across his chair, which had somehow become her chair, and it was useless engaging her in simple, polite conversation let alone bargaining for a share of domestic real estate. He had learned to walk quietly in the last couple of weeks and kept his voice pitched at bedroom levels. He was more than fed up with the situation, but until he found a solution for her problem, it was best to dance lightly around the pool for fear of upsetting the waters and earning himself a case of soaking wet ass.

"We're eating!" Barbara's guileless voice reverberated brightly across the kitchen tile and up the foyer stairs. Ken admired her enthusiasm for mundane family activities. He also admired the way her breasts had adopted an elegant droop over the years, but there was no way he could say it out loud. Every wife of twenty-plus years likes a compliment as long as it's not from her husband. In the first decade of marriage, while wives take note of every bit of sagging and count every new crease in their face, their husbands' opinions mean everything. But there was a finite amount of deflating arguments a couple could have before it was clear neither really did it for the other anymore. Compliments become a means to an end—a thinly veiled offensive towards exacting a selfish agenda—and the trick was to save a few for public ears in order to maintain appearances. Nonetheless, there was always a twinkle of hope in Barbara's voice—hope that things would revert to kind before all was irrevocably lost—and if he wasn't mistaken, he admired her for that, too.

"Coming!" said Kenny. The boy barreled down the stairs and made a hairpin turn at the newel post, barely acknowledging his father's presence. There was the briefest moment in his descent where the lines were open and some meaningful contact was possible, but both had let it pass. If it were urgent, neither would have waited until the opening made itself known. There would have been a preemptive fusillade of fine details regarding the emergency *du jour* before the other had a chance to prepare. It's how things were anymore: pragmatic, functional and impersonal save Barbara's saccharine salvos of lightly toasted platitudes. She was holding it together, or trying at least, and the rest of them were letting her because it was working. Barely.

Ken Sr. tossed his glove at the stairs with the intention of nestling it squarely on the third step from the bottom. Instead, his throw found the front edge of the fourth step and the glove went tumbling end-over-end to the slate foyer. He left it where it lay, recalling how as a boy he hadn't dared do such a thing.

You snatch your little victories where you can.

⛤⛤⛤⛤

Barbara lifted Kenny's mostly empty plate from the table, stepped to where her husband was sat, and lifted his away, as well. She noticed he had helped himself to an extra large serving of mashed potatoes, but barely touched the canned assorted veggies. He was clearly depressed. He always went for the starches in large quantities when he was under the strains of a fascist melancholy. That's why she had tried baking him cookies: a straight sugar high might have unlocked something in his psyche or flipped a switch in his temperament, and it would have been a pleasure to see her man virile again if only for a while. But just as she had done with the cookies, her culinary rescue had failed. A woman was supposed to be able to use her domestic wares to loosen up her family, but at the moment they were tighter than knotted apron strings. The canned veggies may have been a costly shortcut.

"Anyone for dessert?" she asked, her voice cracking on the last syllable. "I've got Jello!"

Kenny shot out of his chair and grabbed the PlayStation PSP resting near his unfinished glass of milk. His fingers began working the buttons before he even opened his mouth. "No thanks, ma," he replied, "Jello makes me gag."

"Alright," said Barbara, "honey, how about you?"

Ken Sr. worked a weak grin and scratched the front of his straining jersey. "No thanks, Barb…makes me gag a little, too."

"Fine," she clipped, and stomped into the kitchen with her hands full of plates.

Ken Sr. called after her: "Did you ask Amanda Jean? She's got to be hungry." He didn't get an answer.

Kenny looked up from his game, never stopping his fingers. "Can I—"

"Yeah, go on," said Ken Sr. "But don't forget to put that thing down long enough to finish your homework."

"It's Friday," said Kenny, his voice cracking like his mother's. "We're going to Grandma's tomorrow, remember?"

Ken Sr. tucked his chin into his chest and stared at the

crumbs that speckled the ruby tablecloth like dim stars. The truth was he hadn't remembered. Despite playing ball every Friday for the past month, he had blanked on the day of the week. Lots of men confuse Tuesday for Wednesday, or Wednesday for Thursday, but losing track of Friday? Maybe he was just tired.

"Right…never mind, then," he grumbled. "Go on."

Kenny heard a blip of digital doom and looked down at his game. "Shit."

"Hey," shot Ken Sr., "can we watch the language, please?"

Kenny pressed a button, stopping the noises. "Sorry." He dropped his hands to his sides and ambled out of the room.

Ken Sr. worked the situation over in his head. He needed to pack. He probably needed a shower, too, as he anticipated an early start.

He needed to try and be nicer to Barbara.

⛤⛤⛤⛤

Barbara slid the plates into the sink and pushed on the left faucet handle. The warm water hissed down in a soft, solid column onto the assortment of dishes and flatware stacked high in the deep steel basin. The steam lent an eerie atmosphere, clouding the thousand-mile stare she had going at the faux marble splashboard. The moist heat tickled her nostrils and soothed the headache that had begun in earnest behind both eyes.

She thought about Satan and how he represented the concept of evil—a word, she was delighted to learn, that spelled "live" in reverse—rather than the dark, brooding suitor that sometimes visited her and chased away that Other Guy.

She wanted to share her thoughts about the subject with her family, but wouldn't dare try. She could with J.D. because he had lost everything and was forced to keep his mind open. It didn't matter if she felt her family needed to explore new ideas, they would say she was awful for even bringing it up.

The water level reached halfway and she pulled the handle closed. She grabbed a bottle of dishwashing detergent, squeezed a few drops into the water, and instantly her thighs began to tingle. This was always the way it happened: she would allow Satan to creep into her senses and instantly her mind turned to sex. It was as if his presence vanquished the watchful eyes of propriety, like a prince of darkness who had struck a deal with a pious village to own the night. As long as he was given free rein when all were meant to be sleeping, his transgressions would be endured. Obedient to tradition, the people surrendered the streets and hid quietly behind their shutters. With them went her inhibitions, pulling closed the latch and dimming the lights, leaving the rest of her to dance under the stars, awaiting his touch.

She lowered her hands into the hot water and inhaled deeply, absorbing his presence and igniting her own. Safe under the soapy water her thoughts were free to swim, thoughts made dirty and delicious and devilish, for sure. She would remain this way until her fingers pruned and started to hurt, and then, usually, a few minutes more. Pain, she recently discovered, was not so unpleasant as emptiness.

⛤⛤⛤⛤

Everyone had gone to bed except Ken Sr., who wanted a few more moments in his chair. He'd waited until almost eleven for Amanda to yawn herself out of it, and he thought he might check the weather.

There was some overly cheery chatter about a local family who raise their own turkeys, before meteorologist Samantha Berman, wrapped snugly in a golden pantsuit, strutted in front of the three-dimensional map of the Delaware Valley and pointed to a patch of green. Sunny, cool, some clouds, she said, with the possibility of a little late night snow. Samantha looked at Ken Sr. and told him to keep warm. Ken Sr. thought he would like to try with her help, and closed his eyes.

He must have been sawing wood for all he was worth when he woke himself up in the early morning to hear the anchors repeating the turkey story. This time it was cut short for a special news bulletin about a group of convicts who had killed a couple of guards and escaped in a transport van. It was violent, manly stuff that wrung a few authentic drops of agitation from the overly tan newscaster, but Ken, half-asleep from the heavy starches, didn't remember a word of it.

Barbara sat quietly in the passenger seat of the Outback, hands folded neatly in her lap. Classical music—Mozart's "Piano and Wind Quartet," according to the dashboard digital display—filtered through the hum of the wheels. The only other sound was wind forcing itself through a sliver of open back seat window that reflected Amanda's blank expression. Barbara knew her daughter often got carsick, and she and everyone else in the family had grown accustomed to the noise and frequent uncomfortable temperatures. When Amanda was a baby, Barbara had to crack the window ever so slightly during trips longer than thirty minutes, or her daughter would panic. Amanda's moving out at a young age (young for the times, anyway) connected her interest in outside air to escaping the smothering confines of their beleaguered family. When Eldren abruptly ended their holy union and sent Amanda back home, Barbara once again saw her daughter's proclivity as a need for personal space—enough to do whatever she wanted, whenever she wanted.

She snuck a peek at her son, who was also utterly miserable. His father had forced him to leave his PSP behind, and because he had taken apart his iPod and failed to return it to working order, he was stuck listening to "old people music". It also prompted him to do something Barbara found highly disturbing: minutes after they were on the road, he'd trapped a fly that had taken up residence inside the van to escape the chilly autumn air. She didn't want to stare, but a few sideways glances saw him pull off its wings and shake it in his hands until it was stunned. The last time she looked he seemed to be waiting for it to wake up so he could repeat the whole barbaric process. She thought to crack his window from her door controls and have him throw the insect away, but then thought better of it. If a fly had to be tortured so she didn't have to, so be it.

Free from torture though she may have been, she couldn't calm her nerves. She already had in her possession the house key given to her by her mother before her passing, but they were heading to the bank where her grandmother had left her a single item in a safety-deposit box. Once that task was completed, they could head for *zee hills*. The diversion would last but a few minutes, but banks always put her ill at ease. It had nothing to do with withdrawals or deposits. Those were black and white issues that required only a few slips of paper, and most of the time could be done without prolonged interaction with another human being. It was the idea of being watched as she dealt with an unfamiliar procedure that unnerved her. Banks were notorious scenes of crime of all kinds, fraud and robbery being the most common. But the matter of interpersonal delicacy she was about to face in the austere environs compelled her to do something obscene the moment she stepped inside. She wanted to rip off her blouse and scream "Hail, Satan!" at the top of her lungs—anything to unseat the lords of the chilly body politic. Those who observed their subjects remotely and electronically, and assigned class distinctions based on paltry accruals, shameful overdraws and dormant accounts, deserved to be shaken up every once in a while. In fact, they would be watching her the moment she entered the building—looking into her soul, if they could—so why not just give everything away and be done with it?

Ken Sr. stopped the car at the curb in front of the bank, switched on the hazard lights, and put the gearshift in park. In terms of the building proper, Barbara didn't find Harvest Community Mutual to be all that intimidating. That didn't change the nature of the activity inside. They would make a concerted effort not to be stuffy, which would only make things worse. The fact they were parked out front like The Dalton Gang didn't help.

"Aren't you going to pull into the parking lot?" asked Barbara.

Ken Sr. threw an arm around her seat and asked, "What for? Should only take a second, right?"

Barbara hid her reaction and looked away from his

penetrating gaze. He didn't want to discuss it, and as with all things he didn't want to do, he would do whatever it took not to do them. What really irritated her was how he would willingly expend far more energy avoiding the issue than it would require to appease as customary a request as pulling into the stupid parking lot.

"Yep, just one second," she said sharply. "I'll try not to stretch it to two so no one has to wait." She removed her seatbelt and pushed on the door. With a stretch, she touched her foot to the curb and held it there. "If you get arrested for illegal parking, be a lamb and leave a note, will you?" With that she climbed out the rest of the way and shut the door firmly behind her. Several defiant strides later, she was inside.

Much to Barbara's relief, most of the employees were too busy with other customers to take notice of her entrance. She took a few moments to master her composure, and crossed the lobby to the teller area where a young girl was finishing with a customer. Barbara clasped her hands in front of her, swallowed hard, and held a smile until the girl was ready.

"Hello," said Barbara.

"Hi," said the girl.

"I'm here to receive an item from a safety deposit box that I understand was parceled to you a few days ago."

The girl typed something into her computer. "Can I have your name?"

"Barbara S. Ducharme." She was careful to enunciate each syllable clearly.

"Pretty," said the girl, dragging out the word. She typed some more and crinkled her nose. "Hmm…that's not coming up."

"Isn't it?" asked Barbara. "There must be some mistake."

"Do you have an actual middle name?" asked the girl. "Maybe that's why."

Barbara swallowed again and said, "Szubanski. It's my maiden name."

The girl tried it. "Hmm...that's not making it happy, either. Anything else?"

"I guess there's the name I was given at birth," replied Barbara, her voice twittering and dry.

"Okay, let's try that," said the girl, her fingers hovering eagerly over the keyboard.

Barbara cleared her throat and said, "Barbara Streisand Szubanski." She squinted a bit and saw the girl stifle a giggle. "Is something wrong?"

The girl turned down her mouth and straightened her ruddy cheeks. With a quick swipe she sent a lock of hair behind her left ear and said, "No, ma'am, not at all." She hit a few more keys and her eyes registered success. "That's the one. Just wait here a moment and I'll get your box." Barbara thought she heard the girl giggle again when she was out of sight.

She returned in less than a minute with a small box, laid it softly on the counter, and held out a tiny key.

"Excuse me," said Barbara, plucking the key from the girl's smooth fingers, "but shouldn't I be speaking with someone of higher authority?"

The girl's eyes went blank.

"You know what I mean dear, don't you? A lawyer? Someone who handled the estate?"

"Oh, right," said the girl, looking a little out of her league. "He's dead."

"Dead?"

"He died about thirty years ago. We received the details of the will from the company that purchased his assets several days after Mrs. Phlegming was—" she checked her tone, "after Mrs. Phlegming was declared deceased. It's all on record if you'd like to check."

"No, no. I'm sure it's all in order." Barbara pulled the box towards her and slid the key into the lock. She thought she felt a slight vibration travel up her arm as the mechanism slid open. She excused it as nerves and lifted the lid.

What she saw inside was not at all what she expected. Then again, she expected little more from a visit to the bank than a slight chill, a middle class exchange of currency, and a lot less oxygen than she preferred. She retrieved the item and closed the box, leaving the key in the lock.

"Anything else I can do for you today, Mrs. Ducharme?" By this time, the girl's affected concern had risen off the charts.

Barbara raised her eyebrows, cocked her head, and opened her mouth to speak. But the words—a litany of hateful vituperation delivered in an unmistakably patronizing tone—never made it past her lips. She closed her mouth into a smile, shook her head "no," and turned away.

Barbara exited the bank to find the car still parked and waiting. She could see each member of her family lost in their own private hells. No one noticed her until she opened the front passenger door, climbed inside, and slammed the door shut. Without a word, she pulled on her seatbelt and faced forward.

"Everything okay?" asked Ken Sr.

"She laughed," said Barbara, and expelled a sigh that fogged her side of the windshield.

"Mom's favorite songbird, again?" asked Ken Sr. with a modicum of sympathy.

"The nerve," said Barbara. "And they call themselves professionals."

Ken Sr. looked down at his wife's lap and saw a piece of stiff cloth rolled in her grip. He figured he would wait to ask her what it was until they had been on the road awhile. Then he switched off the hazard lights, and drove into a lull in the traffic.

CHAPTER 2

A Lower Authority

Jasper Dix rubbed his shoulder and adjusted his bald head to catch the yellow light trickling down from the ceiling like electric piss. Using two homemade mirrors, he inspected his new masterpiece: "BARBARA" was tattooed across the lower part of his brainpan in thick, capital letters. The spacing had taken forever to get right, but the end result was impressive.

He picked up the writing pen sporting a needle made from a piece of wire and a tiny crank made from an old eyeglass frame and dipped it into the bottle cap full of homemade ink. The shampoo and soot mixture worked well, and both were in generous supply—for now. If the guards discovered he was using a lighter and a razor to make the black particles that would eventually end up in his skin, they would take both away leaving him with another unfinished outline. They had already snatched all his soaps. *Morons…what could be dangerous about a bar of fucking soap?*

Jasper considered himself an artist, created like all great artists throughout history—by the system. With plenty of time left on his five consecutive life sentences, he had also begun to study philosophy. One of the other inmates—a white supremacist who had taught him how to tattoo—had turned him on to German hard thinker Gottfried Leibniz. Born in the 1600's, Leibniz believed in revolution, and had a few nice things to say about evil, as well. Himself of German descent, Jasper had worked up a few universal theories of his own. So far he had come up with the idea that the world wasn't real at all, and that if he wanted he could control it through focused thought. Being it was Thursday and he was scheduled to take part in roadside clean up detail, he was itching to test it.

He could hear the guards making their way down his end of solitary confinement. With fewer moves than it takes to wipe your ass, he had the needle back into the leg of his cot and the knot in his shoulder nearly undone.

He heard the jingle of keys at his door. "Open her up, boys," he said, "can't wait to make America beautiful."

⛤⛤⛤⛤

The white transport van stopped along a heavily littered stretch of two-lane highway that fed into a short overpass. Other than the abundance of garbage, there was nothing at all special about the location: no houses, no lights, and not a single piece of roadkill. Just paper, pavement and pine as far as the eye could see.

Two guards stepped out of either side of the front cabin and circled around back. One of them opened the rear doors of the vehicle, while the other looked out for oncoming traffic.

Four convicts emptied out in single file, each holding a large brown trash bag. One by one they formed a line in the grass that edged the shoulder like a flat snake. Jasper took his place among them and inhaled the carbon monoxide, drumming his hands on his orange vest.

"Hell of a day, ain't it boss?" He was looking at the guard who was just then closing the doors.

"Wish I was fishing instead of watching you boys," said the guard, "but y'all will probably catch more out here than I would on the goddamn lake, such is my luck." He turned his attention to the front of the line. "Lawn, up here, please." He waited a few seconds before adding, "Phineas, I'm talking to you."

A Mexican mix with graying, shoulder-length hair and a wiry handlebar moustache quit staring into space and squinted into the glare off the street.

"Sorry, Officer Bent. When you said 'lawn', I thought you were talking about the grass."

The other prisoners broke into laughter.

"That's enough," said Bent. "Not like it's his name, or anything."

"Everyone calls me Phineas."

"Not everyone. Come here."

Phineas bobbed across the grass with a hairy grin on his face.

"I want you and Stanton to get started under the bridge," said Bent. "I want every cigarette butt, condom and beer can taken out and replaced with your loving touch, *comprende*?"

"Under the bridge?"

"Yep, under the bridge. Kids have been at it again. You'd think they'd go someplace else to screw around. The cemetery, or whatever."

"The cemetery?" asked Phineas.

"Yeah, why? Where'd you go?"

Phineas swept his hair out of his face and said, "We did it in a bed, Holmes. What, you got some kind of necrophilia shit running in your family or *sometheeng*?"

The other cons roared at his thick accent, clearly put on for their amusement.

"Alright, ladies, don't wet your panties," said Bent. He turned to Phineas with a weary expression. "Cut me some slack, willya?"

"Just *keeding*," said Phineas, and shuffled back to the line where he got a clap on the back.

"Ain't it dangerous under the bridge?" asked Jasper. "What if they trip or some shit? They could roll down the hill and end up under a truck."

"I'd feel sorry for the truck," said Bent, waving his head in exasperation. "And if I were you, I wouldn't worry too much about them."

"Why's that?" asked Jasper.

The guard faced the overpass. "Cause you and Frosty are gonna be topside."

Jasper looked at the obese black man standing next to him. "Me and him? Out there?"

"Uh-huh."

"The shoulder can't be more than six inches wide!"

"Calm down, cupcake. Officer Rundquist will be up there slowing everything down, and I'll be over here keeping an eye on your boyfriend. Feel better?"

Everyone laughed, and Jasper forced a snicker. He liked clean up detail and didn't mind the guards all that much, but any good sportsmanship on display was merely a matter of biding his time. It helped being a good boy inside. They looked the other way with things like new tattoos and the cardboard and toothpaste tools you needed to carve a bar of soap into a convincing looking dung beetle. But he was outside now, and as long as he didn't tip his hand, he figured the rules were definitely open to interpretation.

Jasper and Frosty took their designated positions on the bridge and got busy serving the community. Eventually, Frosty returned to the van complaining of shortness of breath and Jasper was left on his own. A good hour passed without incident or much in the way of traffic. At one point a school bus crawled through, and he could see the kids in the back cracking jokes at his expense. It was no more than he expected. If he were one of them he'd probably have done the same. Probably showed a finger or two, too.

Sore from looking down, Jasper took a break and leaned into the chain link fence that separated the rail of the bridge from a fall to the road. As he stretched his neck, he examined the barbed wire that lined the top edge of a section of fence on the opposite side. Someone had cut open a gap approximately two feet wide and it appeared as if the edges were bent out. They must have really wanted it to end, thought Jasper. *What would make someone want to die so bad?*

He shouted for Officer Rundquist who was posted at the far end of the bridge. Rundquist sighed, spit, and started in his direction. Jasper could see him watching for cars every few steps, looking back like he was being followed. When he got close, Jasper pointed to the damaged fence.

"Huh," muttered Rundquist, before spitting again. "Looks like someone really needed a ride."

The two men laughed, their large frames bouncing in sync.

Rundquist carefully crossed the street and stood under the hole, using his fingers to trace the jagged edge.

"Damned kids," he said.

"Why's it got to be kids?" asked Jasper. "Might've been a grown up."

"Nah...grown people don't do this kind of thing. If I wanted to kill myself, I'd just use my gun."

Jasper shook his piece of fence and asked, "What if you didn't have a gun?"

"Pills, I guess. Or hanging."

Jasper imagined the officer swinging from a bar in his cell and felt his head go light. "Guess you should call it in."

Rundquist pulled his radio from his belt. "Yeah, guess so. Keep a look out behind me, will ya."

Jasper was already on the job. About a hundred yards away a UPS truck was barreling in their direction. He focused on the driver behind the large windshield and could just about see his face.

The truck's brakes hissed; the driver had spotted him. His tattooed head, orange vest and striped jumper must have provided a pretty major distraction on such a narrow stretch of pavement. With a lock on the driver's gaze, he began waving him through—first slowly, then picking up speed. The driver did what he was told: slowing first before hitting the gas to squeeze by. As Jasper listened to Rundquist report the hole in the fence, he kept his eyes on the driver, smiling as he closed in.

That's it, right this way.

The driver aimed the truck between the two men and revved the engine for a burst of speed—exactly the time Jasper stepped into its path. The driver reacted, cutting the wheel hard to the left. The sound made when the front fender knocked Officer Rundquist to the pavement and mashed him against the low wall reminded Jasper of an old folding chair he once threw into a prison trash truck. He liked the way the chair came out looking nothing like it did when it went in; all scratched confusion and compressed rage. At the time it made him want to sculpt something into the shape of frustration, but knew he could never do as good a job. A look at the dead officer's broken body made him wonder if that were still true.

Beneath the overpass, Phineas dropped to the ground and grabbed hold of the grass. He thought for sure the bridge was collapsing, although hugging the dirt would hardly protect him if it were. Regardless, he couldn't think of anything else to do. He looked over at Stanton who was still standing upright and said, "Get down, asshole!"

Stanton looked back, dropped his bag of trash and ran up the hill.

There was shouting. It sounded like two men—no, three. One was Bent. The other voice, Phineas couldn't place—Frosty, maybe. Then he heard a shot and the sound of a vehicle pulling away at high speed. He covered his head until things went quiet.

When he looked up he saw Stanton leaning under the bridge looking back at him.

"You coming?" he asked, obviously in a hurry.

Phineas didn't answer. He just got to his feet and started running.

⛤⛤⛤⛤

Frosty sat wedged behind the van's steering wheel with Stanton to his right in the passenger seat. In the cage behind them, Jasper and Phineas held on for dear life.

Jasper pressed his face into the chain-link safety partition and saw the speedometer reach 70 mph.

"Faster, Frosty."

"Where the fuck we going?"

"Nowhere yet, just don't stop."

"Well, I need to know, motherfucker. The driver needs to know where the fuck he's going if he's in a hurry to get there, you see what I'm saying? Otherwise we're going nowhere fast and I was already doing that in the joint!"

"Turn here," said Jasper.

Frosty steered the truck onto the exit ramp and accelerated into the curve. The centrifugal force sent Jasper into Phineas' lap.

"No offense," said Phineas, "but you're not my type."

Jasper ignored him and returned to his side of the van: "Head down this road and make a right past the next clump of trees. Then sit square on the speed limit. Lots of cops on these little roads and they hunt by radar. We'll go a few miles and find somewhere to park."

"And then what?" asked Phineas.

"*Think,*" said Jasper, in such a way that closed the matter.

Frosty did what he was told and before long they found themselves on a patchy road lined with yellowing oaks.

Phineas smoothed down his moustache and said, "So does somebody want to tell me what the hell happened back there?"

"I didn't see shit," said Frosty. "I was draining the monster."

"You saw," growled Jasper. "Don't even try it."

"I saw you shoot Bent, but I didn't see Rundquist get his."

"You shot Officer Bent?" asked Phineas.

"Just once," said Jasper, annoyed.

"Should've shot Rundquist, too," said Stanton. "Just to be sure."

Jasper wiped his mouth with his sleeve and said, "Fuck him." With an angry burst, he ripped his orange vest over his head and threw it into the back of the van. The others followed his lead.

Phineas folded his vest, fixed his hair, and stretched his legs. "Sure would like to ditch these stripes," he said with a chuckle. "They make me look fat." No one laughed and he observed Jasper, deep in thought. "You know, Jasper, I always wondered…how'd you get inside? You were just a kid when they locked you up, right?"

"Got caught robbing some old lady's house when I was fifteen."

"That's it?"

"That's it."

"So how the hell did you get life?"

"Killing convicts."

From the corner of his eye, Phineas could see Frosty struggling to get his vest over his head. His fat stomach wouldn't let go and he was starting to get worked up.

Stanton saw it, too. "Settle down, fool," he said. "You trying to get us killed?"

Frosty quit and left his vest bunched up around his chins. "What if I pass a fucking cop, huh? He sees a big, black motherfucker in an orange vest driving a transport van he's going to shoot without bothering to light up the cherries."

Phineas leaned forward and spoke through the cage.

"He's right, we better ditch this van pronto. Cops are probably looking for it everywhere."

"No."

Phineas turned to Jasper, who was still deep in thought. "What's the matter, having second thoughts about the killing you did?"

"Fuck you. Let me drive."

Frosty pulled over and he and Jasper switched places, the round man hoisting his large frame into the back with impressive speed. Jasper adjusted the driver's seat and fastened the seatbelt. Seconds later, the van jerked forward and rocked back onto the road. Phineas checked the rearview mirror and saw Jasper staring straight at him. Something about his eyes told him to get strapped in, so he did.

"What's with you?" asked Frosty.

"Better safe than sorry," said Phineas.

"Well, you're making me nervous. And I'm about as nervous as a motherfucker can be, right now."

The van continued to pick up speed. Frosty's fat jiggled like a misaligned tire and his face went blurry. He craned his bulging neck to the front and said, "Yo...ain't you going a little fast? Talk about me, you driving like you *want* to be—"

There was a collision, sending Stanton through the windshield. Frosty tumbled into the cage, flew upward and rebounded off the roof leaving a dent the size of a moon crater. Phineas stayed put, but felt his brain shake inside his skull like one of those snow globes he had as a kid.

And then he saw nothing at all.

A sign just inside the front door of the Weeping Willow Funeral Parlor read, "Memorial Services for Phineas Lawn". Satisfied he was at the right place, The Visitor strode across the marble foyer, stepped through the double doors, and entered an empty, paneled room full of plastic flowers, electric candles and cafeteria chairs. He couldn't tell if he was early or late.

He walked a gauntlet of strangely scentless floral arrangements that marked the path to the casket, and stood at its side. There lay Phineas, handsome as ever. Someone had bothered to dye his gray streaks the color of his eyes. *Phineas would have liked that.*

He saw a podium with a microphone and a compulsion to say a few words came over him like a fever. Phineas had been, after all, his best and only friend.

He tested the microphone with a jab of his finger and looked out at the few dozen empty chairs. It didn't matter that no one was there. Things needed saying, and he was going to say them. Besides, no one really listens anyway.

He cleared his throat and leaned in:

"Phineas Lawn grew up with money. More than he knew what to do with, at first. His old man owned a one-pump gas station just outside Flagstaff—the kind that had one of them vending machines with Coca Cola in real glass bottles. Being it was just the two of them after his ma got crushed under the old lift, Phineas would help out by pumping gas, keeping the windshields clean, and checking the dipsticks now and then. When his old man wasn't looking, he helped himself to stuff from the customers' cars, too. Nothing expensive at first: change from under the mats, stick of gum, the occasional dangling this or that from the rearview. Seeing as he never could go anywhere—and he already lived in the middle of nowhere—he saw what he took as souvenirs of a life passing him by. He never meant anyone any heartache or harm, really. He was just being a kid.

"One hot Arizona day, his old man came down hard on him after catching him red-handed with a plastic Holy Mother dashboard figurine and Phineas cracked him alongside the head with a tire iron. He didn't even remember doing it. One minute it was in his hand, and the next it was in his daddy's head. Unsure of what to do next, he figured he could keep his daddy in the refrigerated vending machine and just carry on as usual until a good idea came to him.

"A few days later a letter arrived. It said the gas station, lo-and-behold, stood now on some pretty valuable property—a pig–rich supply of platinum, to be specific. It went on to explain…"

The Visitor pulled the old, crinkled letter from his back jeans pocket and laid it on the stand. He read over the details to himself:

- All the platinum ever mined would produce a cube 17 feet on each side, less than 5,000 cubic feet.
- It takes up to 10 tons of ore to produce one ounce of platinum, more than twice as much ore than is typically needed for an ounce of gold.
- Platinum also comes from cars.

Deciding to skip the mathematical specifics, he went on to explain that car manufacturers use platinum as a catalyst in the catalytic converter, and no matter how technologically advanced the car may be, all catalytic converters are gradually losing the stuff by blowing it out the exhaust pipe. So, after almost three generations of cars crossing the family lot, Phineas found he had a big lump sum of it under his boots. What's more, the government was prepared to pay for every last, shiny speck.

The Visitor removed a bright red hankie from his front jeans pocket, blew his nose, replaced it and continued. "Being not as dumb as he looked, Phineas pried the old man from the box, laid him in a hammock and told the official-looking people who come to visit that he was mightily ill. They bought it—although it's probably worth mentioning it was too dang hot to argue—handed him a check, and seeing as no one in town bothered to look into Lawn minor's handling of the paperwork on account they knew his father and his father's father, he deposited the money in the bank, taking a little out for personal expenses.

"It came to four-point-five million dollars," The Visitor told no one at all, and went on to say it cost Phineas around five grand to bury Lawn senior once they scraped him out from under the very same lift that had taken the boy's mother.

The Visitor stepped away from the stand and walked to where Phineas lay in the casket, looking pretty as always.

"From there it was whores and gambling until it was all gone, which took about four years seeing as Phineas always was terrible lazy and things were pretty cheap back then. Broke but accustomed to good living, Phineas took up highway robbery. Then one day, at the tender age of twenty-two, he got busted for fucking a girl six years his junior and it took them less than twenty-four hours to link him to the robberies. The court appointed him a lawyer, as they do, who talked him into confessing about his father, using the trauma of the event as a defense against his wicked ways."

The Visitor returned to the stand and smiled, "And as it goes, his smarts finally caught up with his looks. May his soul rest in—"

⚝⚝⚝⚝

Phineas woke to the smell of smoke and Jasper undoing his seatbelt.

"Come on," shouted Jasper, sweat streaming down his bald, tattooed head, "unless you want to burn to death."

Phineas dropped and crawled to where Frosty lay blocking the exit.

"Fuck him, he's dead," said Jasper, already outside and fidgeting impatiently.

Phineas felt himself cooking so he climbed over Frosty and slid out the rest of the way. Once clear, he got the chance this time to see what he had missed.

Jasper had driven the van straight into a thirty cubic-yard, roll-off commercial dumpster and set fire to the whole damn thing. With any luck, Jasper told him, the cops would think every bit of burning trash—flesh and otherwise—was destroyed in the blaze. According to him, luck was on their side, and he told Phineas he was going to start calling him "Lucky", and not just because he thought he had something to do with their recent good fortune.

To start, he hated the name Phineas, and Lawn reminded him of something that brought up bad memories. Phineas thought to argue that he really wasn't all that lucky anymore, but it seemed like a bad time—especially when he considered what Jasper was feeling the most lucky about. It had nothing to do with his surviving the crash, or coming up with the idea to burn everything, or even being free in the world. All that, Jasper figured, was down to his putting his mind to it. What made Phineas a good luck charm was that Jasper had successfully sneaked a lighter out of his cell by shoving it up his ass.

Lucky had nothing against that kind of evidence.

CHAPTER 3

TRIPPING

The Ducharmes had been on the road for over an hour, yet no one had made a sound since they left the bank. They were either following Barbara's lead, or each had their own, pressing reasons for disappearing. The truth was probably somewhere in-between, which is why Barbara didn't bother searching for them. Gone was good and missing easier, for now.

As the van wound its way up the mountain one foot above sea level at a time, an unhealthy serving of mashed potato clouds covered the sun. The temperature on the dashboard's display read 51 degrees, which, despite Amanda's window being open, shouldn't have felt as cold to her as it did. The higher the altitude, the chillier it became—a phenomenon not all that unusual and one she had experienced before—but in combination with the emotional temperature inside the car she almost wanted to turn up the heat. She could have asked

Amanda to close her window for the remaining hour, but secretly banished the idea. Again, there was a bearable stasis that freed her mind to think. No need to get greedy.

She looked down at the object in her lap. At this point she doubted anyone had the energy to quiz her about it, so she unrolled it and laid it over her skirt. It was a tapestry of sorts rife with needlepoint, and its design was intricate and arcane. When she spun it around a few times, she recognized it to be a map of some kind; one that lacked a proper key, unfortunately, so the stitched squares that marked the inner divisions of what appeared to be a large and complex structure seemed indiscriminate and arbitrary. She considered involving her husband in her study of it—he practically read blueprints for a living—but she wasn't in the mood to hear him explain what he thought the various shapes were if he didn't really know. And every time he explained something to her, he did so as if she were a silly, naïve child. It was at those times she thought quitting school for him all those years ago was a monumental mistake.

She traced the lines of the map with her fingers, but dared not follow with her eyes for fear of her headache returning. Long trips in the car always gave her eyestrain if she tried to read a book or do a crossword puzzle, so she usually ended up with her lids pressed comfortably together, dreaming of her destination. Only, this time the dream felt more like a nightmare. She fully expected they would find the place entirely uninhabitable once they arrived, and was convinced they would spend the night in a nearby hotel where she would end up feeling even more trapped.

Grateful on this occasion for something else to occupy her, she continued her tactile examination of the map. It had been stitched with a silky kind of string of some sort. Some areas were bumpy, others smooth. One spot felt extremely soft, like a patch on a bunny's ear, and she found herself rubbing it like a cherished pet. It was as if it was responding to her, offering the kind of reassurance one associates with such a thing. Surely her overtiredness was warping her senses and enticing her further out on a crooked mental limb, but what was important, especially now, was that she wasn't being forced there. This time she went willfully.

She stopped rubbing and risked a glance to where her finger was resting. It appeared to be in the center of a small, round dot, approximately the size of a dime. It was dark in color, and it, too, was strangely inviting. She recalled the vibration she had felt in the bank, and wondered if this all wasn't an assortment of symptoms provoked by carpal tunnel syndrome. She had been using the computer a lot, lately.

"You okay?" asked Ken Sr.

Barbara sensed a hint of irritation in his voice, and chose to respond as she had done thousands of times before: "Of course, dear."

"We're almost there," he said. "We made good time."

"Good, darling," she said, and carefully rolled the map. She had thought to do it when he first spoke, but a part of her hadn't wanted to release its friendly touch.

She tucked it into a bag that lay at her feet and took a deep breath. They were almost there, he said.

Jasper said he needed a place to have a think. Phineas said he needed a place to have a drink. Before they could do either, both needed out of their prison issue jumpsuits and into some disguises.

Well inside a minute, they stumbled upon the rear entrances of a shopping plaza, and Phineas thought it looked like the kind of place he'd seen on television back at the prison. Finding it had been easy. Once they'd left the burning van and walked a few miles through the woods, they followed the sound of a road and spotted the complex looming over the horizon like a cut-rate Oz. But as easy as it had been to find, it was twice as hard to get to. They had to wade through a huge, man-made pond and right about the middle Phineas was sure they'd be shot like a couple of striped mallards. Fortunately, they made it across without drowning and found themselves ringing out their jumpers behind an overflowing dumpster.

Once dry enough to risk electrical contact, Phineas hot-wired a rusty old junker he found abandoned in one of the parking spaces. It was littered with parking tickets and the dust-covered headlights and dented bumper were smiling away like it was asking for a date.

Jasper jumped into the driver's seat and kept his reflective head low. Phineas got into the back and thumbed through the shopping section of a newspaper he'd spotted through the window. Before long, a costume place was identified and off they went in search of it.

After stopping for some discount duds at a Salvation Army collection bin, they found the place they wanted, just where the complimentary reader said it would be.

"Hurry up," ordered Jasper.

"I'll try," said Phineas. "Looks bigger than it did in the picture, though."

"Get something scary, too."

"Scary? What for?"

"Because I ain't dressed up for Halloween in over twenty years."

"But Halloween's still a few— "

"Don't give a shit, just do it."

"Alright, alright…didn't realize you were so nostalgic."

"So, what?"

"Never mind."

"No!" Jasper slammed his hand on the dash. "Tell me what you said."

Phineas examined his eyes and saw he meant business. "Nostalgic," he said, careful not to condescend, "means you're touchy about the past. No, not touchy—*fond*, I guess. As in, you like remembering."

Jasper sat up and stared out the windshield with a big vein near his temple twisting like an earthworm. His jaw got working and he gripped the steering wheel like he was fixing to rip it out. Figuring it might be a good idea to leave him to ponder in private, Phineas said, "Just try and stay out of sight." With that he slid out, careful not to look back in case there was fear in his eyes.

The place—Party Poopers, it was called—was genuinely enormous and chock full of all manner of visages. Phineas figured if he wasn't so thirsty, he could spend the whole day checking the place out. He hadn't thought at all about what he might do once he was free. It never occurred to him that he would be. He wasn't exactly the break-out-of-jail type, and as far as he knew, today was on its way to being just like any other day. Now, an urge to explore every square inch of modern America was kicking in with both boots.

The more he thought about Jasper's plan to burn them

out of existence, the more he liked it. He'd been spared a horrible death, and suddenly the thought of being a good luck charm greatly appealed. When they were in the middle of that weird pond, Jasper told him not to worry because they were invisible—or maybe it was *invincible.* Either way, that was how he felt at present, and it was better than anything he had felt in over thirty years.

Just when the feeling of freedom had spread all the way to his toes, his cellblock senses started tingling as if he was being watched. He was only ever able to catch someone—or something—out of the furthest corner of his eye, so he made his picking quick: two masks, both ugly. After carefully considering the wisdom of walking out without paying, he thought he might try and talk whoever was working the register into letting him have them instead. "Lucky", he reminded himself, was good like that.

He walked up to the glass counter that held within its cabinets hundreds of assorted costume accessories and placed his choices down. As he waited, he couldn't help but stare at the nubile and sparsely dressed young female that had apparently been given sole responsibility to watch such a place. Her gently curved back faced him as she hung a hairy gorilla mask high on the wall with the others. He figured she'd be easy. Never been a woman on God's green earth could tell Lucky "no", and although out of practice, like a bike and all that, he said, "Umm...excuse me?"

She turned and gave him a start. On her face was one of them shiny, plain-like masks that reflected the lights in the ceiling. As far as Lucky was concerned, those types of masks were scarier than any one of those rubberized things hanging up behind her. The world was full of people with no expression, hiding their true feelings and intentions. The fact that this one was kind of a babe only made him more suspect. He couldn't afford to be squirrelly, though, so he pulled himself together and just came out with what he had to say.

"I got no money for these."

Boy, was he ever rusty. The only way he could have done worse would have been to stick the word "bitch" in there somewhere. She just stared him down; a disinterested cat on a dead spider. He tried to look a little meaner and said, "You deaf, or something?"

"I heard you," she said, her mask not moving the slightest bit.

Lucky got the jeebies but refused to quit: "Then I'm gonna take them and be on my way." With that, he picked up the masks and headed for the door.

"I heard about you on television," she said, smooth and cool like melted ice cream. "And we've got cameras."

Lucky looked to where she pointed. Sure as writing is hard, there them cameras were, looking down on both of them.

Lucky said, "I reckon you want something, then." He didn't mean money. He didn't really know what he meant. She didn't seem scared and hadn't reached for an alarm or nothing, so he just stood there like a dick waiting on her answer.

She made him a deal: take her with them to wherever it was they were going and she wouldn't say a word to anyone. She'd be finished her shift in an hour, she said. Then she said a few more things. Unfortunately, Lucky got to staring at her perky little titties, so instead of absorbing any of the remaining finer details, he just nodded like a slack-jawed mongo and told her he'd be back for her at the appointed time or thereabouts. She thought that was fine, so off he went.

When he got back to the car, Jasper was plenty agitated. When Lucky told him about the deal he had made, Jasper got even more agitated. But no amount of agitation would compare to what they both felt when they came back later and the girl, dressed in a naughty cheerleader costume, scooted her pretty little legs into the backseat. 'Cause it was then she told them her name—Delilah—and showed them what was hiding under that mask of hers. Later, when they were alone, Jasper would tell it like it was: nobody'd ever seen two more hardened criminals turn any whiter than them two then.

⛤⛤⛤⛤

So there they were, cruising up the interstate, not a word spoke between them. A few miles into their trip, Jasper gave Lucky one of those looks that said "do it", and Lucky gave one back that said "you do it". It wasn't because she was up to anything particularly offensive; on the contrary, Delilah had been helpful with directions and free with her money. Killing her seemed the thing to do only because of her face, or lack thereof. She hadn't explained why she didn't have one, and neither of them could muster up the mettle to ask her about it. The sad truth was, even after all they had seen in the joint, they were so freaked out they hadn't bothered to ask her why she wanted to come along in the first place.

Instead, they decided without saying so to place the matter aside and discuss how they presumed to preserve their newfound freedom. Jasper said he had an idea where they could hole up. Then he lifted his right pant leg and showed them a tattoo on the side of his calf. Phineas looked closer and saw that it was an address to a funny sounding place.

"Hellhole?" asked Phineas

"Yeah, it's a place," said Jasper.

"Duh," said Delilah.

Jasper's fuse was lit, but he didn't explode. Understanding when to leave good enough alone, Phineas thought better than to call attention to how horrible his idea sounded. Jasper, on the other hand, went on about how he had had lots of time to think while Lucky was in the store, so he felt pretty confident things were going as planned and pursuing this location was the way forward. Through total silence, they all agreed to think about it.

Lucky's interests lacked complication of any sort: he wanted to get drunk and have some fun, the wilder the better. He had been denied his God-given right to express himself, just the same as Jasper had, and the opportunity to "tie one on" was highly irresistible. To him, they weren't convicts anymore but artists and performers, and a performer isn't worth his weight in wheat toast if no one is watching him do his thing. So that was why he eventually agreed they should head to Hellhole—wherever or whatever it was—and stop for provisions along the way. Delilah liked the sound of that, and that was that.

The next few miles went under the car without incident. Everyone was getting along and keeping their mouth shut, except for Delilah who every once and awhile spoke up to tell them where to turn. Finally, they reached another super-sized building called the Liquor Barn, and Lucky wondered if everything in the world had doubled in size since he went in the joint. Seemed he was the only one who cared, though, as Jasper turned in and found a spot in front of a blue sign sporting a wheelchair cartoon. Her door already open, Delilah was gone before they came to a full stop and was in and out of the place in three minutes.

Back inside the car, she reached into one of the store bags and handed Lucky a bottle of Maker's Mark. Then she retrieved a cold can of Bud for Jasper, but he didn't want any. Without missing a beat, she raised it to her mask and took a sip. If Lucky had to wager, he was pretty sure Jasper was as impressed as he was with the way she pulled on that brew without spilling a drop. Not killing her was starting to look like a wise decision.

They got back on the road and didn't go two lights before Lucky started feeling the whiskey. It was a glorious moment for him. Each of us surely have our own definitions of freedom as no one man could claim the final word on it, but for his money it meant driving down the road with a fresh bottle on your breath and an eye open for trouble. Before they could get into any, Jasper said he could hear somebody's stomach rumbling and thought it might be his. Fortunately, they were in a part of town where there were plenty of places to eat. Delilah chose one called Bojangles' Famous Chicken and Biscuits, and Jasper pulled into the drive-thru.

He eased the car up to the talk-box and rolled down the window. If Lucky was being honest, it made him feel a sight better that their driver couldn't be seen.

"You remember how this bullshit works?" asked Jasper.

Lucky looked over the large, lit-up menu board and smoothed out his moustache. "I guess you pick a number that corresponds to what you want to eat and let 'em know which one it is."

Delilah giggled.

"Hi, may I take your order?" asked the man in the talk-box.

Jasper made a face like he was offended. "You can when I'm fuckin' ready. You got so many fuckin' things on that fuckin' board I'd need an hour and a nap in between to figure it out."

Delilah sighed loudly and raised her voice, "Two Tailgates, a grilled filet sandwich, an order of Bo Berry biscuits and a diet Sprite, please."

The talk-box crackled a bit and asked, "Will that be all?"

"Yeah," said Delilah, fishing some money out of her purse.

"That'll be $36.79," said the talk-box. "Please pull around to pick up your order."

Jasper looked back at Delilah, back at the talk-box, and back to Delilah again. "Y'all know each other?"

"Just pull around, moron," she moaned.

"What'd you say?" asked Jasper.

Lucky saw red spread through Jasper's artwork like spilled wine on an old atlas. He leaned back into his seat and prepared for the worst.

Delilah straightened up. "Pull around," she said, her voice crackling behind her mask like a talk-box on fire, "and try not to speak. Actually, try not to breathe, either."

Jasper put the car in park just as another car pulled in behind them. "Listen, you ugly fuckin' bitch—you better give me one reason why I shouldn't kill you right now and you better make it quick."

Delilah held up a fistful of cash. "You want to feed your stupid hole? Yeah? Well, shut the fuck up and do as I say."

Jasper shook the scariest fist Lucky had ever seen. "See this? Means what's yours is mine. And I already seen plenty of places to dump a body."

The car behind them tapped the horn. Jasper rolled down his window and stuck out his head. "You wanna die, too, motherfucker? Keep it the fuck up!"

Delilah slapped Lucky's shoulder and said, "Will you get him in here before we're the ones that end up dead? People around here don't ask permission to shoot, you know. Or call the cops."

Lucky leaned towards Jasper who was staring down two teenagers in the car behind them. "Come on, man," he said, "let's just get our food and get the hell out of here. Hellhole, remember?"

"Yeah," taunted Delilah. "Hellhole, asshole."

Jasper jabbed his finger one more time at the two stunned boys and pulled his head back into the car. He turned to Delilah and said, "And you—quit the name-calling or I'll peel the rest of your damn skin off. Got it?"

Delilah froze and gave no sign as to what she was thinking. Lucky had to admit he felt a little bad for her. But maybe he shouldn't. It was pretty obvious she had balls bigger than Jasper's head. He concluded they were all just a little hungry and that things would calm down once the food came. It took a few minutes to get it into the car when it did, as not all of it was ready when they got to the window. Once the last of it arrived, Delilah reached over and handed the Oriental girl with the headset a fistful of bills. Lucky couldn't help but see some of what was going on behind her mask and *like that* he lost his appetite. Jasper looked to be feeling the same after she leaned on him. He hardly touched his food when he got it and Lucky reckoned that, like him, Jasper might have got to thinking about how she was planning on getting hers in.

In hindsight, the whole drive-thru thing was a mistake. Still, Delilah didn't seem to care nor carry a grudge. She looked damned good from the neck down and she knew it, making it easy enough to believe she made her way in the world just fine. But if that mask was coming up so she could eat, so was any food he thought of swallowing. Booze would have to hold him, which was fine after quite a few years without it.

With Delilah smacking her gums in the back seat and Lucky cooling his whisky out the window, Jasper continued in the direction of the tattooed address. He did mention he got it from one of his letters; a lady who'd been sending him stuff had emailed it to him. He seemed to think this woman was agreeable to his just dropping by, but when Lucky questioned him on it some more he got the feeling she didn't mean to give him the address proper. In other words, it sounded to Lucky like she had passed it on in error. Delilah said no woman would be that stupid and that seemed to end it.

As they drove out of Saturday morning and into Saturday afternoon, Lucky figured whatever they found when they got to Hellhole would be good enough and they'd go on and have at it.

The Outback turned into a narrow drive that inclined so abruptly, Barbara was sure the entire front bumper would scrape off. She wondered how one could possibly manage in these mountains when it snowed and the passage was slippery with ice. In those conditions, going up was probably impossible. Coming down was probably just as dangerous, perhaps more. They had yet even to see the house, and Barbara had already made up her mind that if it was this difficult to get anywhere, it probably wasn't worth getting there in the first place.

"We there?" asked Kenny, waking up from a short nap.

"Yes, honey," answered Barbara. "Wherever there is, that's where we are."

After a meandering climb to the summit fraught with sudden slips and dips, the Ducharmes emptied out of the car and took in the high, eroding eaves and weathered wood siding of their new vacation retreat. It looked positively malignant, yet much to her surprise, Barbara felt an instant kinship with the dilapidated monstrosity. Watching her own eaves and siding weather over the years may have had something to do with it.

"Well hello, pretty lady," she said, her tone that of a hair salon confidante, "let's see what we can do, shall we?"

For starters, the half dozen or so beehives hanging from the porch roof could be relocated. Perhaps patching up the crumbling chimney was also in order, as was chopping off the tree limbs that had literally grown through one of the windows. It wasn't at all fit for a modern family, but seeing as it was situated in a nice, rural area—or near a nice, rural area—and the various lakes and ski spots were but a sled ride down the hill, across the river, through a few miles of sticker bushes, and over the dented highway rail, her family may have been a decent enough match.

Ken Sr. put his hands on his hips, took a deep breath and said, "Location, location, location."

Barbara stood beside him with a determined smile. "According to the letter I received from the title company," she said with some cheer, "Grandma Phlegming built as far up the mountain as necessary to escape paying property taxes."

Ken Sr. raised his eyebrows with such force they almost

flew off his forehead. "Property taxes? When this place was built they probably hadn't even invented property taxes. Can't imagine they're all that high today."

"Well, that's what it said," volleyed Barbara. She removed the map from under her coat like she had seen many a contractor do and opened it with an authoritative snap.

"What is that thing, anyway?" asked Ken Sr., leaning over for a look.

"A map," answered Barbara. "I think."

"It's ugly."

She ignored his negativity and studied the bizarre layout drafted in the stitching. The first thing that struck her was an elongated figuration that seemed to extend the entire length of the central, main structure. Upon closer inspection, it appeared to be attached to something that resembled a set of steps. She rotated the map until they were now at the bottom.

"There—that's better. Right behind those bushes is the porch."

"Where?" asked Amanda, finally paying attention.

"Behind those bushes," repeated Barbara, but even she wasn't completely sure. The entire house was not only under attack from the surrounding fauna, but an infantry of angry-looking nettles appeared organized around the perimeter to fend it off.

Amanda surveyed the area and said, "Forget it. I'm not going through there."

"We can make it," said Kenny, on his way to investigate.

"Maybe you can, but I'm staying here."

"Oh, no you're not, young lady," said Ken Sr. "We're all going in. That's why we drove all this way to get here. There has to be a path somewhere, but if there isn't, we'll make one."

"Found it," shouted Kenny, halfway into the tangled mess. "It's pretty narrow, so you have to be careful."

Negotiating the path meant scratches on freshly scrubbed skin and pulls on perfectly pressed clothing. But they forged on, each doing what they could to maintain the level of enthusiasm required to finish the job. Determined to lead by example, Barbara ducked through the snarl holding a gloved hand to her hair. As she did, she thought of J.D. and sympathized with what must have been a daily routine of being trapped, prodded and provoked. His only guard against such intrusions was his belief in evil—the variety that unshackled the soul—and he'd told her not to be afraid of it. When you finally realized how necessary evil was for balance in the universe, you made it through the tough times more easily. She had hidden that email in a file with the clever title of "church business", meaning to print it out and bring it with her. But like the fate of so many exciting ideas that had found their way into her mind, the pick and pull of suburban life had robbed her of every opportunity to bring them to fruition.

Kenny made it through first, and waited for the others to arrive at a small clearing in front of the moss-covered stairs. Once they were all together, Ken Sr. carefully scaled the dozen or so steps that led to the top of the high porch and crept gingerly over the sagging, creaking floorboards to a large and uninviting front door.

"S'alright," he reported with an explorer's swagger, "she seems pretty solid."

None entirely convinced, Kenny and Amanda made their way up behind Barbara, each retracing their fearless leader's steps and eliciting the same creepy protests from the wood.

Once they were all safely at the top, Ken Sr. put out his

hand and Barbara retrieved a single, rusty key from inside her purse. She handed it over with a touch of ceremony and felt a pinch of disappointment as he bungled it into the lock. After failing to turn it in either direction, she watched as he adjusted its depth of penetration several times before finally getting it to go. *If only,* she moaned in her heart. Then he turned the knob and pushed on the door. It opened with an abominable squawk, swinging freely until it met with something solid on the other side. A musky current of air wafted out as if desperate to escape the dim and dank interior.

Ken Sr. turned to Barbara and said, "Honey—would you like to be first?"

"How generous, darling," she said, lacing her words with sarcasm, "but no, thank you."

"Okey doke!" He took a deep breath, stepped over the threshold, and continued in a few feet. The remaining Ducharmes stood together outside, awaiting further instruction.

"The Ducharmes have arrived," he announced. "All creatures great and small are welcome to stay as long as they clean up after themselves."

Barbara heard scurrying and thought she saw a pair of beady eyes, but dismissed it as a cruel prank of her imagination. Her husband must have heard and seen the same thing, as he slid his left hand into his pants pocket and rooted around. She knew his dressing habits well enough to know what he was doing: feeling for his penknife. But they were old habits; he hadn't carried a penknife since airports stopped allowing them.

"Seems safe enough," he said, loudly so they could hear—louder still, Barbara guessed, so he could believe it. "No reason to be scared."

Once again, the others followed his tracks and took in the eerie, sprawling expanse. The foyer, covered with moldy, marbleized tile, hinted at a considerably spacious enclosure, and there appeared to be several arched entryways leading into a number of adjoining rooms and hallways.

Barbara acknowledged a surge of optimism, even as she crept uncertainly across the fetid flooring. For better or worse—an avowed phrase she'd repeated often in times of duress—the place was hers. She joined her husband and gave his chest a rub, smiling (she would later learn) a bit of lipstick onto her teeth.

"Well, honey," she said, "what do you think?"

"I'll tell you what," said Ken Sr., throwing an arm around her waist, "you three grab the bags, and I'll have a look around."

⛤⛤⛤⛤

Due to a lack of working electricity, Ken Sr. never made it very far. The remaining daylight was simply no match for the sheer size and complex organization of the house's inner structure, and Barbara's map was nearly impossible to decipher by the light of the oil lamps they'd found. The only option was to pore over the labyrinthine stitching with a weak flashlight that was of such limited use they actually thought to leave it in the car.

They decided to confine their operations to a kitchen they were fortunate to stumble upon right away. Barbara didn't dare try the water yet, but she took the room filled with antique appliances dating back to before electricity was discovered as a poor omen. The discovery of a wood-burning stove that also served to heat part of the house came as something of a pleasant surprise, and with a fully functioning lighter at their disposal and plenty of firewood growing around them, it lent their circumstances an air of security.

They had also been fortunate to find a cluttered but cozy den complete with a fireplace, located just a few short steps from the kitchen. Jutting from its far end was a dark hallway that stretched conveniently towards a twisting staircase, which in turn led to an upper floor. There, Kenny had discovered a full bathroom in working order and a relatively small population of resident vermin. Once the fire was lit, all that was left to do was secure some sleeping arrangements. After a few missions into the belly of the house, they found some old furniture that would suit all requisite accommodations. The den itself presented them with a long sofa that looked as if it could hold the kids, so all in all, Barbara's domestic demands were reasonably satisfied.

The spatial essentials out of the way, it was time to secure the hygienics. While the Kens were off hunting for wood, the girls took their positions in the two facilities that required the most sterilization and began concerted efforts to take them up to Ducharme standards. Barbara announced she would start on the kitchen with some Lysol, and her daughter adjourned to the upstairs bathroom with a steel wool scouring sponge.

Amanda got to her knees and scrubbed for all she was worth. Veritably quarantined in the rustic and ramshackle outpost, a part of her was glad she was far away from the "real world", and more importantly, Internet access. She was pretty sure her brother had seen her performance, but her parents didn't even know how to "log on," as far as she knew. Tainted though she may be, there seemed little point in reminding herself of it.

Scrubbing the old, peeling tile was proving therapeutic. She buffed and scraped until the faces she imagined in the patterns of gummy filth were both gone from the floor and erased from her mind. How she wished she could apply the same effort to life's mistakes with similar results. Regret and bitterness, she was convinced, had transformed her smooth, pore-free skin into a blemished mess and stolen her blush of youth. *Someone would pay,* she vowed. For now, it would be the stains on the tile floor. One day, she hoped, those marking humanity would get theirs.

They hadn't yet been there an hour, thought Barbara, as she squeezed the hair-trigger of her Lysol bottle with rapid-fire precision, and they were already beginning to look like a different family. She attributed the bulk of the shift to the dramatic change in environment. Gone were the din of local news and the pungent stench of another burnt offering in the trash. "Good riddance," she said aloud, as she scrubbed away the bug carcasses that had collected behind a rusted old breadbox. In another hour or so the sun would drop behind the wooded hill, and Barbara silently invited the shadows to swallow what was left of their previous lives.

And as sure as there was devil in their toil, she knew a fire would soon be raging.

CHAPTER 4

SAWED-OFF BASTARDS

It had been a long while since the Kens had spent any quality time together, with Sr. working on his handicap, designing new concrete abutments for the center of this country's more frequently travelled highways, and perforating an endless supply of torso targets. Not to be outdone, Jr. had been diligently keeping to his obsessions and hobbies, locking himself away for hours to hyperventilate over the state of his clothes, or tinker tirelessly with the help of a small toolbox he'd bought his father for Father's Day but never actually gave him. So the sight of the Ducharme men approaching an encroachment of nature onto their rightful property armed with nothing but a couple of lamps and rolled up sleeves was one few expected to see.

A meddlesome red maple had barged through one of the upstairs bedroom windows by force of growth and gale, and Kenny remarked that it looked like a network of bursting arteries. After a few moments quietly contemplating this slightly disturbing observation, Sr. removed his watch, stuffed it into his pocket and got a hand around one of the branches. He cleared away a few of the leaves, focused his eyes on the wood and pushed. The branch snapped and crackled as he pumped it like a well handle, and he found the whole business deeply satisfying. He kept at it, injecting rich supplies of oxygen into his brain and sending fat beads of sweat to the floor.

Studying his father's technique, Kenny unbuttoned the top two buttons of his neatly pressed shirt and found a smaller branch on the other side of the room. He wrapped his fingers around a vulnerable crook near a cluster of new growth and broke it off with a single push. By identifying other easy targets, he worked his way towards his father and made it a race. He committed to working non-stop and was determined to impress. If he failed in the end, at least he would have won the lion's share of dismemberment.

Like that they worked until the offending limbs were beaten into pulpy submission. Not once did they exchange a single word. They said nothing when salty sweat stung their eyes, nor offered so much as groan when their white-hot muscles went limp. It was all push, pull, twist and wrench until each section of tree had been duly punished.

As he worked, Sr. could feel a digging into his abdomen. He knew what it was, and that it was aiming at his lower intestine. *Gut shots hurt the most,* he remembered reading. Or was it a movie that taught him that? *Movie,* he concluded, and knew his son had seen it, too. It had been in the DVD player in his bedroom when the boy had borrowed the machine to take it apart. It was one of the few things that still worked after being returned, but he could plainly see the scratches around the screws. Every part had been accounted for and replaced, which was the reason he'd never brought it up. It was one of those secrets that two people shared but only one of them knew it, and he didn't know why but he liked that.

⛤⛤⛤⛤

Still a few hundred miles outside of Hellhole, Delilah had the boys turn off the highway and into a place called Zeus' Military Surplus, Firearms & Archery Warehouse. The sun had all but gone down, which seemed to relax everyone; especially Lucky, who had begun to worry that his out-of-time appearance was drawing some unwanted attention. He eventually concluded that if Delilah hadn't said anything, it was probably all in his mind. She had treated them right up to now, so he had no reason to distrust her. She'd gassed up the vehicle, tried to feed them, and bought them booze with a fake I.D. Now, she was fixing to outfit them with some ballistic protection. Soon enough the Feds would cotton to their ruse, and she figured a few tools to preserve their freshly unwrapped freedom might come in handy.

Since they had crossed into a state that allowed anyone over the age of eighteen to purchase a gun, Delilah assured them that buying weapons would be as easy as buying smokes. She said if she wanted she could buy a gun a month and never once need a permit. She also eased Jasper's anxieties by saying there weren't any limit on knives. She said she would get him something nice, something that felt good in his hand. Lucky could see she was determined to put their animosity behind them, so he felt confident she would come good on her promise.

Some country, thought Lucky. He had gone into the pen back when a B-B gun required your daddy's signature, and now you could buy a shotgun to kill something and a whole set of steak knives to eat it with without showing your face. A few more sips and he would stop caring, but he wasn't sure anymore if he was still a big dog on this planet or one of them nodding Chihuahuas in the back of an El Dorado.

Delilah came out with a bag under her arm and a shotgun over her shoulder like she might have been shopping with an umbrella. She got in the car and suggested they get back on the highway because they needed a hacksaw and a few other things. Then she said they shouldn't worry—she'd dealt with guns before.

She said, "And I don't make the same mistake twice."

Barbara had to accept the kitchen was as clean as it was going to get without tearing down the walls and repainting from the pipes out. Everything needed to be replaced except for the stove, which she got going by setting fire to what was already inside. At least the rat droppings were gone. She had expected to be attacked by one of the prickly-faced creatures when she was sweeping them up, but much to her surprise, it was a snake's molted skin just inside the back door that affected her most, and not at all in a way she would have expected. She had no idea what a molted snakeskin looked like, but this one must have been there for several years. The thought that it might have been born of an ancient evil made her picture a large serpent closing around her naked body, blinking its emerald eyes and flicking out its long, penetrating tongue. At that point cleaning anything was next to impossible, so she threw down the sponge and quit.

After organizing every drawer and throwing away anything that looked permanently unsanitary, she sat at the kitchen table and unrolled the needlepoint map over the cracked plastic veneer. The years had discolored the mesh so it was difficult to discern many of the shapes. There were no words assigned to the house's various nooks and crannies, nor to any of the surrounding property, but there were a few clues as to some areas being more important than others. For one, it appeared as if a different type of thread had been used to outline a stairway that led from the pantry to the attic, bypassing both upper floors along the way. Barbara found that a little bizarre.

In fact, the longer she stared into the workmanship, the more she noticed other unusual things: expansive dining rooms with domed ceilings, odd crawl spaces and improbably large storage areas. From the outside none of these structures appeared possible, but her growing fascination with all things unusual only drew her closer. She was aware that her head was likely filled with cleaning product fumes, but she sensed an organization to the house that felt—she didn't have an answer. In fact, all she had were questions. Why did she feel protected in this crumbling castle of secrets? Did it have anything to do with why lately she found herself embracing all that polite society considered awful and strange? Was she losing her mind? Quite the opposite, she felt as if she were gaining it. Sadly, she could never share this revelation with the children or Ken. Other than some unfortunate incidents involving erectile dysfunction, unexpectedly terminated relationships, and chronically stained sheets, everything about their lives was perfectly normal. She would have to conceal her exploration of the forbidden and dark while on the outside championing the permitted and light. She was a mother and a wife, after all, and personifying the heights of propriety despite overwhelming urges to the contrary was her duty.

But were the two interests mutually exclusive? Her role as doting housewife wasn't in danger if in its place she was being called to solve the puzzle before her. A relative she had never known had left her this house. Her own mother—a woman who must have spent great amounts of time within these walls—had never spoken of the place in any real depth, always referring to it as "Witch Mountain" or "Haunted Hill". She, herself, had called it "Hellhole" in her correspondences with J.D., and from the outside it certainly fit the bill. The inside hadn't disappointed either, at first. After a few hours, she was forming another opinion against her so-called better judgment.

She was reminded of a time decades ago when she met her husband and they had confessed to each other a crippling fear of society's deviant underbelly. They had bonded over a mutual disillusionment with popular culture brought on by the Jonestown massacre, the serial killings of Ted Bundy, and the long-ignored dangers of lawn darts. So frightened did they become, they spent the remainder of his studies shivering in a Siamese embrace and wasted no time getting married immediately after graduation. There was little doubt fear of an arcane world had rushed them into nuptials, but had it now transformed into something resembling morbid curiosity? There were ways in which murderers and bad men were described that inside rang true and untrue. Was that what she had been doing in the church parking lot: un-ringing a bell?

She loved her family, that much she knew. But how could she really if they were in a limited contract with the right hand of God and she was praying to the roving hands of Satan? If she were honest with herself, it wasn't as much praying as "bargaining", and when she did it, she felt alarmingly sexual. That facet held the most mystery for her. Sex was an important component of life, marriage and society, but it had its place and time. The problem was, she had begun to want it everywhere and all the time—and doggone, it felt right.

Barbara rolled the map and bound it with a rubber band she found behind the stove. There had been what looked like a wine rack in the corner of one of the map's images, and if her bearings were correct, it appeared to signify the basement. She would go down to see if she were right about that before taking the stairs to the attic. Then she would consult the map again and respond to its direction, dutiful wife be damned.

⛤⛤⛤⛤

He knew he had filled his thermos with coffee this morning for good reason. There was work to be done. Through wisps of steam he watched the car turn into the drive and ascend the path that lead to ground zero. He tested the liquid with the tip of his prayerful tongue and figured they had to be kin. The timing was perfect. Pennsylvania law considers a missing person dead after a seven-year period, so in all likelihood this group had come to collect what belongings remained stashed in that cauldron of deceit. After all the years protecting the surrounding town from the deviltry stewing atop that cursed hill, he couldn't imagine there was anything worth saving but the old woman's soul; and of that he thought very little. In fact, he hoped to the pit of his pious heart it was simmering in the fires of hell.

After the passing of her husband—rotting old codger that he was—the old woman had maintained a quiet existence. She was rarely seen in town except to collect the odd provision, and most of the surrounding community assumed she raised her own food. He had seen nothing of the sort when ordered to check on her from time to time, but he'd seen plenty else. He'd also received a ferocious tongue-lashing in repayment for his kindness, and despite filing several reports to the effect he was obligated to return every few months for more of the same.

Her reputation as a witch was well deserved. There were rumors of mysterious ceremonies and reports of strange sightings all in the vicinity of her residence. A few had even testified to seeing the old crone frolicking in the nude—a sight the good Lord had spared him, *praise His name.* Not an image one forgets easily, nor makes up for fun, most likely.

It became of the collective opinion that she had contracted some kind of old age disease. It was believed Alzheimer's ran in the family, and the theory that she'd wandered off and gotten turned around prevailed over others that suggested she had been kidnapped or whisked away by spirits. No one knew exactly how old she was, but her appearance according to anyone unfortunate enough to have laid eyes on her put her in her late eighties or early nineties. Such advanced age invited any number of natural causes, so it was with a degree of deliverance that he cited her missing after one of his quarterly check ups, and for the first time in his thirty-seven years on the force he'd doctored the report. It had cost him his job, but he had had his reasons.

Anyone with common sense knew that Ivetta Phlegming

had stopped her daughter's heart. The coroner demonstrated an allegiance to the town's tourist trade by diagnosing a defect in one of the woman's ventricles, but he needn't have bothered. Folks made up their own minds as to how other folks died up in these mountains. *Fear*, they said. That's what it was.

But he knew it was witchcraft.

⛤⛤⛤⛤

Amanda Jean studied the hard plastic packaging that held the possible key to her salvation—otherwise known as her purple, iVibe Jack Rabbit vibrator. She had been given it as a gift at her bachelorette party, and due to the predictably hysterical nature of the event, its appearance was none too subtle. The packaging mentioned the device was designed for performance and not representation, and true to its word the object looked nothing like a normal man's penis. It was shaped like a penis and the tip certainly looked familiar, but the shaft was filled with silver metal balls and the whole thing sat atop a little black box with buttons that could have easily been mistaken for a miniature TV remote. The buttons had direction arrows on them, and the casing accepted four AA batteries which for some reason seemed excessive. Jutting from the base of the shaft was a smaller, more curved shaft made to look like a rabbit in a straitjacket. There was only one reason it was there, and it wasn't to hold extra batteries.

Needing to sit, she rested her butt on the lid of the toilet and quietly shut the bathroom door. She slid the tip of one of her finely manicured fingernails between the outer ridges of the plastic case, and the two halves came easily apart. She hadn't actually meant to remove it, only to test how difficult it would be to do, and it hadn't turned out difficult at all. She inspected the fake skin of the savage looking item and could now see it had ridges and something approximating veins. It looked alive but unreal; not human, but more than just a toy. Without batteries it weighed about the same as her travel hairdryer. Only this appliance, she concluded, required the user to do the blowing.

A flush reached her face that left her feet cold. She had packed the hideous thing at the suggestion of a friend who thought it might help her get over the sanctimonious ass that was her ex-fiancé. She couldn't say she was having second thoughts about the whole nasty business because she hadn't actually had any first thoughts. It was more like she had stuffed it in her bag and forgotten it was there.

A loud THUMP from above gave her a start. The Rabbit would have to run later, if at all. She placed it in the vanity cabinet, keeping the packaging together, and suddenly wondered if she hadn't been the first to check it out.

⛤ ⛤ ⛤ ⛤

Amanda set off to investigate the noise. Here she was, in the weirdest of places surrounded by all manner of intrusive nature, and yet she felt oddly at ease. She hadn't a clue what she might find, but that didn't bother her in the slightest. She really just wanted to know what could have made such a noise.

She took the stairs to the second floor and heard what sounded like grunting and heavy breathing. She followed the sounds to the end of a dark, dingy hall and peered into a corner room at the most curious sight: her father and brother were hanging on a thick, gnarled tree branch that had no intention of breaking. A pair of oil lamps lit them from the floor casting warlike shadows on the ceiling, and she watched as they clung desperately to the twisted, red arm of the tree. They were covered in chlorophyll from collar to cuff and their hairstyles jutted in several directions, not unlike the remaining branches trying in vain to escape through the open window. She had never seen either of them so determined, deformed, and to some extent, deranged. Sensing she was there, they froze and spun their heads in her direction, eyes wide and teeth clenched. Indeed, they might have been insane.

Amanda dropped her sponge, ran into the room, and leapt into the air, crashing down on the branch and snapping the last, resilient tendrils of its arboreal resolve. All three collapsed onto the floor in a hail of twigs as the trunk shook violently before coming still against the damaged pane. The beast was done, defeated. Its bones lay strewn across the floor ready for collection by the conquering tribe who lay slumped in a circle, catching their breath, ingurgitating the scent of sappy wounds.

Amanda turned to Kenny and asked, "You touch my stuff?"

"Sometimes."

"Well don't, please."

"Okay."

Their father stood up and said, "Here's an idea—what do you say we get this wood downstairs and build a nice fire."

Together they gathered the driest pieces and went off to do exactly that.

CHAPTER 5

They Might Be Giants

The ride up to Hellhole was uneventful—if riding with Delilah didn't count as an event. Her face alone assured excitement, and Lucky was having a hard time drinking it out of his mind's eye. Then there was her manner, which reminded him of a red-tailed hawk. She would circle high above a situation or conversation like she wasn't interested, and then dive in when she saw a chance to strike. More often than not, she came up a winner.

She'd been working on that 12-gauge pump she got for "two fifties" for the last thirty miles. First, she measured it and marked the barrel with duct tape. Then she used a hacksaw to make shallow cuts around the circumference of the business end. She had a steady hand, Delilah, and kept the gun still by holding it between her legs. Lucky couldn't deny being moved by the sight. Her legs were slender and smooth, and she had what might be described as "shapely knees". Like the perfect fender design, they were strong, pretty and useful. And once she had the barrel cut to Federal legal—eighteen inches to be exact—she filed down the end and rubbed it with something called Cold Blue. When she was through, she held the cut piece of the barrel to her eye and looked straight at Lucky. It unsettled him a bit, and he made up his mind that as much as she had been helpful, she was also a provocative little cunt.

Having crossed the Pennsylvania border about fifty miles back and with fifty miles still to go, Delilah napping in the back seat cradling her custom piece of iron, and both boys eager to stretch their stiffening stems, Lucky suggested they pull into a miniature 1950's model village attraction he saw advertised on a billboard. The town was called Shartlesville, which to Jasper sounded like another word for shitting yourself. It didn't sound all that promising to Lucky, either, but it was the first interesting thing they had come across since the giant, fiberglass Humpty Dumpty back in Natural Bridge, Virginia.

Jasper pulled into a spot near an SUV besieged by redheaded brats and cut the engine. That's when Delilah sat up and said she had another surprise. She reached into her skirt pocket and brought out a small bag of white powder, holding it up and flicking it with her finger. Lucky had long-since refrained from considering himself an expert on matters nefarious, but even a dozy 1950's housewife could tell it was grade-A, bathtub-cooked, trucker-loving methamphetamine. Trying not to think about how Delilah was planning on getting it into her system, he watched her cut a few lines on the stock of her Class-D felony and offer it to Jasper. One look at the big cracker and you knew right away it was the last thing a man of his temperament needed. But Lucky figured if he got into trouble it was better to have him sharp on the stick, so maybe it wasn't that bad of an idea in a fucked-up kind of way.

Jasper rolled a bill into a make-do straw and shoved it halfway up his nose.

"Careful," said Delilah.

"Why?" asked Jasper, sounding a little like a red-nosed reindeer.

"Cause it burns, stupid. We don't need you popping your nasty dome through the roof like a jerk-off in the box."

Lucky could tell Jasper wanted to squeeze her head like a zit, but he was reassured by the big man's admirable demonstration of restraint. He must have realized going off would have proven her right. It was getting so they were like family.

Jasper sucked up the line and pinched his nose. His eyes got moist and he scrunched up his face, but all the while he stayed mum.

Lucky was next and a few grains fell into his mustache. Without asking, Delilah reached over the seat and brushed them out before taking her turn. Yep, like family.

"Shit, that sucks," she said flatly. All Lucky could think about was how much it must have hurt. The way she didn't squirt but one tear would have earned her at least a carton of smokes in the joint.

Tweaked to Jupiter, all three exited the car and did a quick scan for cops. Lucky was pleased to see Delilah had chosen to enter unarmed because he didn't feel like a debate while the drug was bumping his mood. Better yet, Jasper looked surprisingly friendly with a gap-toothed smile in his head, giving Lucky even more cause for optimism.

They set off the dangling bells, cleared the small foyer, and gasped a little at the sight: six-thousand square foot of midget, middle-of-nowhere America stretched from wall to wall like a bad dream. What made it worse was the kids. Lucky hated kids. The only good thing about prison was the lack of fucking kids. Suddenly, there were packs of them, carrying on, setting off buzzers, blowing whistles and flicking lights, and more than once he had to fight the urge to boot one of them up in the air.

Around the top of the building was an observation deck of sorts where parents with their own buttons and switches toyed with their filthy offspring in a game of "who can make the most goddamn noise". Lucky figured it was like hell, or like hell ought to be if it was going to work: kind of interesting at first, and then you wanted in the worst way to get the fuck out of Dodge.

Delilah seemed to take to the children better, which Lucky took as natural. Those kids must have thought she was part of the act as they held her hands and escorted her around the little fake neighborhood. Jasper, on the other hand, got a look on his face like he thought of something he might want to try, and Lucky had a feeling it wasn't going to have anything to do with quietly observing the keen craftsmanship therein.

Then, most unfortunately for folks of gentle constitution, the lights went out. As was expected, the kids got to screaming their sticky little faces off. Not expected was a projection machine's light coming on and landing squarely on Delilah, herself having been in the process of fixing her mask. Those who weren't aghast in frozen silence began to scream. On and behind her, slides showing typical life in the 50's—cars, poodle skirts, drive-in movie theaters—continued their parade without undue concern.

That's when Jasper pushed a few folks out of his way

and jumped into the display. He kicked over houses, trees, government buildings, and at least one hospital. Before long, the entire place was screaming as if the ghost of Elvis himself had entered the building. Delilah let out a shriek of joy and followed suit, putting one of her pretty feet through the roof of a schoolhouse. Not wanting to be pegged as a spoilsport, Lucky hopped in and stepped on a few cars just as Jasper lifted an entire train station over his head and threw it up to the observation deck.

A shot rang out: small caliber, from the sound of it. Lucky looked up to see a sunburnt-to-hell dirt merchant holding his peashooter in the air. Apparently he thought he would save the day by putting a hole in the ceiling fan; such was the breadth of his wisdom. All he managed to do was get a gut full of shot and put a few pellets in the faces of those nearest to him. As it turned out, Delilah had brought the gun in after all. Lucky hadn't the foggiest where she'd hid it, and hoped he would never know.

Jasper grabbed one of the moms around the neck and pulled her to his chest. His eyes were a couple of pineapples in Carmen Miranda's fruit hat, but in thinking back later Jasper probably knew what he was doing. Seconds after he'd made his move, the man who had shot first shot again and the bullet hit the woman in the purse.

Not one to let an opportunity for mischief pass quietly, Delilah pumped and fired once more, and once more hit her target and then some. The shooting man, another man and his fat wife came tumbling off the deck ass over teacups. Lucky reckoned he would never forget the sound the wife's head made when it split open on the four foot water tower—nor the sight, as it was pretty disgusting in a humorous sort of way.

Delilah pumped the gun again and shot up a stretch of Main Street before backing over the prone bodies of some panty-wetting toddlers and bolting for the door. Pretty good going, all things considered.

The three of them burst from the building and kicked a path through the kiddies to the car. Before their doors were closed, Jasper floored the junker in reverse and accidentally creamed a half-dozen touring bikes. Lucky got to laughing so hard he started snorting like a pig. Jasper said he'd been skeptical about risking a stop but had to confess to its worthiness as a spectacle. Delilah, as it turned out, had her own observations.

"Talk about a corporate bonding exercise," she said.

Neither he nor Jasper knew the difference between a bonding exercise and a set of yard pull-ups but somehow they caught her meaning.

"Fun sure do bring folks together!" said Lucky, and he shook his hair into his face. Delilah laughed real loud, so he must have read her right.

They would probably need to keep going now, though.

⛤⛤⛤⛤

The den's fireplace emitted a healthy roar as the Ducharme family took their seats at a small table and started in on dinner. Barbara was pleased everyone was too busy tearing into the food to engage in even the smallest conversation. She wanted them on full stomachs before broaching the difficult subject of her interest in Satanism, and so far that part of the program was going to plan. She had only brought a couple of cans of Spam, a box of Ritz crackers, and one container of bean dip for the occasion, but none of it ever stood a chance.

They had all worked very hard getting their designated areas of the house in clean and serviceable order. The den that now served as their dining room had looked like an abandoned pawnshop when they first arrived. More than a hundred tchotchkes needed arranging and rearranging before there was a minimum of space to move freely. Amidst the items were appliances that may have come in handy had the electricity been working, but like the rusty old generator the Kens had discovered in the back of the property, they were doomed to remain husks of former utility and nothing more. So no radios, no TV, and no cell or landline phone service to alert them if the world had somehow ended while they were gone. All they had was the lighter, the wood, a few days' worth of food, a dozen or so oil lamps, one incomplete deck of cards, and each other.

Barbara was determined to make it to the attic, but now that the sun had set, she didn't want to go alone. Before she could invite company, she felt everyone needed to air out their issues. Again, it was an impulse born entirely of her new surroundings and possibly her earlier study of the needlepoint. If that section of the house—the one that had been delineated with the strange thread—held some volatile energy, she needed to be sure she wasn't dragging any excess baggage in there with them.

Her study of Satanism had taught her to release violent and destructive energies through something called "psychodramatic ritual", which basically meant throwing a fit. In order to get her family to cooperate, she was going to have to explain where in the world she got such a crazy idea. She had sworn only yesterday never to speak of her outlandish ruminations, but somehow she had found the courage to try. If they reacted harshly, it could all go horribly wrong. On the other hand, it could be just what the situation required.

"Everyone?" she started, as unassumingly as she could. Amanda and the Kens paused mid-chew, bits of food dropping from their chins and fingers.

"Has anyone here ever heard of...," she tried to make it sound casual and innocent, "Satan?"

Their reaction wasn't what she expected. There were nods, mostly, and more chewing, but none of the gasps and groans that she had played out in her head. Not wanting to lose the impetus of the moment, she reached under her chair and produced a bottle of wine. She had procured it earlier from the basement, a place that held far less drama than she had hoped, but finding it had increased her confidence in the map. And there was more: the bottle had beckoned her by being the only one with a finger streak drawn into the dust. She assumed it was her grandmother's—an attempt at contact beyond the grave, perhaps. Nothing could be discounted. Still, the idea that she was meant to share the wine with her family came from more than just an assumption; she had been directed by an instinct both maternal—and to borrow from the Satanic lexicon—*infernal*. Therefore, her pouring wine into each of their glasses was more than just a gesture of familial camaraderie; it was as if she was taking the first of many steps towards shattering a false mirror.

Amanda immediately lifted her glass and sipped. Kenny was next, testing the dark, red liquid with a sniff before using it to wash down a forkful of Spam. Ken Sr. took it down in a single gulp and held his goblet out for more. She refilled his glass halfway, and placed the half-empty bottle in the middle of the table where the fire ignited its ruby hues. Bolstered by their cooperation, she continued.

"I suppose some of you have noticed we've been missing a few decorative soaps around the house, lately."

They looked at her blankly, as if swirling the statement around in their heads.

Amanda broke the silence: "I just thought they were being used."

"Me, too," said Kenny.

Barbara looked to her husband, whose nod made it unanimous.

"Well, you're all right in a way. They *are* being used…only, probably not how you think." She took another sip of wine and said, "I've been sending them to someone. A man. He's an artist and he uses them to carve things. They're beautiful and he's sensitive and I think there are some people in jail that shouldn't be there. Anyway, now you know."

Ken Sr. swallowed a mouthful of wine and said, "You're sending soap to someone in jail?" His tone was calm and not the least bit accusing.

"Yes. And there's something else." They surrendered their utmost attention and it seemed to Barbara as if the fire popped more loudly than before. Before she could chicken out, she said, "I've been studying the basic tenets of Satanism put forth by Alistair Crowley, and I must say they make a lot of sense."

Her audience continued to stare, excavating the insides of their mouths with their tongues.

"Now, before you all start in, I want you to know that it has nothing to do with stabbing people with pitchforks or taking over the souls of little girls or anything like that. Satanism extends the philosophy of treating people with respect and basically becoming your own god. Well, there's a little more to it than that, but that's the gist."

"Who's Alistair Crowling?" asked Amanda.

"Crowley," corrected Barbara. "He's the founder of the Satanic Church."

"Is he in prison, too?" asked Ken Sr.

"No, he's dead," said Barbara, "but others have taken over his teachings, most notably a man by the name of Anton LaVey."

"Is he in jail?" asked Kenny.

"No, he's dead, too, but that's not the point. Aren't I getting through to any of you?"

Ken Sr. wiped his mouth with his napkin, reached across the table, and took his wife by the hand.

"Barbara, it's just that…it's a lot to take in at once. I'm sure everyone here is trying their best to understand."

"I know, I'm sorry," she said, reaching for her glass. "I'm a little nervous, I guess."

"Why?" asked Kenny.

"I'm afraid of what you all might think of me." She could tell they were waiting for more. "Do you remember that map I picked up from the bank today?"

They nodded.

"Well…I believe it's been speaking to me. Not with words or anything, but I'm getting messages from it. I know that sounds insane, but I need you all to believe me."

"Okay," said Ken Sr., looking to the children, "say we believe you. Now what?"

She went on about the needlepoint and how it was drawing her to the attic. It made her anxious to be speaking so honestly, but it also felt good in a way. She still wasn't convinced her family wouldn't shun her eventually, but because they seemed willing to listen she couldn't stop herself.

"So once the dishes are cleared away," she went on, "I thought we might all go together."

"I'll go," said Kenny. "I heard Satan worshippers sacrifice animals."

Barbara pointed a cold finger at him. "That's not true, so put it out of your head." She withdrew the finger and placed it inquisitively on her chin. "Now, anyone else?"

"Yeah, sure," said Amanda with a shrug, "why not?"

"Okay, that's two. Honey?" Barbara squeezed her husband's hand.

"Umm…will it take long?" he asked.

Barbara's heart sank a little. "I don't know. I'm not sure why we're being asked to go."

"Just seems a little silly for us all to go if you don't know why we're going." His voice was mild as milk.

"Honey, please," she implored. She felt close to tears but didn't want to start crying. He clearly didn't catch how important it was to her, and she didn't want him to think she was making a scene just to get attention.

He pushed away from the table, slapped his thighs and said, "Alright—let's get it done." At that, he began to rise and Barbara held fast to his hand.

"What's wrong?" he asked.

"We've got to do something first," she said.

"Oh Jesus, now what?"

"Please, Ken. It's important."

He settled back into his seat and gestured for her to continue.

"We're all a little…tense," she said, "and I have a feeling it's because we're holding in some disruptive energy that maybe we should get off our chests." She tried to gauge the aptness of her statement by their reactions, and to her surprise all tipped their hand one way or another. "Right. You see, it's important to get it out before we proceed."

"Why?" asked Amanda.

"We'll get to that later, but for now I'm asking you to trust me. Can you do that?"

Kenny stood up out of his chair. "I'm sorry I've been breaking a lot of stuff around the house. I don't know why I do it, but I can't help it. I've also been touching myself a lot lately. I can't help that either. I'm sorry if it's been a problem."

He sat down as suddenly as he stood, and looked directly into the remnants of his Spam.

Barbara stifled a gasp, but it would have been more from his abruptness than from anything she didn't already know.

"Thank you, Kenny. But before we go on, I want you all to know my intentions are not to work a confession out of anyone."

"Now you tell me," whined Kenny.

"You didn't really give me a chance, honey." She looked at the other two and asked, "Anyone want to go next?"

Amanda coughed a little and laid her hands on top of the table. "Kill them."

Silence.

"That's what my fingernail polish spells," she explained. "According to the medieval rune alphabet, anyway. I don't know why I do it, either, other than it makes me feel better—like I'm casting a secret spell on the world. I do it on my customers' nails, too."

Barbara was intrigued by her use of the word "spell". The definition and context was obviously very different from the way she had been using it lately, but words held tremendous supernatural power if employed correctly. Before she got too lost in the thought, she asked, "Why so angry, Amanda Jean?"

"The video, right?" asked Kenny.

Amanda slammed a hand down in front of him. "I will cut off your balls and feed them to the squirrels if you say one more word, do you hear me?"

"Sorry, I just thought we were—"

"Shut it!"

"Alright, alright," said Barbara, trying to restore peace. "Like I said, this isn't a confessional as much as a chance to release a little anxiety. Well done, Amanda."

"Thanks," she said quietly.

Ken Sr. jumped from his chair as if imitating his son and dug madly inside the front of his bark-stained trousers. Just when Barbara thought he might pull a muscle, he withdrew a handgun and laid it on the table.

"Thank God or Satan or whoever," he said, "damn thing was starting to give me a rash."

The fire popped a few more knots and Barbara said, "I'd be happy to have a look at that later, dear." Then she fanned her face, got to her feet and asked, "Would anyone like dessert? I think there's an unopened box of Entenmann's Chocolate Pop'ems still in the car."

⛤⛤⛤⛤

Each member of the Ducharme family carried their own oil lamp. The glass chimneys were much better than candles for blocking the warm breeze that was coming from somewhere inside the house. Barbara was convinced they had been left where they could easily be found for that purpose, and had nearly said so. The idea that it might have been too much, too soon, held her tongue.

For a chilly late October, she was surprised how well the modest wood-burning stove kept the drafty old home reasonably toasty. Then again, she had noticed her brood's collective breath made a mist hers did not. Not having died—as far as she could tell—rendered that little detail a bit peculiar. Whatever the reason, she was certain of one fact more than anything else and that included the love her family felt for her: if there was a breeze in that house only she could feel, she was being called to its source.

She led the way to the back stair in a silent procession. Only the scraping of tree branches against the siding could be heard over their tentative footsteps. She was relieved her family had taken the news of her Satanism rather well, although it was obvious they were still mired in their own personal dramas. Discovering the nature of their secrets caught her a bit off guard, but it put their reactions into perspective. It also eased the tension, which could only be a good thing. She longed for an opportunity to explain the true meanings behind her new interests and hoped one would present itself soon. Like most people, Satanists, Pagans, and others of their ilk embraced darkness to better understand life and love, not to celebrate death and torture as a few miscreants and the predominant mainstream media would have the world believe. Of course, this new person she had become was so different from the exterior she had projected her entire life, a healthy degree of skepticism was perfectly understandable. At least she was learning in more ways than one—in more *places* than one—that she wasn't alone.

The Ducharmes of 27 Heaving Meadows Place were

not who their neighbors thought they were. Or were they? Despite their efforts to fit in—efforts she assumed everyone was making and which explained all the tremendously dull formalities they were forced to endure like bake sales, herb drying parties, and the incredibly bland conversation one often found over backyard grills—she had always gleaned a vibe of ostracization from their social contemporaries. Raucous laughter became instantly muted the moment they arrived at a function, and she had endured plenty moments of suffering watching her children spend weekends alone, staring at the TV or surrendering to some other time-destroying activity. Even her knight in shining armor—a man who hit well over .250 in his softball league and who sought to make the world safe with his ideas—rarely got that call to be a last minute "fourth" on the golf course. To be brutally honest, the phone never rang unless it was one of those marketing robots trying to sell them something.

And that was another thing: quality and service for hard-earned American dollars was becoming harder and harder to find. Her husband was constantly trying to track down this company or that manufacturer who had promised this quality of product or that convenience in service. It didn't matter that he had put out a great deal of his own money into completing a project, money that could have been allocated to improving their lives at home. To her, his resourcefulness and dedication meant everything.

She had met her husband at the one and only fraternity party she had ever attended. He had been throwing up in the front bushes of the massive, mock Tudor mansion that housed the "frat", and she spent the entire night fetching him damp paper towels. He proposed a few hours later over runny eggs, and she promptly dropped all of her courses the following afternoon. Ken may have been something of a socially inept binge drinker at the time, but he was ambitious and clever enough for both of them. In light of these indisputable facts, not wishing to put a strain on the marriage by flying her own flag, she relinquished her goals. He was a good man, better than most, and she would concentrate on being the best wife to him she could be.

Amanda Jean was better than most, too. She had a decent job and did it well. She was always on time, and polite to her customers and co-workers. Now she was back home and her "stock" had dropped precipitously according to the whispers in the aisles of the local supermarket. Anyone with eyes and a fully functioning moral compass could see she was a pretty girl with adequate values, so it made no sense to Barbara why all the men her daughter's age were shunning her as if she were an aging spinster.

Her son also had some appreciable skills, possibly, but what were the chances of his being able to leave the roost and start a family of his own before he was thirty? He certainly had the physical ability to start one—this, she knew. It was almost a blessing girls didn't find him attractive, otherwise she might be up to her earrings in diapers. But as his mother, she knew better than anyone he was hurting inside. His knack for taking things apart and putting them back together positively screamed for help. Why couldn't he just blend in like the rest of the children his age? Did he grow three heads and turn bright green when he left the house?

Barbara also knew the pain of the outsider label. Whenever she volunteered to help at a school-based function, it was always she who ended up doing the bulk of the work—only to learn later that they had dropped the original idea and gone in some other direction. Did she have "sucker" written on her forehead? Did they all give off some kind of pheromone that marked them as doormats, or worse, *infected* in some way? It was becoming a bit too much to handle, and as embarrassing as it was to admit, the whole business had affected her love life worst of all.

Since accepting the blame for the lack of sex she was having with her husband, and assuming the responsibility for all the problems her family was experiencing, she was ready to burst into tears at every waking moment. She had no idea why she now found the opposite of the kind of life she once considered appropriate volcanically orgasmic. Was she psychotic? Maybe she was just angry. Or were they the same thing? She felt more relaxed in that old house than she had anywhere in a long time, and the creaky old money pit was practically a National Geographic gatefold from floorboard to floorboard. That ought to tell her something.

Then at dinner—*gosh*—the very thought of her husband hiding a gun inside his pants nearly made her faint with a piping hot need to touch him, herself, the Spam, the bean dip, and finish herself off with a fiery log! How could that not be psychotic? At last, she was looking at him through the eyes of the man-eating cougar both of them wanted her to be, yet she still had to restrain the expression of her desire.

And here they were, walking in single file up to an old attic that was sucking her in with a hot breath only she could feel. She knew without a shred of doubt she was the center of something grave involving her family. The needlepoint had told her as much, and she was trusting her intuition to follow its cryptic messages with her family's lives. Because no matter what they may have thought about her new beliefs, she was beginning to see they'd been dying all along. Worse, it was something they had grown to accept. Her only hope was to win their trust even if she was wrong about the box of donut holes in the car. She could have sworn she'd seen them. *Oh well,* she thought, the wine had been enough of a surprise.

And she knew fathoms deep in her waters that the real dessert was yet to come.

⛤⛤⛤⛤

Lucky fumbled with his mask but couldn't get it to go on straight. If he could see through one eyehole, the other was down near his cheekbone or stuck up someplace on his forehead. He realized putting such a thing on in the woods at night was a lot harder than it looked. If you got it wrong, it was darker than having your head jammed up a steer's colon—only having your head up a steer's colon probably smelled better. A rubber nose clamped over a real nose full of meth snot didn't smell like no decorative soap, he was willing to wager.

At the costume store, Delilah had rejected the masks he'd picked and chosen two of her own. She said she'd based her choices on what she thought he and Jasper were most afraid of. How she could know such a thing, Lucky couldn't say. She only had a peek at either of them before she came out of the store, and there can't be much to learn about a man just from his looks. Even Jasper with that comic book stapled all over his body wasn't exactly an open book. At that moment, he stood with the headlights lighting him up, wearing what looked like a man whose eyes and nose had been sewn up with string. Lucky looked like an old coot with nails in his forehead and spider webs for hair. If Jasper was afraid of not seeing or talking, maybe she hit it square. But if she'd guessed Lucky right, she would have bought him a mask that looked like hers or the mess he knew was underneath, which wouldn't have been much of a mask at all.

He meant on telling her the first part, only she was too busy casing Hellhole through the trees and gnawing on some little round donuts she said she had found in the driveway. Lucky thought they looked like eggs, and was hoping real hard she was hatching a good plan to get in because it looked damn near impossible from where he was standing.

⛤⛤⛤⛤

By the time she had scaled the entire length of the narrow stairway, Barbara wasn't at all surprised to find the doorknob to the attic stuck fast. They were embarking on a dark mystery, and her memories of novels and films of that ilk told her these sorts of obstacles were commonplace. She just hoped she could keep the act moving long enough to keep her audience. She was afraid if she didn't get to the heart of the matter fast she was going to lose them, and it was pretty clear that over the years, despite appearances, she had been doing exactly that.

What was a little stranger than anticipated—and what Kenny was first to point out—was there was no keyhole to be found, either in the knob or the actual door. This meant it was locked from the inside; a subtle revelation alerting Barbara to body hair she didn't know she had as every bit of it stood on end and tickled her polyester blend. But she knew the others were following her lead and gauging their own fear on her reaction. So like a good leader adept at hiding her true feelings when necessary, she smiled and said "hmm", as if nothing more alarming had occurred than the can opener breaking halfway around a container of cranberry sauce.

Seizing an opportunity to include her audience, she said, "Kenny, why don't you have a look and see if you can find a hidden latch or something?"

Kenny stepped up and examined the entire perimeter of the door with both hands.

"What are you doing?" asked Amanda.

"Feeling for structural anomalies," Kenny explained. "Or a draft."

Ken Sr. raised his eyebrows, but Amanda wasn't impressed. "Why a draft?" she asked.

"Air rushes through keyholes all the time. It's the quickest way to find one in the dark."

Barbara wasn't sure whether to be proud of her son's advanced faculty for intrusion or concerned, but she kept the conflict to herself. "Anything?" she asked, determined to keep them focused.

Kenny scratched his sandy blonde head and said, "Nope… nothing. She's sealed up real good."

"Are we done here, then?" asked Amanda, using both hands to hold the lamp. "My arms are sore and I'm kind of cold."

Barbara looked at her face and the faces of the other two and recognized identical expressions of discontent. They were of the same genetic map, of that there was no doubt; she only wished she could get them on the same page.

"I won't keep anyone who doesn't want to be here," she said, failing to mask her frustration. "If you want to go, go."

Amanda turned her mouth down—a mirror image of her mother's at times of distress—and left.

"Anyone else?"

Ken Sr. switched his lamp from one hand to the other and said, "Kenny, have another look, would you? There's got to be something."

The boy retraced his exam, reversing the sequence several times.

Barbara understood what she was seeing wasn't a union of purpose but a pantomime. Before long they would bow out politely like a round of reverse musical chairs until it was only she left standing, questioning her sanity along with the rest. At dinner, Barbara had nearly won them over. Now, there was a danger they might reject her revelation and retreat back into their shells. The black cat was out of the bag, and if she didn't produce at least some proof she wasn't totally mad, they would likely go so far away as to never be heard from again.

Delilah dug inside one of the bags in the backseat and handed Lucky something she called a "pick mattock". It looked to him like something used to break rocks—small ones, at that. He gripped it strong and swung it a few times, wondering if he could wake a sleeping possum with it. *Never mind,* he thought. *It'd do, probably.*

Then she pulled out a nifty-looking box and handed it to Jasper. He lifted the lid, and the headlights reflected off a large, Swiss Army knife. It was twice the size of the ones you usually see that held a few blades, a small pair of scissors, a nail file, and if you knew where to look, a pair of tweezers.

He knew because he'd stolen one once and used the tweezers to jimmy a few locks. When Jasper opened the different tools one by one, Lucky saw a selection of blades all big enough to carve a steak off a bull—or a bar of soap, as per one's affinity.

"What do you think?" she asked. Lucky thought he might have heard a touch of sweetness in her locution.

Jasper didn't answer, but the way he was fingering the knife's design gave Lucky the impression he was appreciative of her efforts. It was a moment, no doubt about it.

"It was the biggest one they had," she said. "I didn't read the whole description, but I'm pretty sure it's got whatever you need to do whatever you need to do.

Yep, thought Lucky, *she's sweet on him.* How the hell she went from hating his guts to wanting to swing on his vine, he didn't know. But he could bet that behind her mask—if you ignored the mess—there was some serious blushing going on. There was no telling what was going on behind Jasper's, though, and she seemed to want to know.

"Well...say something, you big dork." There it was, that unique brand of Delilah charm. Only, Jasper's posture didn't indicate a pending retaliation like Lucky thought it would. He just looked away into the night sky as if trying to remember how a human being was supposed to react on such occasions. Then he folded up the knife until the biggest blade was left out, and got to carving on a tree. And damned be we all if he wasn't making a heart.

Lucky thought Delilah might piss herself laughing.

⛤⛤⛤⛤

Jasper may have been at a loss for words only moments before, but the cusses sprung from his mouth like water from a busted fire hydrant once those stickers got to sinking into his neck. He was bear-crawling towards Hellhole with Delilah behind him and Lucky after her, and there were words said that would have made the devil blush. Sometimes cutting wasn't fast enough for Jasper, so he tended now and again to lead with his head. He was good with his new knife and he knew it, and wasn't about to quit over a throat full of thorns.

He caught another sticker in the top of his hand and Delilah shushed him before he could react. He simmered down almost immediately. Again, it was the way she had done it—all motherly and soft-like. Lucky thought his pick might come in handy in front, but it didn't seem right to split them two up and he sure as hell wasn't going to leap-frog to get there. So he held his place and got to ruminating: the way they were communicating with each other—it was like the masks had awakened their insides, making their outsides less important. Not for Lucky. He didn't like digging too deep. He liked things to look nice and natural, and it bothered him a little that he had to wear that stupid smelly thing over his head. It was like where those two were made stronger with something covering them up, he felt the opposite. At present, he was looking through the nose holes and thought he might as well take the damn thing off. He could make up a story about one of the stickers getting it, and tell them when they reached the window that would be their entrance. He didn't much care if they didn't like it, and by then it would be too late to do anything anyway.

When he saw that pretty young girl through the glass, he made up his mind that his face was a much better weapon than any limp-dick pick. Even if he was getting up in years, he knew he could still make it work with a little sweet talk. Since winding up in prison, he found he could get most people to do and believe whatever he wanted—with the possible exception of a certain judge and jury. But he reckoned he could convince some little girl to let him in if given half a chance.

Lucky reached up and took hold of the rubber nose.

"Leave it," said Delilah.

Cunt.

⛤⛤⛤⛤

Amanda sat by the fire drinking straight from the bottle. She thought of Eldren, and how he had annihilated her entire life with a single, thirty-second phone call. She remembered dropping the cell phone from her ear, and how her knees beat it to the floor. Instantly, she was transported into a nightmare from which she had yet to awaken. At that very moment, thousands of pervs were watching her skank out on their flat screens and he was somewhere with someone talking about all the things they were going to do once they were married: how many kids they would have; what their names would be; what kind of pets they liked; where they would go on their honeymoon and anniversary; where they would be buried when they died, together, in the comfort of each other's arms. The whole time he would be touching her soft skin and telling her how "pure" she was. He would say that word over and over and make her feel like Snow White on a pink cloud soaring over a glittering rainbow. And then he would lean in and kiss her, his tongue making promises he would soon keep as long as she stayed that way: *pure.*

Amanda started to cry, tears finding their way into the

corners of her mouth. She didn't want to spend the entire night miserable, and had stopped in her room for some nail polish remover in case the wine had filled her with inspiration. If it did, she wanted to have ten clean little canvases to work on. Before she got caught up thinking about Eldren, a wave of creativity had come in on a tidal surge, its crest lifting her spirits. But the tears were winning, and the only creative thing she could think to do was take a final swig from the bottle and throw it in the fire, shattering the glass to pieces like the remains of her broken heart.

Something made her jump. It sounded as if more glass had broken elsewhere and it seemed to come from the front of the house. It was difficult to tell, but the noise had definitely come from behind where she was facing. One thing was for sure: it was no echo. The breaking had sounded much different, and had broken, she guessed, for much different reasons.

⛤⛤⛤⛤

Lucky hadn't expected it to go like he wanted it to, and to be honest he was a little disgusted. By the time Jasper had reached the window, he was too covered in bloody scratches to suffer any negotiations. With a swing of his elbow he busted the pane sending a shower of glass into the house. It must have made him feel as better as it made Lucky feel worse.

No matter, they had made it. They were in Hellhole.

Let the games begin.

PART TWO
ON

CHAPTER 6
INSIDE

Amanda calmed immediately after her start and decided to investigate the noise. There were so many innocent impositions onto the old place she wouldn't have been surprised to see a squirrel twitching near a broken serving bowl offering her an after-dinner nut. The last time she went searching for the source of a large thud the experience had been cathartic, if slightly bizarre. Discovering the origin of this latest intrusion would at least get her mind off her troubles. She didn't feel the need to alert the strangers she called her family. There was still an entire weekend to go, so making a new friend that wasn't deeply unstable sounded like a good idea.

She rose from her chair and strolled with a neutral curiosity in the direction of the foyer. The casual way she held the oil lamp—down by her hip as if there was little more to fear than a sharp draft—made her wonder if the wine had numbed her senses. Even without its help, "numb" was a state with which she was quite familiar. Adopting an impenetrable veneer was an important ingredient to functioning normally, and the blank slate of her face levied no undue tax on her customers. When they spoke, nothing they said penetrated further than the thin membrane of her eardrum. She was friendly enough and skin deep, and luckily for all concerned, people having their nails done tended to like their nail techs that way.

Nails on her mind, she realized the nail file was still in her hand. What was she planning to do, clean the claws of an owl? File the cuticles of a raccoon? *Old habits,* she thought, even if she wasn't old in the tax bracket sense. Still, something inside her—the last, remaining piece of twine holding her sorry shit together—planned on getting her there.

As she neared the entrance to the living room she glimpsed something fairly large cross the floor. She wasn't sure if it had been light, dark, hairy, or covered in feathers; no option could be trusted. Now that it was gone, she could barely believe it had been there at all. Then she saw a pile of glass on the floor directly beneath the serrated remnants of a window, which now presented an unfiltered view of the overgrown sticker bushes surrounding the house. The horrid things shivered in a wind picking up speed over the mountain, sending a chill over her wine-flushed skin that shook her entire body.

"Listen," she said, adding a nervous chuckle, "if you're a bear, all we've got is Spam."

The sound she heard next made her wonder if bears could laugh.

⛤⛤⛤⛤

Barbara watched patiently as her son searched high and low for a way to free the door. That he would persevere with such diligence when it was obvious there was nothing to find warmed her heart. But she reminded herself she was already a little warmer than both of them and it shouldn't shock her in the slightest if they called it quits and joined Amanda by the fire.

"Let me see that map again," said Ken Sr. "We must be missing something."

"Now, there's a new trick," she said, "the husband asking for directions." He took it from her without acknowledging her joke and pulled it open as if it was a blueprint for his next big project.

"I don't get it," he confessed, and it clearly pained him to do so. "No one makes a door you can't open from both sides."

He continued to scan it carefully, dissecting every corner. Convinced his search would fail, Barbara closed her eyes and tried once again to connect with the sensation that had called her to the door in the first place. Surely, the answer to their puzzle lay within.

"Wait a sec," said Ken Sr., "what's this?"

Barbara and her son convened at the map and looked to where Ken Sr. was pointing. There was a circular shape stitched onto the delineation of the attic door. The door in front of them held no corresponding shape.

"Maybe we got the wrong door?" asked Kenny.

"No," said Barbara, "this is the one. I can feel it."

"What do you mean you can *feel* it?" asked Ken Sr., his voice tinged with parched impatience.

With the index finger of her right hand, Barbara made contact with the circle. When she discovered Satanism, its study had led to the further discovery of an enormous, dark iceberg underneath. Just a tiny taste of its mystical power had driven her to search feverishly throughout the Internet for more information. When she surfaced, she came away with the knowledge that nearly all forms of Paganism believed in magic. A few spelled it with a "k" after the "c" to distinguish it from the stuff one saw at children's parties. There were a number of ways to perform a number of different "tricks", utilizing all manner of symbols and special objects. Perhaps the map was one of them? If so, the circle on the door might be directing her to a specific action—one she had read about many times.

Careful not to remove her finger from the map, she handed her lamp to Ken Sr. and stood at the top step. With the index finger of her other hand she drew a circle on the door, retracing it several times while mumbling something about entering the room. It started out as a simple repetition of "enter here", but soon grew with the addition of more words until it sounded closer to a cohesive message.

As her mantra took shape, she sensed her husband and son fidgeting uncomfortably behind her. A quick glance confirmed her suspicions, as did their nonplussed expressions. As long as wife and mother appeared to know what she was doing, they would let her take the lead. But it wouldn't last long before they zoned out, their thoughts seeking refuge in the life they left behind: a lonely, green fairway and the broken spokes of a disconnected bicycle wheel.

⛤⛤⛤⛤

Amanda went stiff at the sound of the laughter. She would have fallen over like a knife on point if not for an apoplectic right knee that quivered her back into balance. Was she hallucinating? *How strong was that wine, anyway?* Whatever the answer, she thought it best to about-face and get going.

She turned with a half-pirouette, took a step, and stopped. Someone was definitely behind her. Just the possibility would have sent most girls (and more than a few boys) screaming into the hall, but in her mind it was always the more frightening prospect to run from something undefined, as it soon became the worst thing imaginable. So she repeated her half-pirouette and faced the room.

At the faded edge of the lamplight stood a figure. The first thing that sprung to her mind was a trapeze artist—or any lithe, young woman with too perfect skin and a horrible, fixed gaze. It was probably a combination of her appearance and the weightlessness of Amanda's legs that brought the image to mind.

She squeezed the nail file, bending it to match her new reality. "Who are you?" she asked, her cracking voice mimicking the old plaster above.

"I'm the bear," replied the woman, tonelessly.

Amanda could hear the oil lamp's glass chimney rattling in her hand. She wanted to ask this person what she wanted, but realized she might not want to know the answer.

"Where is everyone?" the woman asked, taking a soft, deliberate step forward. She was sneaking in plain sight and playing it for laughs.

Amanda could see her better now and the news wasn't good. She was wearing a mask, which explained the fixed gaze and smooth, porcelain skin, and at that moment the young divorcee knew the wind of her evening—or her life, perhaps, far more than recently—was dramatically changing. This time, instead of stinging and hot like a desert sandstorm, it was icy and bitter, leaving her stranded atop the world's highest peak. And like all wind, it mindlessly sought a destination, behaving as it liked along the way. There was never any way to stop such a wind; there was only the possibility of staying in its good graces. To do so meant figuring a way to address it, harness it, redirect it to a purpose, or as her father was so good at doing, seek shelter against it.

Her father—what she would do to have him there with her now.

"I think I'll go get my dad," said Amanda.

"Can we come?" asked the woman. She took another step forward and Amanda saw a gun by her side. *Was that what she meant by "we"?* Again, she pleaded for an answer and no answer at all.

If the woman meant to give her one, she didn't wait for it. She blew out her lamp, whipped herself around, and moved as fast as she could into the void. Navigating by memory, she hoped in her relentlessly pounding heart she was going the right way and that her little brother had found a way beyond the attic door.

⛤⛤⛤⛤

Lucky listened as the slapping of bare feet faded into the sound of the wind. He had missed the chance to use his charm, and the situation was such that he may never have another shot. Even worse, Jasper's breath had consumed the last whiff of the girl's powdered sweetness, and the thought made him madder about the idiot's choice to break in. Adding injury to insult, he had slipped coming through the window and cut his knee. The wound wasn't deep, but it distracted him something fierce. And in the pitch dark having just announced their presence, it throbbed like a handful of toad. Had the other two listened to him in the first place, they might have gotten invited in like guests. He could have said he was lost, or maybe looking for a wayward hound. But the chance was lost once Jasper got in his mood from the stickers, and Lucky figured it had less to do with the pain in his neck and more to do with how they had scratched up his precious "vision".

The truth was Delilah had his dick in a headlock and his head in a dicklock. When they had begun this trip, all that walking billboard wanted to do was carve a few bars of soap and kick off a little chaos like in Shartlesville: innocent stuff that wouldn't stick to them much if they kept moving. Now, the big lummox was showing off, and if they didn't get to that little girl right away the hornets would be stirred up for sure. *Ain't no fun in scaring something if you can't watch it be scared,* he complained to no one in particular. Their control of the situation was deteriorating rapidly, putting them in serious danger of fucking the whole thing up. That's what he planned on telling them eventually, with all due respect.

Until then, it was time to assess their circumstances and make the best of them. The lamplight they had been fixed on like miller moths was gone, so they would have to get about by moonbeam. Dirty windows in woods thicker than pine tar meant they would be hard pressed to find them folks by dawn. By then, they would have likely been scared to death.

Sure as shit on your shoe, Delilah had a solution. With a

click her mask came into view, and Lucky could see a tiny light of some sort in her hand.

"How'd you do that?" he asked her, waving his hand over the tiny bulb.

"It's a keychain light. I stole a few at the surplus place." She dug into her tight skirt pockets and with a cute wiggle produced two more and handed them out.

"Why didn't you tell us before?" asked Lucky, trying to keep his voice down. "We could have used them in those friggin' needle bushes out there."

"That's why," she said. "You would have turned them on and ruined our surprise."

"And Chief Breaking Glass didn't do that anyway?" Lucky realized he'd let his manners slip and hoped he wouldn't lose a few teeth as a result. To his relief, "Chief" was too busy shining his new light at all the surrounding junk to hear.

Delilah covered Jasper's bulb. "Careful, we don't need to give too much away. She's only seen me and there's no need to let on as to how many we are. I say we split up, but head in the same direction. And we'll have to come up with some kind of signal for when one of us finds one of them."

"We could blink our lights," said Lucky.

She shook her head and said, "This place is bigger than it looks from the outside with at least three ways to go in deeper. Light makes us too much of a target. No—we'll need to do it by sound. Let's each pick something, but nothing so loud that it spooks any more prey."

Lucky bristled at the word "prey". It might have been because it reminded him of her eating biscuits. Or maybe it was the idea of one of them getting to his little girl before he did. More than likely it was due to the fact they were involved in a hunt, which awakened a competitive spark he hadn't felt in a dog's age. He would need to move fast. A head start wouldn't hurt, either.

Lucky nodded in agreement to the plan and they hashed it out some more. The idea was to play with their food before eating it, stretching the fun to its maximum return. In that spirit they chose their various signals: Jasper would give a short bird whistle, Lucky would throw some change, and Delilah would pump her gun.

Satisfied they had a plan that would work, Lucky slipped the midget pick into his belt and went off to find them little bare feet.

Amanda tried moving quietly, but it was impossible. Her lamp now cold, she was forced to use her free arm to guide her while being mindful of her steps. It was as if she were on a frozen pond being chased by cracking ice. Her eyes remained fixed on the faint glow of the fireplace that bent around an unknown number of walls before coming into view. As she feared, she was heading back using a different route, so it was all new territory for her. She might as well have been dropped in an ever-changing maze.

Things fell over all around her—floor lamps, vases, picture frames—and at one point what sounded like a stack of little cages. Those had made the most noise, and in all her terror, the absurd image of hiding inside one came to mind. The more noise she made, the faster she felt she needed to go. It was a vicious cycle of blind flight and bartering space and she was paying the price with her shoeless feet. For everything she disturbed, several smaller things followed. She wanted to scream in pain when an errant footfall found a plug or a piece of glass, but as nonsensical as it sounded, she didn't want to give away her location. It was one thing to be leaving a trail of antiques to track; it was quite another to be alerting someone that she was heading in their direction, possibly injured and completely out of her mind.

She poked her head around a corner and did well to control her breathing. There were other things to consider, and she needed as clear a head as possible to work them out. She was almost to the den, which meant the hall to the attic stairs was just the other side. Once through, she could take the familiar route past the kitchen and into the long, and mostly empty, corridor. It was a relatively straight shot from there, meaning there was a good chance her family would hear her if she called out. Doing so, however, might give them away. She had to decide if it was best to tread lightly—assuming they would be safely inside the attic by the time she arrived—or stay quiet and take her chances alone.

There were other considerations, as well. If she were being pursued, she was certainly closer to her family than this visitor who, as far she knew, was the only crazy person in the house whose last name wasn't Ducharme. Perhaps the woman would decide the contest wasn't worth the trouble. If the "bear" turned out to be some neighbor's daughter with a toy gun and a demented sense of humor, it might all be laughed off as a stupid prank in the morning. A little money exchanged for the window with a few choice words of warning and everyone would go back to scrubbing floors, trimming trees and breaking entirely with reality.

But one stubborn detail lay wedged in a primitive fold

of her brain: she might have brushed against someone as she turned to leave the foyer. She took small comfort in how it could have been her imagination in cruel cahoots with the wine. Not only were her thoughts racing from the shock of the events, she had managed to drink the dusty bottle totally dry before sending it to its doom. As she covered another precious length of hallway, a new set of conflicting thoughts gnawed at her resolve: if one small woman had come all the way up the mountain just to spook a bunch of strangers, she might be crazier than she looked.

Amanda caught a lucky glimpse of glass and barely avoided slamming into a door. A profound sense of security washed over her when the doorknob turned easily. Pulling on it, she found out why: the door was freestanding, attached to nothing and leading to nowhere. Her stomach knotted tightly and she vomited a teaspoon of hot bile into the back of her throat.

There was a whistle. She held her breath and waited to hear it again. As quietly as she could, she tiptoed around the door and flattened herself against the wall behind it.

There was another sound. Despite being utterly incongruent with the circumstances, she knew exactly what it was, having heard it hundreds of times at work. When one of the coins rolled into her right big toe, she thought it might have been a dime.

Kenny could hold it no more. He would have to leave now and find the bathroom or risk having his bladder burst open like a water balloon. Not only that, after sitting on the steps for what seemed like an hour, his butt cheeks had gone totally numb. It happened while he was concentrating on what his mother saying, over and over as if in a trance:

Satan, please hear me
Enter this dimension-ahhh
Hear me, sweet Satan
Hear this communication-ahhh.

He didn't know why she was trying to get Satan on the phone, but he wasn't picking up. Her words did sound kind of cool echoing in the stairwell, but at last he could announce it as official: his family was batshit insane. This undeniable fact explained why he always felt a few cards shy of a full deck, and why other kids called him "Special K". It also explained why he did crazy things like operate on small animals. He had to admit he sometimes felt bad for the furry little creatures, like when they wriggled helplessly beneath their miniature restraints. There were times when animal suffering made him feel sick—like in one of those wildlife documentaries when a lion or crocodile dragged some large, bellowing animal away from its herd and chewed it to death. But as far as a chipmunk here and a red robin there, to him it was all in the name of science. One field mouse had actually lived for a few days after he had sewn it up, marking a breakthrough in his understanding of the central nervous system. If that meant he was bouncing reality checks on a daily basis with the rest of them, so be it. There was no need to prolong this particular banking session any longer.

"I gotta pee," he said, breaking up his mother's call like a bout of bad reception. "Sorry."

His mother looked at him out of the corner of her eye. He could tell she was annoyed, but there was no arguing the matter; he honestly and truly had to go. Which is why he said, "When you gotta go, you gotta go!"

"Be careful when you flush," said his father. "In fact, just leave it for now. Or go outside."

"Maybe I'll just go out the window," said Kenny.

"We don't have to act like animals," said Ken Sr.

"Sorry," he said, and started back down the stairs. As he descended, he thought about how it was all very confusing. It was like, ever since they came to this house the world had begun rotating in the opposite direction. He barely recognized his mom and sister. He knew Amanda Jean was a slut—or *used* to be a slut—but he thought most sluts were happy. He sure would be. Only, she had stuff about killing on her nails and that didn't seem normal—not that he should talk. And his dad had actually brought his gun to the dinner table. Kenny couldn't believe it when he pulled it out of his pants. *What the heck was that about?*

He reached the bottom and made a left down the corridor. His lamp cut a soft swath for him to follow, closing up behind him as he went. It was like being zippered inside a body bag, or what a crawdad might see under a flashlight.

The thought made him wonder: could his father have been planning to kill them up in these woods? Is that why he brought a gun without telling anyone? He couldn't imagine why he would show it to them first and then leave it out on the table if he was planning on using it on them later. It did seem like he was in a perpetual state of disappointment with everyone, especially Kenny. Not because of anything he said, but more what he didn't say.

Whatever the truth, the wine was making his head feel funny, and now it wanted out. There was a simple solution to that problem. If only everything in life were as simple as getting your dick out.

He stopped off at the second floor and wound his way to the bathroom. If there was a haunted room, this one was it. The cracks of paint, loosened by years of moisture, hung down like giant flakes of skin. It stunk like wet garbage, too. But there wasn't time to be scared. He really had to go and was starting to wonder if he would make it to the toilet.

He balanced the oil lamp on the edge of the sink and walked as fast as he could to the porcelain throne at the far wall. His best buddy already in hand, he slammed the lid against the tank and let go a laser that roared into the water. Relief washed over him as he stiffened his legs and tightened the muscles around his bladder. He loved peeing. He didn't love it as much as the other thing, but both were pretty much the only comfort he could find in an adolescent duel between trying to fit in and trying to look like you didn't care. And with a new pimple showing up every other day, there was really no other way to put it: being a fifteen-year-old leper sucked major donkey.

Jasper had seen the boy leave the hallway and enter a room. Judging by the sound he was hearing, it must have been the bathroom; either that or he was watering a really big plant. He gave a whistle and hoped one of the others had heard it. He sure as hell heard a few things—stuff falling and crashing, mostly—but it wasn't until the money hit the floor that he knew what any of it was. He willed the upcoming encounter with the kid to be a twofer: a shock for the fuck up and for him, a treasure trove of art supplies. *Goddamn,* he loved being free.

⛤⛤⛤⛤

Kenny shook off and put it back. Then he pulled it out again. *Screw it—it'll take a minute, tops.* He had been pretty busy up to now, but that old familiar urge returned the instant he'd laid a hand on it. The floor was a disgrace, as his mother used to say—*why did she have to come up?*—so he stayed on his feet, closed his eyes and started pulling.

He thought about the video of that lady on the shopping channel who had accidentally flashed her panties to the camera. She was at least ten years older than his mom—*get out!*—but she was still kind of pretty. He liked older ladies, probably because they were always nice to him. And he really loved YouTube. He could spend all day there, and practically did, once. That was when he saw the video of Amanda Jean—*crap!*

Kenny gritted his teeth until they hurt and realized his quick jerk wasn't working out like he had hoped. More frustrated than he thought possible, he opened his eyes and saw the shadow of a large figure on the wall in front of him. He zipped up so fast he almost chopped it off.

Too late—he was caught. There was nothing left to do but bow his head and suffer the world's most humiliating case of shrinkage. Now his dad would know he was a filthy little pervert and be even more disappointed in him, if that were possible. All the guns were out of all the pants, now.

"Don't quit 'cause of me, kid," said a voice that made him wonder if Satan had finally answered his phone. "You see it all day long in prison."

Amanda smelled the stale stench of whiskey only inches from her face. The effect was total paralysis. Her body refused to exhale, and she could feel her lungs burning and ready to burst.

"I know you're there, Luscious," said an oily, muffled voice. "Mind if I call you Luscious?" Amanda pictured crusty lips mashed against a shower curtain. "Name's Lucky. Lucky and Luscious...*Mmm*, don't that sound nice?"

She surrendered a cry, and a hand found her mouth, rooting her head to the wall like a trophy doe and pushing her lips against her teeth. A finger traced her jaw line.

"Don't get excited, now. I'm not the hurting kind. Just don't provoke me, okay?"

Amanda nodded.

"No screaming, no knees to the nuts—nothing like that, you hear?" His mouth was at her ear now, and she could feel something rubbery against her cheek. "Just want a little company, is all."

Amanda groaned as he leaned into her, his scrawny thigh applying pressure against her groin. She had a clear shot at his testicles and considered going back on her word. Not that she could have done any harm; she barely had the strength to stand.

"What's the matter?" he asked, and leaned back, releasing her pelvis. Amanda was considering an answer when a bright light sliced through the blackness and fell onto the face of an old man with two large nails protruding from his forehead.

"Is it this?" he asked. Then he pulled at a part of his neck and let it go with a "pop".

Amanda hit the floor, nail file still tight in her hand.

⛤⛤⛤⛤

Kenny turned to see a hulking silhouette blocking the door. Instinctively, he backed up and went butt-first into the toilet. As the piss-water swirled around the bowl, he watched the figure take a few steps forward and stop in some moonlight filtering through the window. He knew he would have peed his pants at the sight anyway, so it really didn't matter that he was soaking in the stuff.

"I'll be damned," said the monster, inspecting the walls and ceiling, "looks about the size of my cell—eight by eight by twelve." As if jarred by a sudden memory he looked to the sink and said, "Ah-hah!"

He picked up a bar of soap that had been laying in a shallow indentation on the rim and held it in front of Kenny's face. "You mind? I'm sure your ma's got more."

⛤⛤⛤⛤

Barbara felt a hand on her shoulder. She had resumed chanting after her son left, and continued now at the door for a few more seconds before accepting her husband's conclusion and leaning back into his burly chest. His quiet support was comforting, and she hoped their moment of unspoken understanding wasn't lost on him. He didn't need to tell her he wished her chant had worked, just as she didn't need to vocalize how grateful she was for his patience and compassion.

She refused to allow her failure to overwhelm her, preferring to concentrate on progress made elsewhere. In the last hour or so, she and her husband had behaved more like committed partners than in perhaps all of their thirty-some years together. She was sure that, to the outside observer, there were times when they may not have looked remotely interested in each other's company, and now and again over the course of their relationship that had been exactly the case. But up here in the mountains, far removed from the trappings of their agreeable, suburban caricatures, they were free to settle into who they really were. As a result, each accepted the other without question or explanation. A trust existed that superseded—subverted, even—the roles they had been given to play and at which, quite frankly, they were failing miserably.

And yet, she realized it was all they knew. So there on that step, alone together, marked a sort of beginning. They would have to venture into this new world together, fording all streams, summiting all summits and traversing all deserts one at a time. To start, she would have no problem exploring why her newfound sexual desires seemed to correlate with her interest in the occult. And she would do so freely if he inquired a bit about his children's complicated lives instead of simply seeing them as one right angle to his perfect square. The corners were coming loose; she could feel as they pulled apart and settled along the curves of her body. Their lives were taking on a new shape, and while it was more difficult to define, it was infinitely more sensual.

Barbara swayed her hips and placed her hand on the front of her husband's pants. She thought of the gun he had brought with him, with its long barrel and densely coiled potential to explode. With a whisper, she asked, "Where do you put it, darling—the gun, I mean?"

He swallowed hard and said, "Inside the waistband of my briefs."

She spun around and kissed him full on the lips. Their teeth endured a moment of uncomfortable contact, but it only served to raise her temperature as she wiped them down with her tongue and started again. She was through being a good wife. From this point forward, she would be a very, very bad one. She would show him things she had learned while he was at work; little tricks that would spend him unexpectedly. To hell with the cookies, it was she who deserved to be tasted. Let them both lay smoldering in the trash, good for nothing and no one. Far too much time had been wasted on pointless and joyless routine.

She pulled away and examined his face, preparing her next assault. Before she could go in for the kill, he said, "Barbara... maybe we should—"

"Yes?" Her mouth hung open in bated anticipation. She was more than prepared to fuck away her failure. He only need say the word.

Ken Sr. felt like he was seeing his wife for the first time, and it got him thinking. He'd always considered himself the President of the Ducharme family, a job he took very seriously. But he had been losing support—not to mention erectile function—and could barely knot his tie in the morning on the first try. His approval ratings were dropping, his batting average was dropping, and worst of all, his Black and Decker was dropping.

"Maybe we should consider a divorce," he garbled, thinking it was time to drop the stock, too.

Barbara tried to rearrange his words into an order that changed their meaning, but no matter what permutation she explored, one word refused to go away.

Then she heard it—it sounded like nothing she could identify: cold, smooth and mechanical, like something had been locked, or perhaps unlocked.

The door! Something her son had done or she had said had finally earned its confidence. The same could be true of her husband, and she would at last prove to him she wasn't crazy. Then, maybe his words would rise into the cobwebs to be easily swept away. Alas, having raised two children made it impossible to mistake the direction of the sound. Whatever she had heard had come from the base of the stairs.

Ken pulled an inch away from her and froze. She could tell he knew exactly what the sound was but couldn't quite believe it in this context. A wife's intuition is often a curse, and knowing he had been taken by surprise filled her with fear. He didn't look behind them when he said, "Did you find something?"

"Uh-huh," answered a woman's voice. "Looks like I found me a couple of love birds."

⛤⛤⛤⛤

Lucky watched Jasper stoke the fire with a leg he'd ripped from one of the chairs without even trying. Then he saw him throw in some kind of map. Apparently the mother had been holding it tight in her hands when Delilah found her. He could see Jasper's eyes squeezed tight as assholes as he poked and prodded the crackling flames, locking in on their intensity. His jaw clenched madly behind his mask, and Lucky knew he was fixing to make a mess. Those other personalities on his skin were itching to see a show and he was itching to give them one.

Delilah was tying daddy's shirt around his head like a blindfold. They had all been done with their shirts. Lucky had been beaver eager to pluck Luscious out of hers, and it had been twice worth the wait. After carrying her in he had awakened her with a kiss and got to ripping and tearing and watching her fret on it. The whole production achieved some limited satisfaction, but made for curious viewing. For every sweet piece of flesh bared, something hairy or pimply canceled it out.

Then came the part that made Lucky nervous: Delilah was cutting the eyeholes. He meant to ask why she covered those folks up just to go and let them see, but thought better of it. Mask party—had to be what she was after. She was in the business, after all. But the way she tore open them shirts with Jasper's knife was a little too careless for his constitution. Guess he should have expected she wouldn't be worried about hurting them in the face. Faces weren't likely all that important to her at this point.

Holes cut without incident, Lucky took over and put the family in their chairs. Nobody put up much of a struggle, which to him was kind of a downer. He knew shock did funny things to people, but these folks just plum flat-lined. They whispered a litany of nonsense, a few tears fell, and then they went about keeping their cool. It wasn't at all what he was after, but the night was still young and the wooded privacy more than kind. If he were a psychologist, he would say they had all gone completely *loco*. It was like you'd poke one after the other and not one of them would care. They just kept rocking back and forth, settling into their thousand-mile stares.

Even if she was a little lobotomized by now, Lucky hadn't wanted to tie Luscious up like the others. He was worried if he piped up about it, he might lose leverage on the other two. You didn't have to do lunch with too many lifers to figure out why criminal "genius" usually ended up rotting in the pokey. "Piss-poor luck" was the easy answer, and one you were mostly likely to hear. It was cast-iron bullshit. The truth was they had trusted somebody, and you could put your best bolo on it having something to do with wanting to get them naked. *Fuck that,* thought Lucky. Anything he was going to do—whether it was locking uglies with Luscious or helping momma with her boo-boo—was going to be in secret. Secrets are what kept a person safe. *Don't tell nobody nothing, never.*

Delilah threw Jasper the knife and right away he held the blade to the fire. When it got hot enough to heat the handle, he pulled away and started into his bar of soap. He worked slow and steady, twisting the blade to achieve the proper contour. It reminded Lucky of the time he and a real life Injun shaped the front fenders of a '62 Chevy Corvair to resemble a pair of tits. They applied the same delicacy to those beauties that Jasper now applied to his soap. By the end, you almost wanted to suck on them. He couldn't tell what Jasper was trying to make, or if it would be suck-worthy, but Lucky had a feeling it would be special.

Delilah threw Lucky the gun from the table, snapping him from his daydream. Then she pulled a rat out of a pillowcase and held it aloft by its naked tail. At first it just dangled there, sedate as a stopwatch. Than she held it over a plate of half-eaten food and it got to twitching like an eel. Lucky figured it was hungry, and as it turns out, Delilah was counting on it. She smeared what he recognized as bean dip on various parts of each family member's body, and repeated her trick several times. There was squirming and moaning, and at one point the rat got stuck under fat daddy's gut. Before long, it ran off with a face full of crumbs and disappeared into a dark corner. Delilah giggled throughout, but Lucky could tell she wasn't through.

Jasper never quit his carving. Every now and then he'd stop to look when he heard someone complain, but for the most part he continued with his masterpiece. Once, when he went to reheat his knife, he noticed the map he had thrown in wasn't catching. He said it must have been made of some kind of *flame-retarded fabric,* and Lucky thought that sounded a little off. Anyhow, he said he was too busy to worry about it as he was very close to finishing the most realistic set of fire ant antennae the detergent industry had ever seen.

⛤⛤⛤⛤

The cobwebs above the attic stair crackled and shriveled from a surge of heat that came from behind the door. It filled the alcove before rushing down the steps, leaving a faint circle of red on the heavy wood.

⛤ ⛤ ⛤ ⛤

When Kenny first felt the rat on his leg, he had an image of all the animals he had ever tortured ganging up to kill him. When he heard his tormentors laughing, he pictured a lawn covered in bushy-tailed squirrels, a tree full of blackbirds, gutters teeming with chipmunks, and giant frogs jumping for joy. But they were more like cartoons than the real thing. Like the guy in the mask that had dragged him out of the toilet and pushed him down the steps, they were coated in cheap paint and set in motion by some artificial force.

He remembered feeling scared when he first saw the mask, but now he could barely feel a thing. Everything that was happening—that had happened since he woke up that morning—was so far removed from any known experience he had no conditioned reaction to it. The world was upside down like a plastic egg timer, inside out like a pair of soiled underpants, and reversing in direction like a poorly reassembled lawn mower. All the rules had changed or been thrown clear out the window. He imagined them like breadcrumbs floating in a pond being picked off by a school of giant carp. Fish had no feelings, or so he had heard. They just did what they wanted and no one hated them for it.

No feelings. *Awesome.*

The girl in the mask put the rat on his shoulder and his skin began to itch. It wasn't that bad, really. Just before it had been eating something out of his crotch which almost had him worried.

Fucking rat bitch. How dare you and your friends laugh at me? Don't you know who I am?

Amanda tasted whiskey on her breath. The man who had hunted her down and scared her into unconsciousness had kissed her, transferring his fetid backwash into her unresponsive mouth. She could see him now, spit accumulating in the hairy corners of his gob. He had taken off his mask and the others hadn't liked that. They said he was trying to undermine their performance. Amanda could tell he had done it because he thought he was handsome. He might have been once—in a Latino outlaw kind of way—but the years were adding ugly by the pound. She wished she could show him somehow, and decided she would. She made plans as the ropes cut into her wrists—rivulets of blood flowing into her cuticles and seeping under her runes. Yet, she felt no pain. The wine had long since worn off, but its effects were replaced by a numbing clarity a hundred bottles couldn't achieve.

She focused her eyes on the glass in the fire and thought about how it had gotten there. *She* had put it there. *She* had shattered the bottle into a hundred pieces and it had felt good to do it. Now, the thought of it brought an accompanying irritation. As the laughing girl lowered the rat into her hair, Amanda tried to pinpoint exactly what the irritation was. It started as a humming in the back of her head that got progressively louder. It wasn't a person humming, but a thing—a machine, of sorts. It made an "eeeee" sound like an electric nail file, only deeper, toothier and infinitely more menacing.

She looked harder into the fire and thought she could hear the machine speaking to her. At last, she was able to identify a pattern of fuzzy pulses that interrupted the constant mechanical stream. The effect was that of an intermittent consonant turning "eeeee" into "feeeed". Did it mean the fire? Possibly. Destroying the bottle that within held the details of her suffering like a rotting old scroll was a damn good start, but she could tell it wasn't enough.

It wasn't *nearly* enough.

Nothing in Kenneth Ducharme Sr.'s life had adequately prepared him for seeing a gun pointed at his family. After decades of designing the strongest cement structures modern technology could produce, and protecting perfect strangers from what was "out there", he had somehow allowed mortal danger to enter his domain. His own gun was being used to torment his wife and children, an event he had made possible. There was only one word for that: failure. The thing about failure was, most would say he didn't take it very well.

If he knew how to read the blueprints of real people as well as inanimate spaces, he might have acknowledged the bulk of his patriarchal issues could be attributed to an adamant refusal to accept the collapse that had been occurring under his own roof. He had always been an "outside" kind of guy, cantilevered over the minutiae that truly defined his family, protecting them but never really understanding whom it was he was protecting. He figured a provisory contribution would establish the retaining wall behind which everything else would fall into place. And fall, it did: with a series of sickening thuds that shook the weakened rafters of the Ducharme hearth.

Even if he did finally understand at the expense of total helplessness, the proper adjustments would have to wait. First, he had to make things right, square, sure, and level. To address the problem sufficiently, he would have to be objective, calculating, studied, and clinical. He would need to begin, as in all things, with the foundation. Foundations are built into the earth, but the earth doesn't move without an obscene amount of convincing. Fortunately, all he needed for his present situation to relent were some facts. He wasn't worth a T-square, plumb bob or pencil without a few, steely facts.

For starters, who were these intruders? Where had they come from? Had Barbara brought them here with her Satanic chanting? *Those sorts of things don't happen—the Devil isn't real.* The concept of evil was invented to explain that which the common laws of nature refused to make clear. As far as he was concerned, the Ducharmes had been plucked for consumption like unsuspecting cattle beset by a pack of jackals, and now it was up to him to keep them from being eaten.

Watching the invading forces degrade the already deteriorating structure of his family, he noticed their faces weren't faces at all but blocks of mottled bedrock. Likewise, their limbs were large root systems that required severing, sectioning and removal and their laughter was nothing more than the rattle in a flatbed full of rebar. It was time to construct something to keep them at bay, or better yet, something that could use their forces against them; something that could hardily withstand their advances while delivering tremendous abuse.

Something that could kill if necessary.

Barbara listened to J.D. talk about his soap, and how he hoped she would like what he was making for her. He said he would give it to her when he was finished, affording her a clue as to how long she had to live. *How sweet.* After alienating her entire family before discovering her husband wanted a divorce, J.D.'s tiny bit of kindness really went a long way.

Of course, she had herself to thank for inviting him here, but she had done it with good intentions, hadn't she? Yes, she decided she had, only she hadn't truly understood what those intentions were. In reviewing her history with Jasper, one might have expected a moment between them when they'd finally met face-to-face, but none was forthcoming. Instantly, it all became clear: a moment had occurred, only it had been between her past and present self. Without realizing it, she'd been serving him lines in her emails like a series of midnight snacks, in hopes that he might repeat them back to her. To his credit, his opportunistic, lizard mind had done just enough to keep her on the hook. To hers, it was actually she who had been the understanding voice at the top of a dark well; the one who truly understood that her imprisonment was enforced not by metal doors, thick walls or high fences, but by the confines of modern society. They were kindred spirits, she had said. When he'd tried to reuse the notion in a later missive, it had taken her a few minutes to figure out what he meant by "kinturd spits", as he was a much better soapsmith than wordsmith. Nonetheless, she had foolishly convinced herself that his heart was in the right place.

His heart. Barbara thought about that blood-swelled organ situated somewhere in the center of his chest, pumping life into his hulking frame like a vulgar machine. She wondered what it might take to stop it.

The sound of her own heart filled her ears. She could see what was happening through the shirt tied around her head, but she couldn't hear much over the persistent thumping inside her ears. Even when the woman had dangled the rat in front of Amanda's face, she could only discern it was screaming by watching its sniveling snout. She had made a motion to shield her daughter, prompting the longhaired man to fire a shot between her legs. Even then, she could smell the powder but the shot itself was silent.

She was a mother, something none of them seemed to understand. It was her job to shield, nourish and heal. Tied to a chair she could do none of those things and that was unacceptable. Normally, the condition of being incapable to serve her family rendered her obsolete. If she wasn't useful to them, she simply disappeared—replaced among the cleaning supplies left to expire on a shelf in the pantry. But *her* heart, larger and louder than ever, was telling her that wasn't true. Still, as it circulated love to the tips of her fingers and toes, she couldn't shake the idea that her version of the sentiment had put them in their current position.

Barbara watched the unmasked man work the barrel of her husband's gun into Amanda's mouth. She loved her daughter, and wanted to yell for him to stop. But what would that do? Maybe her heart was telling her not to love in the way she had loved her entire life? Maybe it wanted her to finally listen and do what she felt was right? Perhaps all of her good intentions needed to be reviewed.

Which must have been what she had been doing the past few months as she pored over Satanic doctrine. She wasn't seeking a dissenting figure to rescue her from her woes; she was seeking a more lucid perspective on being alive. As a result, the meanings of words she had previously held dear—words such as "honorable", "dutiful", "obedient" and "reserved"—were being gradually redefined by the interpolation of four other words. She recited these words in her head everyday, punctuated by the rhythms of cooking, cleaning and class system croquet. They formed a phrase she had read regularly in her studies, but due to her preoccupation with the day's inherent demands, had never really appreciated its significance. With the prospect of all things unthinkable before her, they made sense—perfect and thrilling sense.

She tilted her face to the girl and whispered the words that waited in her head.

The girl looked confused. *Poor thing.* "What was that, ma'am?" she asked. *So polite.* The longhaired man took notice of their exchange and removed the gun from between Amanda's teeth.

"What now?" he asked, blowing the front pieces of his hair forward. "Did I miss something good?"

Barbara saw they were acting like well-behaved pupils, and she, as their instructor, had been given the honor of their undivided attention. Things were already becoming more civil.

She smiled a mother's smile and repeated herself: "Do what thou wilt."

The girl gave a snort, grabbed the gun, and smacked it across Barbara's face. Her upper lip stung with cold heat and she could feel blood trickling over her mouth, down her chin and landing on her bra. She resumed smiling and said, "Do what thou wilt."

The girl hit her again, this time with a punctuating grunt.

Barbara spit out a mouthful of blood and showed a row of slightly loosened teeth. She could see her family was watching the lesson, and it was precisely what she wanted. Because when she said the words again, this time they joined in. Their recitation was uneven, allowing her to hear each one of them distinctly. All were accounted for, and it filled her with a quiet confidence.

Then a warm wind—the same kind that had drawn her to the attic—swept into the room and wrapped itself around Barbara's body like a spool of invisible silk. Again she said the words, and this time her family closely matched her cadence. It wouldn't be long before they achieved Von Trapp Family perfection.

The girl and the longhaired man backed away as the chant grew in power. It was neither loud nor forced, nor weakened by a shred of uncertainty. To the contrary, it was wicked, precise, stealthy and strong like a large fish, a hot machine, a fortified castle, and a mother's wrath. All their tormentors could do was watch, their clothes and hair whirling at the behest of an insistent sirocco. Not one of them moved, because not one of them could.

⛤⛤⛤⛤

The circle on the attic door shone red as the heart of hell.

CHAPTER 7

FEAR TO FERAL

Lucky could hardly believe that family all sitting there, heads covered up, chanting their fancy baloney. At first, he'd thought it was funny. Now, it was jumping on his last nerve with both feet. As if the situation wasn't ridiculous enough, out of the corner of his eye he caught Jasper in a moment of classic prison comedy: his multi-colored chassis thrown out of alignment by the room's sudden change in climate—due, Lucky guessed, to its sharp opposition with how he had willed the events to transpire—Jasper failed to anticipate the effects of ambient heat on soft gelatinous surfaces and dropped his bar of soap. When he reached over to keep it from sliding away, he hit his head on the table and damn near knocked his ass out cold. His thick caveman skull coming up against that flat slab of oak made a sound as unforgettable as it was disheartening. If one pictured a baseball bat going yard on a ripe honeydew, one would be about right. Luckily for him, the knife that went into his leg when he hit the floor didn't sever any major arteries, and actually managed to bring him around faster.

As expected, Delilah went over to check on him and in doing so placed her sawed-off on the table. Not having been cut from his momma a mere twenty-four hours prior, Lucky immediately trained his piece on daddy who was an easy stretch away from obtaining it. Not that he would've been able to do anything dangerous on account of his hands being tied, but Lucky had learned from the guards in prison that no matter how innocent a thing appears at first, it's important to maintain control at all times. Stranger things have happened than a gun going off by accident and perilously shifting the pendulum of the situation.

"There's a lot of blood, but he'll be fine," she said, her voice betraying genuine concern.

"I should hope so," said Lucky. "All he did was hit his stupid head." He returned his attention to fat daddy. "Hey... *hey!*"

The man kept chanting as if Lucky wasn't there. Lucky walked up close and leaned into his face. "You wanna shut the fuck up and tell the rest of your clan here to do the same? I'm asking but I'm not, if you follow."

Apparently, he didn't–which was weird, but not as weird as when the pistol in Lucky's hand decided to approximate the weight of a spare tire. Only a few minutes ago he had been waving it around and using it to take Luscious' temperature. At present, he could barely keep it above his waist. The fatigue it was causing his shoulder was beyond distracting and he started thinking maybe the heat had something to do with it.

He looked at Delilah who held Jasper's mask in her hand and took it to be a poor omen. There they were: him trying to lift a little gun, Jasper bleeding out like a two-dollar oil change, and Delilah kneeling unarmed on the floor next to him. Still, the family kept on chanting. Maybe a little proactive ingenuity would get things back to the way they were.

Lucky glanced back at the father and thought it might be a good idea to shoot him. Just, BANG—*now what you got to say about that?*—and send the rest of them back into their stupor. Besides, he was a little on the big side and not altogether uncoordinated looking. They had no use for him anyhow. The other one they could afford to lose without cramping the evening's festivities was the kid. Jasper had history with the mommy, and Lucky was fixing to make some with Luscious, so it was down to which one of the swinging dicks it would be. Smart money said Daddy but something wasn't quite right about that kid.

Firstly, he smelled like a couple quarts of rattlesnake piss. Secondly, he was about the same age Lucky was when he lost *his* daddy, so popping the fat hairy bastard risked an emergence of empathy that might slow him down. If he shot the kid, a walk down memory lane might cease to be an issue. In a sense, it would be like killing his past and letting him start fresh. *Yeah,* thought Lucky, *let's see how much song they've got in their hearts when their pimply little brat's full of holes.*

Lucky cocked the hammer and aimed at the boy. The others turned their heads in his direction but never quit chanting, never lost sync. The heat in the room continued to rise, and Lucky began to wonder if maybe he wasn't a little overdressed. Then the room started spinning, and everywhere he looked there was a kink in his vision. The contents of the room appeared rooted to a sharp crease in the center of his eye. To make matters worse, what was above the crease didn't necessarily match up with what was underneath.

Delilah squinted and rocked back on her heels. She put a hand to the forehead of her mask and asked, "Jesus fuck…what was in those biscuits?"

"Your eyes all fucked up?" asked Lucky.

"Yeah…something's wrong. *Fuck,* what the hell's going on?"

"I'm burning up," said Jasper.

"Me, too," said Delilah.

"Well, shit, we can't all have hit our heads!" said Lucky. He listed to the right and there started a pounding behind each ear like he'd been struck in the head with a shovel.

"What the fuck are you doing?" asked Delilah, only just noticing what he was up to.

"I can't take it no more," said Lucky, his voice aquiver. "I'm gonna do the fucker."

Jasper rubbed his dome and groaned, "Do the little shit. Do 'em all! They're giving me a fucking headache."

Lucky took a step closer and felt like he was wading in water grass. Everything around him was coming alive and twisting out of proportion, locking him inside a sweaty fever dream. He had grown hotter yet and his shooting arm began to shake, making him think he might actually miss the boy if he didn't get right up on him.

He took another step towards his target and rested the tip of the barrel on the boy's nose. "Shut the fuck up!" he screamed. He knew the kid's family could see what he was about to do, but not one of them would oblige. "Y'all don't cut out that racket, I'll kill him—I swear it!"

The place went quiet save a warm wind whistling in from the hall.

In Kenny's alternate universe, time stood still. A storm approached, turning the midday sky gunmetal grey. With it, the cartoon animals returned, no longer angry as before. They circled him, sniffed him, and ran up and down his legs. The birds above screeched verses of chaos over shivering leaves, while back on the ground a legion of old-souled creatures gave him audience. Kenny scanned the assembled and saw reflections of his face staring back at him. He was here and he was there, in the fixed eyes of those on their backs exposing their viscera and those that stood obediently on hind legs, entrails dangling. From out of the horizon appeared new armies of four-legged familiars, blanketing the soil with fur, feathers and skin. Shells scraped, claws scratched and teeth gnashed in a chorus of sin, sorrow and death.

Goaded by this black song of freedom, Kenny rose from his chair and showed his hands. In them sat the rat, its eyes like burning pebbles of coal, its mouth busy with the feral language of the earth.

In all that heat, Lucky froze. Later, in a world of hurt, he would think back to how it all went to hell and wouldn't for love nor liquor figure out how the boy got loose. He would struggle with accepting the rat had chewed through the twine, knowing it couldn't be. There simply hadn't been enough time for it to happen.

He would learn later how Jasper had inadvertently covered the boy's wrists in soap while tying him up. It had worked itself into the knot and the boy knew a small truth from soaping up screws to put them where they didn't belong: as easy as they went in, so too they came out. All you needed was a strong, flexible wrist to do it. If you were looking for one—the kid would say—you could do worse than calling on him.

Lucky stared down the droop of his barrel and watched the boy remove the shirt from his head and drop it to the floor. Then he looked straight into his eyes and they gave the con a twitch. It wasn't the lack of fear in those dark orbs that shook him; it was the lack of anything at all. Emptier than a shark's eyes, they were, and worse than Delilah's mask for guessing as to what deviousness they was working on. The boy stared back as if daring him to shoot, but Lucky's trigger finger wouldn't budge. Could have been his arm was numb and nothing south of his elbow was working right. He was afraid to think it was because he didn't have the guts. Whatever it was, the boy must have gotten bored because he walked off into the darkness without so much as a "fuck you".

Lucky knew he couldn't leave it this way. He tried leading the little bastard as he walked, but if he had managed to hit him it would've been by dumb luck. His arm was so tired and his legs so heavy, the best he could hope for was to stay on his feet.

"Go get him, asshole," said Delilah.

Unwilling to suffer back-to-back humiliations, Lucky feigned a confident posture and stepped into the adjacent unknown. He wouldn't miss the heat and trickery of the previous room, but he would miss the boy untying his family and removing their makeshift masks. In fact, the boy would later explain how they all missed it—Delilah and Jasper, too. Lucky realized they would never get those seconds back, but then again they hadn't really been there for them in the first place.

⛤⛤⛤⛤

Delilah got to her feet and immediately fell over. She was fortunate to get a hand to the table, which was lucky and not so. It had held her, but she had gotten a palm full of bean dip for her trouble. "Shit, fuck, piss," she said, wiping it onto her skirt. It was a far cry from the "eat, fuck, kill" she had originally planned for the evening.

The remaining three family members sat in their chairs, eyes unblinking as they watched her fall apart. Their expressions were hard and stiff, like an anesthetizing layer of frost, yet Delilah refused to acknowledge the irony. With half her mind on keeping her balance and the other half on Jasper still hunched at her feet, her brain was already plenty busy.

There was a time in her life when even her own family looked at her that way: detached, objective, removed. Her father had been a famous surgeon before his stroke, after which she and her mother had shared duties caring for him. If that wasn't challenging enough, there were her two children to look after. Most would say kids are a blessed chore, but fraternal twins diagnosed with fetal alcohol syndrome conspire to steal every ounce of youth from a pretty young girl with an I.Q. of 190. At the tender age of sixteen, she had had enough and then some.

She made a call. It was supposed to be simple: *the door will be unlocked, so just come in and get them and don't ever contact me again.* Some people will do anything for a few bucks. It hadn't even broken her to close the deal, leaving her with enough change for gas money and new shoes. Unfortunately, just like the night she had gone into that parking lot with the drummer of a local band and gotten herself pregnant, the idea hadn't gone down as planned.

Little did she know, her mother had herself made plans to be rid of their patient before his hard-earned fortune was completely absorbed by medical bills. Dr. Boris Van Vleet couldn't do shit by himself—well, shit was the only thing he could do—and she had seen it in his eyes that he wanted out. Delilah guessed she had labored over the decision, trying to decide if what she thought she understood was indeed what he had in mind. So when her mother drove to the lake that morning as she did every morning—a place her husband often visited and where she would push him around until it was time for his first cleaning—Delilah believed she only meant to drive around the block and return. He wouldn't have put up any kind of fuss when she placed the plastic bag over his head, reassuring his wife she had guessed correctly. All that was left to do at that point was go home and explain how he had passed doing what he loved most, sweetly and quietly, with the ducks at his feet.

But when Delilah's mother arrived home, she would find a strange young man in head-to-toe sweat clothes exiting the front door with her grandsons in his arms. When questioned, the man would hand her the boys and take off running. Seconds later, Delilah would see her distraught mother calling the police from her cell phone.

Wasting no time, Delilah jumped into the car and engaged in hot pursuit, never once noticing her father, several minutes deceased, sat up and sagging in the back seat. She was determined to find the man who had taken her money. Things had gone wrong, and while it wasn't anyone's fault per se, as things stood if the police managed to apprehend her accomplice based on her mother's testimony, Delilah would have plenty to answer for.

About a quarter mile up the road, she would check the rearview mirror and see her father gazing back in her direction. He would have that same, far away fix he always had when he was tired.

"Don't worry, daddy," she told him, "I'll get you back in time for—"

A pair of observations struck her dumb. Her parents had returned too soon, and her mother had left her father in the car. When she took the next turn a little too sharply, her father slumped over on his side.

She wiped the tears from her eyes and focused on the road ahead. Then she saw him. He was laboring to unlock the driver's side door of a Volkswagen Jetta parked facing her on the opposite side of the street. She pressed her foot on the gas pedal and the car lurched forward, growling like a charging bear. He saw her just as his door came open, and hurriedly retrieved a 12-gauge shotgun from the front seat. He pumped it once and turned it on her.

Delilah steered straight into his aim.

The collision was loud, bloody and devastating. By the time the ambulance arrived, they had several pieces of John Doe to collect and one very hysterical young lady.

Later, the report would read the gun had blown a hole straight through the air bag. It and the windshield had reduced the velocity of the lead shot just enough to save the young woman's life. Her injuries, it read, were extensive, but largely superficial. The man in the back had been killed on impact, according to the same report.

Delilah reached for the gun on the table but somehow the father beat her to it. He had done so with such nonchalance, one might have thought he was going for another sip of wine. As far as she was concerned, the only way he could have gotten there first was by reading her mind and perfectly timing his attempt. As she watched him examine the weapon with mild interest, Delilah concluded she could no longer trust her interpretation of the events transpiring around her.

As if to test her conclusion, the daughter rose from her chair and approached with intent. Delilah's vision was still way off—like peeking through a flushing goldfish bowl—so it wasn't until the girl was very close that she could see she was sort of pretty—just as she had been not so long ago.

The girl stood toe-to-toe with her, and Delilah noticed they were the same height with almost identically matching figures. She was her opposite, however, in one very important respect: she was all face and no eyes.

The girl asked, "How old are you?"

"Twenty-one," said Delilah, before adding, "Almost."

"I'll give you 'til twenty-two, bitch, and then I'm coming for your soul."

Delilah kept her response to herself, stepped back and helped Jasper to his feet.

He said, "This…this ain't—"

"Shhh, let's go."

"Did they get done?" asked Jasper, finally upright. His speech was thick and slow and as heavy as the past.

"No," she replied, watching the girl count quietly under her breath. "We did."

She spun him slowly and nudged him towards the hall. When she looked back, all three family members were on their feet. The father had the barrel of the shotgun down the front of his pants, the stock end pointing up and bowing forward with the hairy pot of his belly. His wife stood proudly beside him in her bloodstained brassiere, one of her hands resting coolly on the wood. It wasn't clear who had put the gun where it rested.

Delilah squeezed the knife into the palm of her hand, and with a mother's touch guided Jasper from the room. Before they could completely disappear into the shelter of darkness she heard the girl say, "Eight...nine..."

CHAPTER 8
Hide and Go Freak

Barbara examined her husband's eyes in loving detail. The intruders had recoiled in horror when locked into his deep blues, but to her they were as they had always been: equal parts inquisitive and adjudicating with perhaps a touch more twinkle.

He reached out and touched the bloodstain on her breast, and she held his hand to the spot. They stood that way for a long breath before melting into a passionate, filthy kiss. It was difficult for Barbara to stay on his lips with the gun poking against her chin, but she couldn't deny its effect on her desire.

Ken Sr. pulled away: "Honey…about what I said earlier on the stairs—"

Barbara grabbed his hand and squeezed her breast.

"Later," she ordered.

"Okay," he said.

They kissed again, their hands covering every inch of

bared skin between them. Ken's weapon by birth achieved full girth, and Barbara could feel it seeking her out. They were improper, inappropriate, and as far as she was concerned, a bloody, gorgeous mess.

"Twenty-two," said Amanda, still eyeballing the spot where the girl and the lummox last stood. "Now, if you'll excuse me, dear parents, I've still got some what fucking thou wilt to do."

"Wait," said Barbara. Something in the fire had caught her eye: the map remained unharmed. As remarkable as that was, it was actually something else that had caused her to hold Amanda up.

She hurried to the fireplace for a closer look. There appeared to be something very tiny and very alive walking across a portion of the stitched detail, but she couldn't make out what it was. In fact, it wasn't just one tiny thing but several, crawling from place to place as if looking for a secret stitch by which to escape.

With her husband and daughter looking on, she reached into the flames. The fire was hot but inexplicably bearable, and she feared no burn. As if withdrawing eggs from a nest, she removed the map and placed it on the table. It smoked a bit, but remained in perfect condition. Only the "bugs", or whatever they were, continued to mark its face.

Amanda leaned in and followed them with her finger. "What are they?" she asked.

"I don't know," said Barbara, peering more closely. "They seem to be shadows of some kind."

Ken Sr. put his hand on the gun and said, "It's them—it's those bastards. They came in here to torture, rape and kill us and now they're looking for a way out."

Barbara immediately saw he was right. "We mustn't let them get away," she said, her voice a pleasant shrill. "It wouldn't be right."

"Can I...?" gasped Amanda.

Barbara offered her husband a few capricious bats of her eyes. "Darling?" she asked, as if inquiring about a new puppy.

Ken Sr. snorted and pulled the gun from his pants. "Grab the map, the lamps and let's go. Stick close, and keep a lookout for Kenny. If he's anything like his old man, he's due a good at bat." He cocked the gun, but a shell was already in the chamber. He shrugged and said, "And if he is—dammit, I'd like to be there."

⛤⛤⛤⛤

Lucky stubbed his toe and fired the gun into the floor. Stupid. He hadn't checked to see how many bullets were left, and realized he might have blown his chance to end this whole clusterfuck the easy way.

Fucking kids.

He went to dig the penlight from his pocket, but decided against it for the same reason Delilah had earlier: to keep his exact position a secret. By the smattering of ambient light at his disposal, he tried to determine just how big that old house was. He had continued straight ahead after leaving the den some minutes ago, and as far as he could tell he was still in the same room. One thing about the dark settled his nerves a bit: creased vision was no longer a problem. He didn't know why his eyes had turned against him back in the room with the fire. If Delilah hadn't complained of a similar affliction he would have thought it was the speed playing tricks on his brain.

Things had just started getting interesting, when—

A noise. Like the sound of a door creaking open. The little fucker was hiding somewhere and was clearly set on making Lucky feel around for him. He had a gun and about a hundred pounds on his quarry, so it made no real sense for the idea to scare him like it did. It was just those eyes—he tried not to picture them, but the more he tried, the more he did. Just thinking the boy could be watching him pimpled his skin. And now he imagined himself sinking underwater, further and further into the blackness, vulnerable to the vicious eating machine the piss-soaked rascal had earlier brought to mind.

"Listen, *pendejo*—"

He stopped himself. Maybe some good old southern sugar was in order? Like that time back in Mexico when he was cornered by those three *putas* he had paid in play money. He was fixing to hightail it before they got a good look, only somewhere in the joining of passion he'd forgotten about the razor wire fence. After a double helping of charm they halved the price—a pinch on his *pito* his only regret.

He started again: "Listen, boy…I reckon we're in kind of a stalemate here, so why don't you and I just sit down and figure this out? We were just playing in there, you know…and okay, things got a little rough. But you know how that is, don't you?"

There was another sound, like something heavy being dragged across the floor. Lucky thought of turning back but he wasn't about to tell Delilah he'd been spooked by a little moving furniture.

"I'm sure you crossed the line once or twice in your life and felt bad about it, right? And what did you do? You said you were sorry and you meant it. Well, Phineas Francisco

Lawn ain't above saying he's sorry. Ain't none of them back there above it, neither."

There it was again. Dragging. He stopped and pointed the gun to where he thought the sound was coming from.

Then he had a thought. There was another reason he hadn't gone digging for his penlight, he just failed to identify it at the time. In a moment of highly regrettable irony, he had hung it on the light switch in the fireplace room when he put down his pick. He was so eager to get his hands on the girl, that in his haste to free them he had effectively handicapped himself. He was often amused by how the sleazy side of his brain liked to put him in a spot. He hoped now wouldn't be one of those times, but he was probably already too late.

Click.

With the sound came a handful of sun in his eyes. As quick as it came, it was gone. He fired the gun towards the fireworks floating mid-air and heard the bullet hit glass. Flash blindness giving way to peripheral vision, something flew towards his face. *Sweet Chocolate Jesus,* it had a face of its own with crazy, white eyes.

His head rocked and an explosion of pain engulfed everything above his neck. A second later, his vision shut down, cutting short any hope of an introduction.

⛤⛤⛤⛤

Jasper held tightly to Delilah's hand, using it to keep his balance. His leg was still bleeding and he dragged it behind him like a sack of spuds. In his mind he cursed a steady stream until the words blended into a single, colossal expression of frustration. He couldn't believe how fast things had turned.

Last thing he remembered, he was carving out a prize-winning fire ant when the damned thing went flying from his hand like an ornery pickerel. Caught up in the excitement of the moment, he quickly reached for it and knocked his stupid head on the table. Say it again: *stupid-ass sonofabitch knocked his motherfucking ass out reaching for some motherfucking soap.*

In all his time in prison, he never caught the business end of nothing reaching for no dropped soap and he'd done it plenty of times. If this was what they called "suffering for your art", Jasper was more than ready to take up something else. As he slung his dead leg back to front, he thought about what that might be.

Delilah had been there to witness his stupidity but never once laughed or yelled. Instead, she took her eye off what she was up to and went straight to him, rubbing on him to make it all better. It was like, no matter what was going on or how much fun she was missing, none of it was as important as how he felt. He'd smelled her hot snatch as she crouched near his head, too. It was like apple pie, rare steak and mother's milk all stuffed into one little box. He never had a mother—he was told she'd moved on and he never asked again—so he didn't know if it might be sick to say so. But he wanted to. He wanted to tell her something fierce.

He did have a dad, once, though. Nicest sonofabitch to ever draw a breath on this planet or any other. Bill Dix—not William, no middle name—worked every single day from his thirteenth birthday—when he went by "Billy"—until his death. It wasn't because his family needed money or he was some kind of Eagle Scout or nothing, the man just loved grass. Not the smoking kind, but the kind that grew out front of a house and sometimes up in the back if there wasn't too much sand and you had some topsoil left over. He liked how it smelled and all the different textures and kinds. He even liked crabgrass. He said it was tougher than weeds and would never vacate the earth, leaving her naked where the sun could crisp her ends. A man's lawn was his first line of defense against the Devil, he said, and it made the street pretty just the same as the houses if both were seen to properly. It also kept wildlife close by, and when you had a sprinkler on, brought a rainbow to your door. Bill said nowhere in the world was worth living that didn't have a nice front yard and a few bushes to set if off. Flowers he could take or leave, but grass—grass was the very glue that kept America together as the greatest country in the world.

By the time Jasper's father was in his late teens, he was cutting everybody's grass in the neighborhood. And as the neighborhood grew, so did his business. Everybody thought of him first, he would say, cause he'd done it forever and tomorrow and that was the way it was. Grass didn't take time off, so he would do a few lawns every day depending on who needed it and they paid him straight after. Cash, of course. He didn't need much, and told Jasper (when he was old enough to help with the hoses) that grass was the color it was cause it was all the money in the world. He'd say, "Look there, Jasper—that ain't no yard, that's Fort Knox." Didn't even matter Jasper didn't know what fort he was talking about. Only mattered it made him happy.

When they were done their day's business, they'd load up the truck and get to one of Jasper's bike races and then pizza after if there was time. Bill told anyone that would listen that his son was a great bike racer, and that he planned for him to carry on the business one day. Jasper could tell it made him proud to say those things. Jasper knew the ins and outs inside out, and thought about one day making a bike track with hedges carved into the funny shapes of all the bugs he'd seen working the lawns. He was scary good with the trimmers, so it wasn't going to be as hard as it sounded. And when he did do it, he thought he would call it Big Bill's Green Heaven after his dad and the grass and everything it did for him.

He would tell Delilah about his dad when he got a chance. Right now, she was looking for the window they came in through, but the house seemed to grow a little since they got there. It didn't look like a regular house anymore. The windows had become too high to reach, and there were lots and lots of doors. If that weren't creepy enough, each one they went into seemed to lead away from the outside. Everything seemed to be a way in somewhere. It was like they were marbles spinning around a funnel, gathering speed towards the hole. *Hellhole*—sure was living up to its name.

Motherfucking soap.

Jasper stopped Delilah and stood on one leg. He said, "Let's rest awhile. They ain't gonna find us. Hell, we can't find us."

She said, "Yeah…okay."

They sat on the floor and inched back into a hollow, hunching up close like two scared peas in a very scary pod. Might have been a table they were under, or a bench. Whatever it was, they just sat there quietly, he not letting go of her hand and she not letting go of his. It wasn't the worst time he'd ever had, even if they were hiding. Or maybe they were lying in wait—he didn't quite know. At least they weren't boiling alive back in the room with the fire and the map that wouldn't burn. Things had cooled, and he thought about a drink.

Then he thought about how he shouldn't have given his

father that last beer. If he hadn't, maybe the old man wouldn't have fallen asleep. Maybe they'd still be in that house watching TV and eating pretzels, surrounded by Jasper's bike racing trophies. Maybe they would start talking again about how the BMX circuit was going to make him famous one day, and all the good-looking girls that would be hanging around. If he hadn't gave him that last Bud Light, maybe that stinking Pall Mall wouldn't have dropped from his hand and melted all their dreams away.

They saw that fire clear across town and halfway into the next, according to the nuns at the home. They felt bad, the nuns said. Then they told him to pray on it and Jasper did—day and night until he finally slept—but nothing good ever came from it. At the time them nuns were the only things on earth he hated more than himself. Now, he just hated everything.

Except Delilah. No matter how well he covered himself up, she saw past it. She saw past his bad deeds, rotten seeds, and wicked needs. That's how he knew they would make a plan to get out, and another to keep going. They would be the first real plans he'd made since the last ones all went up in smoke. Didn't even matter that she had no face. Neither did he, when he thought about it.

No sooner had the thought of smoke entered his mind, Jasper smelled a bitter one. He looked into the murk and saw three candles heading in their direction; nope, they weren't candles, they were lamps like the one that little bitch had, like the ones at the hardware store back home—or what used to be home before prison. They weaved from side to side, and Jasper imagined a lazy formation of drowsy UFOs. Each time their positions shifted they would give something away in the room, throwing its long shadow against everything else. Jasper could see the place was big, with high walls and endless rafters that continued out of sight. It was like a big old barn filled with all the junk in the world, or one of them shops that sold old things—things with memories that would eventually fade until they were just "things" again. Things with nothing left to be remembered for.

Jasper needed to come up with a way to defeat the family that now threatened him and his girl, but he couldn't quit thinking about turning that hose on his daddy's house until it melted in his little boy hands. When they brought him back the next day, they wouldn't let him out of the car. All he could see through his singed eyelashes was a pile of smoldering wood, and a small patch of grass that quickly turned to mud.

⛤⛤⛤⛤

Reverse engineering is defined as the process of discovering the technological principles of a device, object or system through analysis of its structure, function and operation. It often involves taking something apart—a mechanical device, electronic component, or software program—and analyzing its workings in detail, usually to make a new device or program that does the same thing without copying anything from the original.

No matter how many times the kid explained it, it still didn't make no sense to Lucky. Neither did the sight of that little statue standing near the table he was strapped to. First thing he saw when he come to was the last thing he saw before he went out: a pair of wide, milky eyes staring out of a shiny, chocolate brown face. He thought his vision had been knocked inside out like one of them picture negatives. The kid said people call it a "lawn jockey", which sounded like an effort to disgrace Phineas' family name—"Phineas", at this point, more fitting a persona than the one Jasper had given him. The kid went on to say something about George Washington, a surprise attack, and some fool nigger holding a lamp so he could find his way home. Before he got to the part about how the first thirteen winners of the Kentucky Derby were black, Phineas' skull really started to pound.

A quick count came to four oil lamps spaced evenly around his head. He could see them in a shard of mirror the kid was holding—one he said the bullet got instead of him. When he turned it, Phineas saw a reflection of his swelled up face. Nothing important got busted, the kid said, but his right cheekbone was shattered and probably real tender to the touch. He showed him by poking it a few times.

He said, "I could try and fix it, Mister. I've got a few loose screws." Then he laughed a coyote's laugh.

"Fuck you," barked Phineas. He tried to make himself like a dog in the street, threatening to bite anything that dared come close, but the kid just laughed and went back to his box of tools. Every few minutes he would return and shine a penlight into Phineas' eyes before using it to inspect the wound.

Phineas was dumb enough to ask, "What the fuck you think you are…some kind of doctor?"

The kid replied, "I'm not interested in medicine."

"So what the fuck *are* you interested in?" He tried to sit up out of habit and his vision went white with a pain that thumped his head onto the oak.

"I told you," he said, "reverse engineering. My old man builds stuff and I want to learn how to rebuild it and make it better. Follow in his footsteps, kind of. Show him he can be proud of me."

"Can't imagine nobody being proud of no kid who'd tie a man down after knocking him out with no nigger statue," said Phineas. The pain was pissing him off.

"I told you that, too," said the kid. "His name's Jocko. Jocko Graves. He was a hero. His lamp shone bright in the dark and he helped George Washington defeat the people who wanted to come and take over. You heard of the British, right?"

"You mean like the Beatles?" asked Phineas.

The kid didn't answer. He just went about removing a pair of needle-nose pliers from the toolbox and moving the penlight over Phineas' face.

"Now, hold super still," he said, "otherwise, the screws might not go in right and I'll have to take them out and start over."

With that, he began adjusting the pieces of cheekbone with the pliers. Phineas tried to turn away but the kid had all the leverage and held his head in place.

"Don't you fucking come near me with them things," said Phineas, his eyes wider than Jocko's. "You do, I swear I'll take you apart."

"Take you apart..." said the kid, and flicked his tongue up and down like an excited lizard, "now that's what I'm talking about."

He placed the penlight between his teeth and grabbed what looked like a serrated kitchen knife from the table. He returned the pliers to Phineas' cheek and looked into his watering eyes.

"I got my dad's gun back, dude," he said. "Don't make me put you under."

Delilah watched her pursuers draw closer. She couldn't understand why they didn't just let them leave. It was pretty obvious she and the boys had deserted their original agenda. You don't chase the people that were torturing you once you managed by some freakish miracle to get free. And you sure didn't do it in your underwear.

The real problem was the psychos had her gun. There were at the most two shells in the chamber, but she knew better than anyone a single shell could do the trick. Normally, dipshit families like this one were easy to confuse, and at first they had been. Like helpless lambs they had offered their necks quietly and allowed themselves to be wrapped up for Christmas dinner.

Then something changed. She refused to accept it had anything to do with the nonsense they were mumbling, but she couldn't deny the palpable shift in reality. It wasn't just she who had felt it. The half-breed had all but flaked to queer dust, and Jasper—he'd been a little clumsy, is all. Still, she clearly remembered the air turning thicker than a Virginia country ham, and just as suddenly, her vision going all bifocal. Before she knew it, she was being hunted by a family of spastics in Fruit of the Loom elastics.

As vulnerable as they were, it felt good to have Jasper near her. He really did have a sweet bone or two in him, but she couldn't let that turn her into some kind of teenybopper dork. She had written off romance long ago and for good reason. In fact, the more she thought about it, the more she understood why she had never had any use for it to start. Men were useless. To wit, most would consider Jasper's hulking presence to be a valuable asset. But he was confused and bleeding out, and if her senses hadn't completely vacated her, he was as shit-scared as she was.

She heard soft footsteps approaching and calculated the best time to hold her breath. If she chose wisely, she could keep herself stone-still until they moved out of range. Any hopes of Jasper doing the same, however, were cruelly dashed when he started babbling under his breath. He was too weak and in too much shock to manage what she had in mind, so it was pointless to try and communicate her idea. Prison: the place makes you hard, but it also makes you soft in ways you might not expect. Having someone tell you what to do and provide three squares a day may not be the best training for thinking on your feet in an unpredictable combat situation.

According to the shadows creeping over her toes, it was time to vanish. She held Jasper's nose and pressed the lips of her mask against his mouth. To be extra sure, she worked her tongue through the slot and slipped it between his teeth. That stopped the babbling, and for both of them, the breathing. She would have lifted her mask first, but she feared the movement would give her away. She was also afraid that, with the darkness all but excusing her deformity, kissing him without a barrier might work a tremble from her heart.

Delilah tensed her body as they passed, and waited a few seconds more before breaking her tongue lock. She slowly pulled out of the kiss, and put her hand over Jasper's mouth until she was certain the family was gone. Only then did it occur to her covering his mouth might have been the other, more simple solution to her dilemma. Refusing to explore any embarrassing implications, she said, "Shhh…not a word or I'm doing it again."

He shrugged.

Before she could warm to the gesture, she said, "We have to get out of here. *Now.*"

More than just a wriggle from a spell of romantic whimsy, she knew her words to be true. As deceptively big as the house was, it wasn't infinite, and something about these people made her think they'd be sniffed out all too soon.

CHAPTER 9

Bonding Sessions

AARRRRGGGGHHHHH!"

Phineas had barely caught his breath before the evil shark-boy went back into his cheek with the pliers. It felt like he was pouring molten lava into his face and scooping it out with a spade. He'd rigged the penlight around his head like some kind of coal-mining accountant, which explained why Phineas had forgotten to take it with him; it hadn't been there to take. The kid must have swiped it during those lost minutes. It was working for him, too, because no amount of screaming prevented him from getting lost in his work.

There was no telling how badly he was being butchered. Screw after screw was added, and with each one the kid looked less convinced. It was like he was working on a model airplane without the instructions. Phineas prayed for one of the other members of the family to show up just to see what their sawed-off little fucknut was up to.

"Crap…it's worse than I thought," sighed the kid.

"Jesus, just quit it, okay? I need a real doctor, now."

"I told you I'm not a doctor! I'm an engineer."

"Engineers drive trains, you stupid moron!"

His quip broke the kid's concentration and he peered into Phineas' eyes. Them holes he was blinking seemed driven right back through his skull and straight into outer space. The evil was like nothing he had ever experienced in his long, miserable life and it made him miss home. He would give his best boots and all the change in his pocket to be back at his old man's garage. He'd straighten up, too. No more stealing. Fixing cars was honest work, and he was just getting handsome. *Life's a scorpion's tail.*

The kid started rooting around in a bucket. It sounded like he was putting the Tin Man through a wood chipper and it made Phineas crazy nervous. "Hey…you know, I used to work on cars," he said. "Engines, brakes, electrical—all of it."

The rooting stopped.

"All kinds, too. One time, we had this souped-up chopper roll in. It had one wheel in the front—"

"No shit."

"Right, right. But the best part was the guy had it rigged up to a sofa."

"A sofa?"

"Hell, yeah! Purple velvet upholstery, all this fancy, ornate woodwork—I'm telling you, it was a sight."

"How'd they keep the sofa from catching fire?"

"They epoxied the damn thing and welded it under the cushions with just enough room for the air to cool it. And either side they had these two big tractor-trailer tires."

"What about the exhaust pipes?"

"Shoot, they had them stuck out the back like cannons on a fucking pirate ship. Must've been thirty of them."

"Thirty, huh?"

"I'm telling you, you ain't never seen nothing like it. Roared like a T-Rex, ran like a Rolls. Spotless, too. Not a mark on her that I could see." Phineas could feel the blood caking on his face and figured he had stopped bleeding. His vision had sharpened a little, too. Best of all, his gab was coming back.

"You said it was epoxied?" asked the kid.

"Uh-huh. With expert precision."

"You mean like a circuit board in a radio—what they use to keep everything together and in one place?"

"Sure, I guess. It's like plastic, but it don't burn for some reason."

"Uh-huh."

The kid was thinking. Normally, that was a good sign, but not with this kid. The silence started in on his nerves.

"What? What's the matter?" He was just about to tell him about the two half-naked chicks sitting either side of the guy on the sofa but the kid was clearly getting ideas of his own.

"I gotta go look for something," he said. "It should only take a second."

"Let me help! I promise I'll be good—one engineer to another. Four eyes are twice as good as two in a place like this."

"That's okay, I know where it is," said the kid. "I think I saw it in the van."

"What do you mean? What's in the van?"

"Bondo."

With that, he ran off; penlight bouncing like a comet on crack. The kid had an idea, all right. He was going to put body putty in Lucky's face.

When he did it a few minutes later, Phineas tried to imagine what was hotter than lava. All he could think about was the sun, and how he wished he could see it or nothing at all.

⛤⛤⛤⛤

Delilah tugged at Jasper's tourniquet until she heard a moan. He had been complaining about shortness of breath, and every once in awhile he would whisper something about grass. It could be he was starting to hallucinate from blood loss and dehydration. If she could find some water she might be able to bring him around. If not, he might do something stupid and they would both end up like Lucky.

She could hear the lover boy's screams. They echoed off the walls and shook the fake glass baubles that hung from a nearby lampshade. Jasper tried yelling back—calling him "Phineas" for reasons he had not yet shared—forcing her to place a hand over his mouth. As much as she was taking to him, she had to consider the possibility of taking him out. It wouldn't be easy, but he was weak and she would only have to ask nicely for the knife. She still had a functioning head, and more importantly, the presence of mind to preserve it.

She knew they were alone in the room and pretty sure as to the way they came in. Retracing their steps should get them back to the den. If she remembered right, there was a kitchen directly next to it. Where there's a kitchen, there's usually a sink with a running tap and a kitchen window. If she could get Jasper hydrated and through the window, there was a chance he could clear them a path to the car. They would have to hurry, though. If all went according to plan, there would be more than just a family of vengeful freaks licking at their heels; the heat would most definitely be on.

Lucky passed again through her mind. For anyone to be doing whatever they were doing to him probably meant he was trapped. That must have been the worst part for him. When she first saw the Mexi-mix with the funky moustache she thought he was sexy in a leering, perverted uncle kind of way. She had detected more than a hint of vanity and had used it against him from the start. Still, the few hours spent with him driving up to Hellhole weren't all that bad in relative terms. He knew what lay behind the mask and yet she could taste the testosterone bubbling up from his nuts whenever she sent a whiff in his direction. She could tell he thought he might get some. His dick—just like every dick she ever met—fooled him into thinking it was he and not the pussy that was in control. Lucky was all surface, like any one of those fiberglass monstrosities they passed along the way to Hellhole. Which meant if those gurgling wails she could hear were any indication, what she was planning to do was really doing him a favor.

With a mighty heave, she got Jasper to his feet and right away he knocked over a stack of serving trays. Delilah held her breath and dug her nails into his shoulder. The crash was loud enough to hear all the way back to the car but she didn't see any lamplight heading their direction. By fortune or fate, the wind died down, and in its place came the din of murmuring voices. They were chanting again. She couldn't determine where it was coming from as it seemed to be coming from everywhere, which wasn't a surprise in a house so full of odd surfaces. Maybe they were having a little family reunion over Lucky's twitching corpse? He had touched the girl in a sexual way and meant to shoot the boy, so it would be natural if most of their anger were concentrated in his direction.

Delilah pictured them holding hands and singing, and supposed they could probably do with a little campfire to complete the scene. If she could get Jasper back to the den without drawing their attention, she would be more than happy to oblige.

Jasper emitted a faint whimper and she withdrew her claws from his flesh. She hadn't realized she was hurting him—that she could hurt him. If somewhere in the back of her mind she was punishing him for bringing them to this place, then a part of him clearly thought he deserved it. He'd been warned, after all, and in saying it repeatedly—*Hellhole, Hellhole, Hellhole*—he'd warned them, too.

"I'm sorry, Delilah," said Jasper.

Delilah clicked on her penlight and saw Jasper's sad eyes peeking out from under a very swollen forehead. His pupils were dilated, and she watched with genuine pity as he rubbed them like a small child.

"Nobody forced me to come along," she said. "Actually, I forced you. Now shut up, stay low and don't knock anything else over. I'm gonna find us a way out of here."

"You're leaving me?"

"I don't have a choice." It couldn't have been more the truth. It was in her nature to abandon the helpless. She had already done it to two children, what was one more?

She reached into his front pocket and pulled out his penlight. It may have looked to the casual observer like she was hanging him out to dry, but in truth she meant to help him. No light meant less to give him away.

"I promise I'll be back," she said.

"What about Phineas?"

"You mean Lucky?"

"His name's Phineas. I called him Lucky 'cause—never mind. Thought having him around would help."

Delilah had wondered how a person in prison could be named Lucky, although he was such a piece of work she wouldn't have blinked if it were written on his birth certificate. One thing was for sure and it flew out of her mouth: "Remind me never to listen to your stupid ass ever again. You hear me?"

He nodded and she stroked his hangdog expression. The stubble there felt wrong on a full-grown man who had become more of a large toddler. Whatever that family had done to them, it was possible his head injury had left him more susceptible to its effects. But if she was ever going to make it out of there, she had to leave him to his own devices no matter how regressed they had become. Regardless of what she might have wanted to believe about the possibility of a future with him, he was of little more use than a steak thrown in the corner of a lion's cage. Forget the tattoos, he had "dead meat" written all over him.

She lifted her mask, held his chin and pressed her mangled lips against his mouth. As expected, he didn't flinch or recoil. On the contrary, he relaxed his cheek into her palm like a dozy Great Dane and wept. *Damn it,* she thought. She might actually miss him, now.

⛤⛤⛤⛤

If he were subject to the review of a panel of plastic surgeons, Kenny would not have been surprised to hear he'd done a reasonably competent job. Once the prodigious amount of swelling had been drained around the carefully reconstructed cheekbone, his patient's face had regained its flattering symmetry. After that, it was a simple matter of replacing the skin flap and gluing it within as rigorous a tolerance as possible. A few swipes with a damp rag and he had to wonder if the man was right: maybe medicine was in his future? The boy felt a wave of accomplishment unlike any he had ever experienced before. If only his father had been there.

He checked the man's pulse. Weak. He had come in and out with such regularity that time must have held very little meaning for him. The thought prompted Kenny to shine his light onto the far wall. Among an array of framed mirrors hung an old-fashioned wall clock. The shiny pendulum reflected his beam, and it felt as if it might start swinging at any moment.

He concentrated on the round face with its hands stuck on the number twelve. It looked as if one of them had fallen off, but as he approached he could see the second hand was neatly tucked behind the hour hand to signify noontime, or the exact beginning of the day; the "witching hour", to be specific. What had his mother said as they climbed the stairs? *Black magic is at its most powerful during the witching hour.* Maybe that was why her chant hadn't worked. At the time it felt closer to seven-thirty.

He focused on the fancy design of the numbers and the intricate tooling of the hands. With a free portion of his brain he thought of his father. The man was practically a stranger. He couldn't think of a single person he knew less and for longer. At the same time, he couldn't think of anyone he loved more. The guy was a winner, as far as Kenny was concerned, and he, sadly, was not. Could be that was changing. Or maybe the work he had done on the man's face was a fluke to be witnessed by no one other than himself—a kind of cap to his growing list of frustrations. No matter how badly he wanted his old man to be proud of him, maybe it was never to be.

"Interesting," said a voice behind him. Kenny turned to see his father holding a lamp near his "patient's" head. It appeared he was examining his face, and not the needlepoint map that was laid on top of the man's stomach.

"Sorry," said Kenny. He had learned to start every conversation the same way, even if he didn't know what he was sorry about. Usually within a matter of seconds he would be given a list of offenses, followed by a reading of his rights.

"Come here, son," said Ken Sr.

Kenny lowered his head and made haste to the foot of his handiwork. "Sorry," he said again.

"Stop saying that, Kenny. You're not in trouble."

"I'm not?"

"No," he replied, still inspecting the face of the man on the table. "What's happened here?"

Kenny told him and left nothing out.

"I saw the Bondo," his father said, his voice rising in interest. "Shattered, you say?"

"Totally," said Kenny.

"Pretty impressive, son."

Kenny put a hand on the man's leg for support. His father was actually impressed with something he did—something of the kind that usually got him grounded and scrubbing oil stains from the garage floor.

"You really think so?" said Kenny.

"As far as I can tell. I'm no surgeon, of course." He walked to the other side of the table, mentioning something about alternating perspectives and how raising and lowering one's viewpoint helped better assess the facial planes. Then he said, "Maybe I should start saving for medical school, huh?"

An explosion of tension burst from the top of Kenny's head like an invisible mushroom cloud. Unable to conceal his glee, he slammed his fist down on the table, accidentally sinking it into his unconscious patient's crotch.

Lucky's world became smothered in an avalanche of pain and he struggled to keep from vomiting. When he finally opened his eyes, he focused on a sight that filled his heart with dread. Over him stood the boy and his father, and they were laughing.

Jesus fucking Christmas, his mind screamed, *they're laughing.*

⛤⛤⛤⛤

The Kens walked side-by-side, Jr. reviewing the map by penlight and Sr. using the gun to sweep aside items reaching in from the shadows. There was a bounce in their step and they cavorted like playground buddies.

"There!" said Kenny, jabbing his finger into the air. He was excited about a wardrobe made of red oak tucked back in a corner like the largest tombstone in a graveyard.

"Can I?" asked Kenny.

Sr. rested his lamp on an old hanging planter and checked the safety on the gun.

"Okay. Go ahead."

Kenny swung open the wardrobe door, using it to shield his body. Inside, slumped amongst a smattering of flattened shoes, was the weary heap of the tattooed man. He tilted his head upward and peeked out from under a giant robin's egg jutting repulsively from his forehead. In his hand was the large Swiss Army knife, one of its blades pointed in their direction.

The man said, "Daddy?"

BLAM!

A flash lit up bits of flesh and skull as they rebounded off the back of the wardrobe. By penlight, Kenny could see other pieces sliding over an unfinished carving in the wood like slugs in a downhill race. Kenny stood fascinated as the concussion of the blast dissipated, with particulate matter sprinkling down through the piles of junk like the last few beads in a rain stick.

When the race was over, he looked in closer and saw that the knife in the man's hand was actually a steel file.

"Huh," said Kenny. "Weird."

"You want him?" Sr. asked. "Might be a project in there somewhere?"

"Nah," said Jr. "I like them alive."

Sr. pulled his son close. He pulled him close like he loved him. He pulled him close like he loved him because he did love him.

⛤⛤⛤⛤

Delilah heard the shot, as did the two crazy bitches mixing eggs in the kitchen. She hoped it would distract them long enough for her to send the whole place back to hell.

She ducked beneath a disintegrating baby grand piano and waited. As expected, she saw two pairs of women's feet stepping casually in lamplight's glow. She refused to move a muscle until her own shallow breathing drowned out their footsteps. It helped that the gun going off did what guns going off often do: silence the world, allowing her to be doubly sure when it was safe to come out.

She assessed her situation: things had gone from weird, to scary, to just plain fucked up. She figured Jasper must have farted or something because there was no way anyone would have found him in the wardrobe so quickly. There were literally hundreds of places to hide in that house.

Maybe she was being hasty assuming he was dead. It was entirely possible the gun had been fired at an errant shadow, or one of the many reflective surfaces mistakenly taken for one of them. She could see how oil lamps played tricks on the eyes, and if these kooks were one-tenth as nervous as she was, it wouldn't be unrealistic to imagine one of them accidentally shooting another. Unfortunately, there was no carrying on to follow and she thought she heard more chanting. It was time to face facts: Jasper had dropped his soap, hit his head, stabbed his own leg, and carelessly created a racket that almost got them both killed. A behavioral pattern existed that defied debate on the matter.

She crept out from under the piano and headed straight for the den. She had planned to enter the kitchen, procure some sort of weapon—a knife, fork or spoon, if necessary—and make a break for a window or door. But so much weirdness occurring in rapid succession has a way of altering one's logic. For example, she could smell something baking—*baking!* It was hard enough to believe a family of squares would pursue three dangerous criminals in a house full of hiding places, but to think they would stop to bake a cake was the kind of information that started one seriously questioning their sanity.

Delilah understood crazy—or so she thought—but clearly it was the other kind; the lawless kicks and wicked violence kind. This downward-spiral-into-the-rabbit-hole shit made no sense to her at all. She and her posse had almost fucking killed these people, for crying out loud. Weren't they scared at all?

Tiptoeing down the hall listening for the slightest noise, she realized the answer to her own question. Most people you can push and they fold like so many lawn chairs. Others had no place to go—not up, nor down, nor left, nor right. They just free-fall inside their heads, breaking rungs down Jacob's Ladder until they smash into midgets on the yellow-brick road. That's why she couldn't take the obvious route. That's why she had to go big or never go home.

She snuck into the den and saw the table had been reset. Possibly more disturbing was how the entire room had been tidied up and decorated. Delilah was pleased to see they had tended to the fire but not bothered to remove the extra pieces of Jasper's rended chair. Also lucky was how the legs were stacked neatly beside the fireplace next to a lighter that stood upright on the brick facade.

Delilah tore a thick strip from the top of one of her knee socks and tied it tightly around the end of a chair leg. Next, she used her palm to secure the metal tip of the lighter on the edge of the brick mantle, and struck down on the plastic end with her foot. The tip separated and she soaked her sock with the unshed fluid. She could have yanked some burning wood from the fire and strewn it about the room, but she didn't want to cook her own goose in there with them. She would bring some fire with her to use, but only when the time was right. It might be necessary to go head-to-head with one of these loons, and in terms of potential destruction, even if she did find a knife it was no match for a torch and certainly nowhere near the bargaining tool.

With a shaking hand, she dipped the sock end of the leg into the fire and it caught with a reassuring whoosh. She recalled more than one monster in her youth fearing flames, and hoped these monsters would prove the same.

She left the room and found the kitchen. There, she saw a cake pan on a wood-burning stove, and in it the ingredients for a chocolate cake. As she absently savored its aroma, she heard the chants once more. The combination made her drowsy and she nearly dropped the torch—which would have been disastrous at this stage. She shook her head to regain her senses and made a dart for the kitchen door. She grabbed the knob and it seared into her palm, causing her to pull away and press the hot flesh onto her skirt. There was no logical reason for what had happened, which was plenty reason enough. She tried using her skirt to turn it, but the heat was still too great. If she had the time, she might have been able to wet a towel or find an oven mitt. But as things stood, the door would play no part in her escape.

The chanting grew louder, their arrival, imminent. She had no choice but to stay put and bargain. Fearing the torch alone would fail to sway them, she snatched a metal spatula peeking out from a forest of water bottles that covered the kitchen counter. The ridiculous arsenal hardly spelled fear.

The mother and daughter entered the kitchen side by side, spewing their secret language. Delilah grew terrified for just the second time in her life. Only this time she wasn't prepared to lose anything important.

"Stop right there," said Delilah, waving the torch and stabbing with the spatula. "I mean it." She knew doing anything useful with the wide, dull blade was highly unlikely, but she would have to keep up the charade.

They continued chanting for a few seconds and then stopped at exactly the same time. Their matching dirty aprons and messy bun hairdos added a bizarre domestic touch to their flat, all-business expressions. And like two den mothers hopped up on hash brownies, their heavy-lidded stares bore into her.

"Here's the deal," Delilah continued, "you let me open this door and get the fuck out of here—I don't ruin your tea party." She had zero scientific proof they had anything to do with the scalding knob, but ever since she gave up on reality it had been a hell of a lot easier to communicate.

The women smiled in perfect synchronization and their expressions warmed to genuine amusement. The mother's lips, still swollen from Delilah's vicious strikes, spread grotesquely across her face before finishing in wicked serifs; she was the Queen of Hearts, The Cheshire Cat and The Mad Hatter all in one.

The daughter turned to her mother as if awaiting permission. The mother faced her, nodded, and looked back to Delilah. Then the daughter walked to the door, paused for effect, and continued straight past Delilah toward the sink. It could have been she was going for a knife that had gone unseen. In a kitchen that size full of so much crap, there were surely several lying about. But that was her old brain thinking again. When she saw the daughter pick up what looked like a Betty Crocker hacksaw, she silently scolded herself for assuming anything.

"What the hell is that?" asked Delilah.

"It's a cake leveler," said the girl, sawing in the air. "It's for cutting off the top of a cake. This one's super sharp, see?" She gave the teeth a tap with the tip of her finger.

"I don't give a fuck what it is," said Delilah, "just keep you and it away from me."

The girl frowned a big, doll's frown. "Tsk…that wasn't very nice, was it?"

"Just open the door or there'll be no cake for any— " Delilah was too busy laying down the law to notice the mother had snuck up beside her. When she finally did see her, the woman smacked the spatula from her hand as if it were a bag of pot she was about to sell her daughter. Then, as nonchalantly as the father had taken the gun from the table, she doused the torch with a measuring cup full of water and placed the empty container on the counter. Delilah's shock wore off just in time for her to see her charred sock dripping into a puddle on the floor. By that time she had neither a chance to make a break for freedom, nor the desire.

⛤⛤⛤⛤

Delilah sat on the mantle in front of the fireplace surrounded by the entire family. On the table was a cake decorated with a pentagram. She watched the daughter light the candles using a tiny branch, before reducing the flame to a fine tendril of smoke with a single blow. Her mother gushed proudly about how she had hoped baking a cake would allow the two of them some quality one-on-one time, but had no idea it would work out so well.

The men laughed. Arm in arm, they laughed. They laughed the same way they laughed when the father had pointed the gun at her and asked if she wanted a "shot". It was an awful joke and they knew it. The kid didn't even get it, but that only made them laugh harder.

The mother pushed her chair in front of Delilah, smoothed out her apron and sat down. Her expression made it very clear she would not be tolerating any more games, and Delilah had no intention of testing her.

"I want to know," the mother said, her voice a layer of black icing, "were you always going to kill us? After torturing us, I mean?

"I don't know," Delilah answered honestly. "Probably."

"Why?"

Delilah made a choice to match the woman's level of sophistication. As brutal as her words might sound, she might lessen their impact by adding a touch of delicacy to her tone. It was her only chance.

"The idea appealed," said Delilah. "Maybe the thought of killing you—and the men raping you and your daughter, certainly—made us feel powerful and free. Perhaps it also made us feel superior—which you have to admit, for two convicts and a young woman without a face, is a pretty attractive notion. I think I speak for the others, as well, when I say there was no small degree of sexual satisfaction to be derived from your torture. Weird, now that I hear it out loud."

"Very weird," said the woman. "Especially since you seem like an intelligent girl. What on earth would make you take it this far?"

Delilah sensed she was genuinely curious. "We were just riding the rush," she confessed. "You know, enjoying what came. We never really discussed the details of what we wanted to happen. Thing is—and from the looks of all of you I assume you'll understand—we don't always know why we do the things we do, do we?"

The woman leaned back and lifted a hand to her cheek as if startled by Delilah's candor.

"No, I guess we don't," she said.

"The important thing is that we do them, isn't it? No regrets."

"Listen to our hearts," the woman offered with a hint of wonder.

"Listen to our hearts," said Delilah, and she thought of Jasper and the babies she gave away. She thought about the people she had shot at the funny place with the fake town. Then she thought about what she would have done if she had managed to escape, and had to be honest with herself—she probably would have turned around and come back. She could imagine standing in the driveway looking longingly at the house, working on a way to get back in. There was nothing left for her at home and she was through hiding. It was probably why she hadn't made any trouble when they frosted the cake right in front of her.

The truth, as incomprehensible as it may have been to normal people and why here it made perfect sense, was she wanted to see what they would do. This family interested her more than anything had in a long time and she was curious as to how it would all turn out. It was the most ambitious thing she could think to do with the rest of her life, as sad as that may have seemed. In the "zero sum" game she and her friends had begun, there was only ever going to be one winner. Now that it was over, she found herself growing anxious. And just as they had been repeating the moment the wheels came off the trolley, she wanted them to do whatever they were going to do and she wanted them to do it now.

"Listen to our hearts," the woman said again, only this time meaning every word.

"Can I?" asked the kid.

"Sure," said his dad.

The boy broke away and removed Delilah's mask as if he were lifting the lid off a shoebox full of champion bullfrogs. All at once, each member of the family inhaled a long breath and held it. Outside, a branch scratched the roof, tickling the moment.

Snapping from her trance, the mother exhaled and spoke: "So...who wants to cut the first piece?"

The daughter held up the cake leveler and said, "I'd better do it—I've had the most practice."

No one said a word as she placed the leveler at the back of Delilah's neck and started sawing. As the teeth ripped into her flesh, Delilah thought of her father's face in the rear view mirror. She was glad he never had to see her like this.

And in a way, she was grateful it was finally over.

CHAPTER 10

On Again, Off Again

Phineas lay there in the smothering blackness like a bored whore under a splayed drunk. And he was fighting a mean itch. It was somewhere behind his right knee, and all he had to deal with it was a clouded and confused mind. Still, all was not lost. He was alive and his predicament had all but cured his troublesome "sleazy brain". No way he'd slobber into any fool traps now. He was as alert as a cat in a fan belt and convinced that returning to his more focused persona would soon see him free. As it happens, a song came into his head talking about "freedom's just another word for nothing left to lose". Phineas couldn't imagine what Kris Kristofferson knew about his being free. The beardy bastard's been a millionaire for a million years and probably didn't know the half of it.

The itch subsided, and then returned with a vengeance. At least it kept him from thinking about his face, which for certain was attracting the kinds of bacteria that would eventually see him pass for Delilah's twin—if he lived that long. He wondered where she'd got off to, and reckoned she'd found a place to tuck in. Somehow that girl always managed to put things on her terms. He liked her well enough, even if she did creep him the hell out. But she had a cool head and a great ass, and if he was right about her survival skills, there stood an outstanding chance she would be there soon enough having at his bindings with that complicated knife she bought for big, dumb Jasper. Come on, D, where you at?

He didn't have to wait long before the room inhaled a faint and dusky light. Picture frames emerged from the void, followed by everything you could imagine that could hold a cobweb. He prayed to God for a woman's voice and he got one.

"Hey there, stud muffin," said the voice.

God, he should have guessed, would be an asshole.

"This seat taken?" asked Luscious. With that she slid up on the table and climbed atop Old Smokey whose fire was well and truly out. She smiled the smile of a hungry cat, licking her lips more than once and looking sexy in the way a lady vampire looks right before she gnaws out your jugular. Phineas thought he would sweeten her up with some compliments, but reckoned it would be best to put it another way.

"Hey there, Luscious—change of heart?" He thought it best to come right out and address the issue of his previous indiscretions. The elephant in the room had not only been identified, it was filled with peanuts and filthy with acrobats.

"Not really," she said, sounding a little indifferent, "but I did want to talk to you."

He could tell she was wearing some kind of apron, and lifted his head to see as much of it as possible. Unfortunately, what he saw confirmed his fears. He thought he'd smelled metal when he heard her voice. Having had a look for himself, he now knew she was covered in blood.

"See…my family's eating cake in the other room," she said. "I tried to join them, but after what I did to your girlfriend, I kind of lost my appetite."

"Now, now…she weren't my girlfriend. You know you're the only one for me."

"You mean it?" pouted Luscious.

"Of course I do, Lu—you know what? I don't even know your real name."

She opened her mouth in mock amusement before saying, "Amanda Jean. Drop the Jean, though, okay?"

"Well, Amanda dropped Jean, I can tell you with flat-out certainty that I have eyes for no other woman but you. And I'll tell you something else—you let me go, I promise to help you and your family clean up any messes we might have managed about the property. We can get to sprucing this place right up."

"Really? You'd do all that for us?"

"It'd be my pleasure, Amanda. Free of charge, of course."

She pressed her bottom into his groin and a wicked wind blew a dirty chord through his organ. She must've felt it, too, cause she started doing something that made Phineas think of a hen covering her eggs. Not only did it make him forget about the ache in his face, the itch behind his knee was gone and a new one had started up inside his nut sack. It was no less frustrating, but about a hundred times more welcome.

She leaned down and whispered, "So, what's *your* name?"

"I, *amor mio,* am Phineas—all the way down and all day long." He realized he was out of his mind from a cocktail of lust and pain, and now she was working on his fly. *Holy Harry S. Truman,* it felt better than sliding buck-naked down a stick of butter.

"Do you have a name for it?" she asked.

"It?" asked Lucky. "Oh, *it*. Well, in prison it was known as "off-limits". But when I was a boy I called it Rascal after a rattlesnake that hung around the station."

"Rascal, huh? Mmm, I like that." She worked her way down his legs and teased the serpent to the surface. "Say, Phineas...you ever seen one of these?"

She let out an inch of wick in her oil lamp and showed Phineas a tool that went by a name he could only guess. It looked a lot like what he really wished it didn't. Last time he saw one it was in an old comedy about a jailbreak. One of the prisoner's accomplices was sawing the window bars in an attempt to spring him. Unfortunately, there was only one thing un-sprung at the moment and that prisoner wanted no parts of any break.

"Aww shit, Amanda...what the hell you doing with that?"

She laughed and said, "It's a cake leveler, lover. You know what it's for?"

"I'm going to say leveling cake, baby. Cake and only cake." A wave of nausea crashed in his guts.

"Tell that to Marie Antoinette," she said, suddenly serious.

"Who?" Phineas waited for an answer but Amanda wasn't listening. She just laid the blade of the leveler onto old Rascal's neck and seated it into the flesh with a wiggle.

"Marie Antoine, *who*?" he asked, this time with pure fear.

"Your ex, you fucking prick. Not sure what you did to her, but it's not exactly something a little makeup can fix, now is it?

"Hell, honey—I don't have a clue what you're talking about?"

"I have an ex, too, so I kind of understand. And if it's any consolation, I wish it was him on this table right now instead of you."

"Amanda, I'm telling you the truth. She ain't never been my girlfriend and weren't never going to be. You got to believe me!"

"All men lie," she said with chilling certainty, "especially about lying. My ex did it all the time."

"I'm nothing like your ex-boyfriend, I swear!"

"Tsk...silly. You don't even know him."

"Well, unless he's an ex-con with a face full of putty and a heart full of regret, I don't need to."

"Just hold still, now."

"Amanda, please...*nooooo!*"

Amanda gripped the saw tightly and pictured Eldren kissing his new girl, his pudgy fingers stuffing her with promises of apple pie and picket fences. *Fuck him,* she thought, *he's her problem now.*

She pressed down and the world erupted into a grand cacophony of madness. Every item in the room—in every room—blared to life. Lights flashed on and off, hands of clocks spun wildly, and toys began wailing and whirring as if possessed by the ghosts of abused children. It was every bit the chaos that big old house and everything in it could manage.

The sudden, violent intrusion caused every muscle in Amanda's body to cramp at once, knocking her off the table and onto the floor. The oil lamp, kicked by her heel, followed her down and drowned under a splash of its own blood.

Just like the brain inside her head.

⛤⛤⛤⛤

Just like the circle on the attic door.

⛤⛤⛤⛤

"Let there be light."

When he had hit the switch on the generator, it had roared to life just as he had planned almost seven years ago. With an enormous amount of pride he listened as the joyful noise filled the interior of the house. The angels had sent their army, their trumpets calling all warriors. To be heralded this way was an honor: not only would he lead his men into battle against a despicable evil, but that evil's power would be severely weakened by the summoning of His bold orchestra.

The time had come for it to end.

⛤⛤⛤⛤

Louis P. Odekirk tucked a thin hat strap under his bottom lip and stood at attention in front of the mirror. It had been a very long time since he had worn the hat for any real purpose, and it reminded him how incomplete he felt without it. Like any good warrior he needed to be topped-off appropriately: the quarterback and his helmet; the soldier and his green beret; the saint and his halo.

He had been all three.

All other insignia and accoutrements had been stripped, but he had convinced them to let him keep his hat. He promised he would never wear it in public, and after recalling twenty-five years of dedicated service that once saw him save a fawn from an iced-over pond to the delight of several television networks, they gave in. For seven years he had kept that promise. Tonight—tonight he simply could not.

Alone in his office, he could hear the half-dozen delinquent boys (ranging in age from fourteen to seventeen) chattering in the next room. They were excited to be in the middle of God's country, crammed inside a real log cabin and out of sight of their respective guardians. The cabin wasn't one of those prefab models the Amish were peddling, either—not that anything was wrong with them—but this one had been built with his own hands. It had taken him the better part of three years to complete it. It wasn't big or all that attractive, but it had been constructed in the glory of His name. To call it a "church" would be stretching the term. But like a church, they had gathered under its roof to praise the Lord Father in the way of the truly devoted: through deeds, not words. If he were to call upon his military background in the Special Forces, he might call it "command headquarters" from which all and sundry would be implemented in an effort to weaken the enemy. The details of these operations comprised the other half of the chatter he was hearing. His troops—rookie drug-abusers and destructive juveniles who had slipped through the system—were eager to act on their training, and more importantly, their hearts.

He opened the door and stepped into the light. The boys immediately dropped to their butts and gawked slack-jawed at his size thirteen boots, following them all the way to the top of his six-foot, four-inch frame. Humbly they looked upon him like one might any natural wonder, and he wasn't surprised.

Having had their hair shorn to shoe-buffering length only a few days prior, it was obvious they were still self-conscious about the way they looked. Odekirk had lost much of his hair already, so taking it down the rest of the way had been a liberating experience. He felt invigorated, virile—*reborn*. He was already in top condition from climbing the trails that snaked up and down the snowy slopes of the mountain, and the boys he had chosen over the last year—those healthy and hungry for combat—were of sturdy build and impressionable stock.

Blessed as such, Odekirk made the best use of them: he took what appeared to be a natural and virulent inclination towards destruction, and channeled it for His divine purposes. His methods would have been considered extreme and severe in the eyes of lesser men, but they had been wildly successful. He had assembled a powerful and deadly congregation, and they had accepted him as their commander and patriarch. So when he entered that room, he could feel a potent energy shift reverently in his direction. As trained, they remained sat and solemn on the floor, waiting for his divine words of wisdom.

"Thank you, gentlemen," he began. "Tonight we'll skip communal prayer and allow our private thoughts to guide His mercy. First, let me say I'm proud of all of you and I think you know that. I've asked a lot—long nights of grueling physical and spiritual training, all in secret—and now I've taken your hair. Why? Well, that answer lies in who we are, doesn't it? And who are we? Who are the Bible Skins of Lake Wallenpaupack?"

One of the taller boys—only fifteen but shooting up like a stubborn weed—unraveled a wiry arm into the air. Joshua was among the youngest, but he had seen the most violence from the time he was a baby. As a result, Odekirk had to be harder on him than the others, but his diligence had paid off. The boy was a lethal killing machine with a cool head, and like a select few of the others, his name had been changed to reflect his considerable skill.

"That's alright, Joshua," said Odekirk, "we all know the answer. I just ask it aloud so you'll remember. Warriors of Christ, defenders of the covenant, destroyers of evil—that's who we are. And tonight I ask you to join me as we embark on a mission delivered directly unto me by our Supreme Commander. I won't sugar-coat it, boys—it will be dangerous. We will face a great and dangerous evil tonight. Some of you will be tested in ways you've never been tested in your young and sinful lives. But I guarantee this to all of you for it has been visited upon me in my darkest hours: that which we sacrifice in His name will be rewarded back to us tenfold. At least. Probably more."

The boys nodded and cast their large eyes to the ground. The earlier excitement surrounding the mystery of the task was slowly giving way to fear of the unknown. Odekirk needed to address it, and quickly.

He directed his words to a young, chubby boy seated in front: "You need not fear God's love, son. When the Lord looks upon you it's like having a tower of strength built inside your belly." He gave the boy a rub on the soft protrusion that stretched the bright blue fabric of his New York Giants sweatshirt. "He knows you risk your life for him and he loves you to death for it. Now, I don't mean "death" in *that* way. Well, okay, possibly I do, but we don't have it to fear if we stick together and watch out for each other."

He adjusted the chin-strap that had slipped over his mouth.

"Listen, boys...I know how you're feeling. I've felt like that myself, many a time. Every time I approached that house of wickedness to check in on that detestable old battle-ax I said to myself, 'I may never return—am I okay with that?' And you know what? At first, I didn't know. Truth is, I wasn't sure. But each time I faced that woman and her windows-to-the-bowels-of-eternal-suffering eyes, I grew stronger. And it became clearer and clearer to me what I needed to do. Forget what they said down at the station and on TV. Forget their decision to retire me from the force. If they couldn't see she needed to be sent back into the pit of damnation from whence she slithered, then let God deal with them on His own accord."

He paced, shaking off the indignation. "Did I lay my hands on her? Yes, I suppose I did. Once or twice at most, but it was because I was *brave*—not cowardly as the papers would have you believe. Did I scare her into the forest so she might one day succumb to His will without the protection of her infernal grotto and all its soul-devouring power? Of course I did. But it was because I trusted my faith, and took it upon myself to serve Him without regard for my own welfare, praise His name. I faced the darkness, and in doing so I dissolved my fear into fear dust. It fell from me like the hair fell from your heads only a few days ago. And like your hair, upon the floor it lay until I vacuumed it up and dumped it out the door." He pointed for emphasis and said, "That door, right there. And you will do the same because it's right. Right?"

The boys nodded.

Odekirk repeated himself: "Right?"

The boys answered together: "Right!"

"Alright, settle down," said Odekirk. "I need to bear witness. You see...I saw it today—the glow of hellfire. Now, don't get excited, I've been waiting for it. It's why I built this cabin in which you sit. I had a job to finish. I knew evil would return to descend upon our town, our families, our pets and so forth—so I took it upon myself to erect this temple in His name. They thought I was crazy, but you've seen it—every last one of you has seen what I've seen. Before your salvation by my hands, you saw those fires burning into your pathetic lives and you wanted to extinguish them as much as I did. You gathered together the burdens of this world—a world, mind you, that refused to understand your gifts—and placed them on your broken backs. At first you didn't understand what you were doing, so you lied. You lied to your parents, to your brothers and sisters, and you lied to each other. You told them, 'I'm going to Nehemiah's house to watch The Lord of the Rings,' or 'Josh just got an Xbox,' or 'Zabdiel needs a hand with his rabbit cage'—"

"Ferret," said Zabdiel.

Odekirk squatted down beside him and said, "They're all God's creatures, son. The point is you lied to exact revenge against those burdens sinful society has forced you to bear. And maybe there were times when it felt wrong, but I'll tell you..." he stood again and addressed the room, "sometimes what's right feels wrong when you look at it with small eyes. But His right—capital 'R'—never feels that way. No sir, His right is the truth—capital 'T'. And tonight, gentleman, we shall set that truth free. And do you know why?"

The boys lifted their heads to him and waited.

"Because of who we are. And who are we?"

Together, they said, "The Bible Skins of Lake Wallenpaupack."

"I'm sorry, who?"

"The Bible Skins of Lake Wallenpaupack!"

"Don't tell me, you little sons-of-bitches, tell Him."

"THE BIBLE SKINS OF LAKE WALLENPAUPACK."

"Well, then—let's get off our idle butts and go do His work."

The Skins grabbed their flashlights and popped to their feet, their hearts filled with a hunger to kill for the man who had saved them.

PART THREE

AUTOMATIC

CHAPTER 11
Express Purposes

The faces of the Ducharmes in the den were covered in chocolate cake when the sound and light bomb went off. Kenny had only just completed another assault on the pentagram frosting, his middle finger stuck in his mouth well past the second knuckle. He was lucky not to have bitten it off.

His father leapt to his feet and grabbed the gun. He pointed it at an old, plastic radio spitting deafening static between a pair of gnome bookends, and Kenny thought he might shoot. Then he noticed the table shaking and saw that his mother had both palms pressed tightly to the surface as if to keep it from floating to the ceiling. She was terrified. They all were. It was time to do something.

He stood quickly and said, "Dad!"

"I'm thinking!" his father shouted.

Kenny sat back down and wiped his frosting-covered hands on his pants.

"The radio," said his father, "turn it off."

Kenny jumped up and ran. As he passed the entrance to the next room, he looked in. As far as he could see there were lamps shining, lights blinking and mechanical parts flipping, flapping, opening, closing and just about every other act of purposeful motion known to modern engineering.

Something near the ceiling caught his eye, stopping him in his tracks: a toy train was chugging away over the exposed beams letting off puffs of grey smoke as it went. Someone had placed it up high where it couldn't be reached. *Why would someone do that?*

"Kenny, now!" screamed his father. Kenny ran the rest of the way to the radio and pulled the plug. When he looked back to the table, his parents were running in opposite directions.

Barbara arrived at the kitchen sink to see water sputtering from the spout in fat, green globs. It was a bowel-clearing sound that always managed to startle her when it happened at home, and this time it was deafening. The old house was coughing to life, and the pained wails of the resurrected plumbing brought to mind a giant mummy awakening from a centuries-long coma.

With a twist of both handles, she closed the faucet and a familiar horror propelled itself into the base of her brain: she was losing control of the situation. Even more terrifying was that the situation in question had yet to be clearly defined. Just a few hours ago she and her family were facing a slow and agonizing demise filled with protracted periods of sheer terror, and somehow she had found the strength to turn things around. Surely, it had something to do with their attackers placing them all together in a single room. Without realizing it, the fools had stacked the deck against themselves. When the chanting began, it was only a matter of time before the scales tipped in their direction.

Now they were scattered, doing what they could to quell the tumult that had erupted around them. She hoped to once again billow the fiery source of their influence, but she was unable to rouse her will while occupied with the tasks at hand. She needed to make things quiet again. Once they were, she needed her spouse and brood around her focusing every ounce of concentration on fanning the family flames. But as the water dripped its last, rancid efforts into the bottom of the drain, its sulphuric assault on her senses doused her confidence all the more.

Barbara noticed her bra becoming heavy and wondered if she was losing her strength. A quick look down brought her around; she had grabbed her husband's gun and stuffed it between her breasts as if it were a small bill she'd spotted on the supermarket floor. A few minutes ago, any accompanying innuendo would have sent a repeating round of electrical charges straight into her crotch. Now, the gun's existence presented just one more opportunity for protection, and her soaked panties held nothing more alluring than the salty sweat of nerves.

She drew the pistol from its fleshy holster and inspected the chambers. She counted three bullets, which she hoped would be three more than necessary when the ordeal proved an innocent, electrical misunderstanding. It was still better to be prepared, so she lowered the gun and spun the cylinder until the first bullet was a simple trigger pull from firing. She had always been more educated about firearms than her contemporaries—her father having been a collector with no sons to bestow the proclivity—so it didn't surprise her how easily one fit into her hand. Holding it in front of her now, she felt completely at ease as she pointed it towards the window and trained the iron sight on a waving pinecone.

A bald-headed man popped into view, stealing her balance. His eyes brimmed with malice, and he held a machete dripping with what she hoped was tree sap and pulpy vegetation. As he pushed his face against the glass, the overhead light illuminated the absurd disfigurement, bleaching it inside her reflection.

The air left her lungs. This was a boy no more than fifteen years of age. What stole her breath wasn't his distorted appearance or shocking youth, but how his expression burned with a hate beyond anything she'd ever seen.

He reared back as if to slash through the glass and she pulled the trigger—*click*. She looked at the weapon and realized she had guessed wrong as to where to place the first bullet. The hammer had found an empty chamber but struck a very raw nerve: she had fired at a young boy and meant to kill him. The same thing had nearly happened to her boy only hours ago. At that moment, she realized she needed to stop shaking, start breathing, and find him.

She slammed the gun on the counter and headed out of the kitchen, shutting the light off behind her.

Then she ran back into the dark, picked up the gun, and ran out again.

Ken Sr. guessed they had somehow set off a booby trap. He had seen such crude precautionary measures designed into facilities that had been hastily constructed without proper emergency specifications, and someone in his family—all of them, perhaps—had tripped something unknowingly. It was all too common in his line of work to spend weeks convincing plant managers that cutting corners at the construction phase would be more costly in the long run. What eventually resulted were additions of one kind or another that drained both financial and human resources. Depending on the client's sense of humor, he would explain it like this: as long as there was shit in this world, some of it would eventually find a fan. If you weren't prepared for the inevitable, you should expect to stink pretty bad.

And stink, it did. As he cleared the first floor stairs, he smelled a horrible odor filling the hallways. Upon reaching the second floor he saw a remarkable sight: a bioluminescent mold of some kind was swelling plaster from the ceiling and paneling from the walls. He had never heard of such a thing existing outside of the tropics, but then he remembered the warm wind and wondered if it were somehow connected. There was definitely plenty of water, and much of it was leaking in, bringing with it the stench of rotting earth.

Running now, he passed the upstairs rooms with their flickering bulbs spurring him on like a gauntlet of poltergeists. POK!—one exploded as he passed, showering shards of glass onto his bare torso which stuck to the sweaty mat of his body hair. They itched his back, and he reached behind to slough them off. As he did, his breathing became shallow and thick. He had been allergic to mold as a child, but the condition had passed. His present reaction must have been psychosomatic, as the mold had always been there, he just hadn't seen it. Regardless, his brain felt swollen inside his skull and it evoked in him strange thoughts about the state of reality, and how in a larger sense, it was more what we perceived to be and not necessarily what was. For example, he had always been slightly overweight—something he had grown to accept. Now, alone in that hall, he was beginning to feel self-conscious. Something fundamental had changed.

He looked down at the shotgun in his hands and felt sick. The fact that it could have easily been used to take his life and the lives of his family may have been why. But they had survived. Having done so should have filled him with confidence, however it had the opposite effect. Perhaps because he couldn't recall how they had done it. He couldn't feel at all the sense of control and courage it had required, almost as if it hadn't happened. He was terrified to think they had preserved themselves for an even deadlier challenge.

He reached the bathroom and shut off the pond water that was filling the tub. As its pungent breath pierced his sinuses, it became clear he had made a colossal mistake. He should have never left his family. They should have never split up.

The first of the Skins through the door was Zabdiel. He owned the ferret, and as these things often go, looked a hell of a lot like one. He had a long, lithe torso with powerful, stumpy legs and a sharp, rat face that jutted rudely from a pointy head. He was the first in because he was fastest through the brush, using his machete to clear only what was needed to reach the porch. The others had swung their weapons wildly in a display of pointless demolition, temporarily losing sight of the goal. He may have looked like a common thief, but Zabdiel was so named for a reason: he was the leader of men. His fearlessness commanded respect, and although barely seventeen years old, he had enough scars to claim hitting every branch in the ugly tree. But, as he was fond of saying, "Y'all should have seen the tree".

Zabdiel strutted through the front door like he was just in time for supper, and wasted no time getting in on the action. As per his instructions, he located the room with the overhead train set and waited on the others while keeping an eye out for demon activity. When he had seen the girl on the floor and the man on the table, he held his ground until he was joined by the other two officers in charge of recon: Joshua, two years his junior but taller and very lean; and Nehemiah, quiet, most likely queer, and head of gaming strategy.

All three reported directly to Lieutenant Odekirk, who observed them in secret as they cleared the hot zone. He favored terms like "hot zone" and "recon" for their effective shorthand, but was careful not to associate too closely with actual military procedure. He was smart enough to realize that kids, especially those prone to outbursts of violence and addicted to stimulation, saw everything in terms of a game. Therefore, terms like "recon" that were serviceably structured yet playfully abridged were favored over their more militarized counterparts. He also knew that if he could hone their skill sets in front of a TV, they would see every challenge as if it was connected to a reset button. In other words, they had been desensitized to reality, including their own mortality. The only thing they knew besides killing was the Lord, and that's exactly how Odekirk wanted it.

When the other two arrived, Odekirk was pleased to see Zabdiel following his orders with laudable precision. He instructed Joshua—so dubbed for his spying and ambushing abilities—to gather "intel" outside all entrances into the room, but to avoid venturing too far. He was then to direct the other warriors entering from various points around the house to what would now be considered "base command." Zabdiel went on to say that, while Joshua was busy carrying out his duties, he and Nehemiah would secure the immediate perimeter and question both the girl and the man on the table. In the event of incidental enemy contact, either with non-combatants or full-fledged, fire-breathing hellcats, all were to be met with moderate prejudice until further orders. The information to be acquired from live targets could prove immensely valuable to the cause, so it was best to engage any and all opposition with intelligence and caution. However, if met with extreme hostility of any kind, they were to act swiftly and depose the threat without mercy—save His, naturally.

Odekirk backed out of his observation point and felt his face blush. Zabdiel—bless his deformed and demented soul—had sounded exactly like him.

With Joshua now deployed, Zabdiel made his way to the girl and saw she was unconscious. He also noticed her skirt hiked above her waist revealing a generous portion of succulent thigh. After instructing Nehemiah to turn his head, Zabdiel steadied his hand and returned her to a modest state. A Wallenpaupack Skin was trained to adhere to the laws of propriety and decency, but it wasn't always easy. She was a looker, by God, and his hand was so close to her—he couldn't think of it. He said a small prayer of contrition and turned his attention to the man on the table.

At first, it looked to Zabdiel as if someone had dripped paint onto his face. But when he spoke, thanking them elegantly and profusely, it became obvious something wasn't right. Nehemiah wasn't leery in the least, and assured the Mexican-looking heathen that everything was fine. But something about that man's face made Zabdiel suspicious. His cheek went lumpy as he talked about the girl and how she had tied him there against his will, and Zabdiel wondered how a petite female like the one at his feet could get the drop on a male of any size. And then there was the matter of his dick hanging out of his pants. It was enough to make the hardest of God's warriors throw up into his mouth.

Had Odekirk not entered at that very moment, straightening his hat and chewing his tongue, Zabdiel would have started to worry about spells. From his training he could tell they had walked in on some kind of demonic sex ritual for which most witchcraft was notorious. But seeing Lt. Odekirk calmed him down. A man like that—one who had dedicated his entire life to fighting the forces of evil—would be able to detect the slightest of witchy vibrations were there any about. And if there were, there would have been orders to commence a second jam operation. As it was, Odekirk looked confident and relaxed, and began yanking plugs on anything making noise. He wouldn't have done that if they needed the jam, so Zabdiel knew all the commotion and light had done its job just like Odekirk said it would.

"Get that man to his feet," said Odekirk, lifting the arm of an old record player that had been scraping its needle against a stone turntable. He followed with a hit of the power switch, and said, "And get him some water."

Zabdiel removed the canteen from his belt and unscrewed the tin cap. By that time, Nehemiah had cut the man's bindings and had him halfway sitting up. Zabdiel tipped the vessel and watched the water spill down the man's chin, still thinking something rotten had yet to be revealed. He wanted to ask a few more questions before releasing him, but now that Odekirk was calling the shots, he would have to accept that he knew what he was doing and there would be plenty of time for questions at the trial.

Amanda regained consciousness in time to see her brother walking among the wooden beams that crisscrossed high overhead. He looked like he was waiting for a train. Then she realized he was.

What the fuck?

She sat up and saw two boys approximately her brother's age freeing the man who had captured her, kissed her, and at last, ended up beneath her prepared for the worst. Eager for an explanation as to who they were and what had happened, she opened her mouth to ask for one but immediately held her tongue. Something told her to look back to the ceiling, where she saw Kenny put his finger to his lips. Thinking better than to argue, she gave him a nod and her view was obstructed by the long face of a middle-aged man wearing a funny hat. She recognized it to be that of a mounted policeman like the one from a cartoon she had seen as a child. If these people were the police, she hoped they were about to cuff the bastard they were now helping so carefully to his feet.

"Morning, hellcat," said the man, managing to smile and frown at the same time.

"Watch him," said Amanda, pointing to Phineas who adopted a lopsided smirk.

"Oh, we're watching him, alright. Looks like the Lord interrupted your sinister plans."

"My sinister what?" She reached for a sore spot on her head and found a lump. After testing it for blood, she rubbed it to work out the soreness and work in some meaning to his words.

"Who the hell are you?" she asked, her voice straining from disbelief.

The man straightened his back and inhaled sharply before exhaling a foul-smelling tempest into her face.

"Hell?" he howled, misting her with black coffee and bile. "Hell don't want nuthin' to do with me, you insolent little maggot! Hell *fears* me."

With that, he grabbed her hair and, giving no quarter, pulled her to her feet.

Ken Sr. took the steps to the first floor more quickly than he should have. The stairwell was dark enough to put you sailing onto your head if you weren't careful, and he'd had to catch himself more than once with the rail. Dangerous or not, he didn't have much of a choice. There were still a few bells and whistles in the house that needed silencing, and he needed it done before the last of his nerves frayed like cutoff denim cuffs.

He reached the final step, carefully slid his foot onto the first floor, and drove a hand into the face of a small person that had to be his son. The push sent the boy backward and it sounded like he and something metal he might have been carrying hit the floor.

"Kenny, you okay?" There was no answer. Still clutching the rail, he waited anxiously for his eyes to adjust and listened for an auditory clue. He squinted knowing full well it wouldn't help, but it was one of those things you couldn't help but do—like feeling the gun in his hand and hoping he wouldn't have to use it.

He could stand the silence no longer. "Who's there?" he asked. His reply came in the form of a cold point in the center of his chest that only just broke the skin. Being that his head was already occupied with the image of his son, he didn't even think to raise the gun.

"I found one!" screamed a young stranger's voice. "He's a fat one, too!"

The last time Barbara saw her husband, he was running down the very same hall she was in now. If she were correct, it would lead to a back stairway that led to the second floor. She wanted to run there too, but thought it best to check the gun and make absolutely sure she had it set correctly. She didn't want a repeat of what had happened in the kitchen. Or did she? If she kept the first bullet a few clicks short, there was less of a chance she would fire on impulse. It had been a single boy—albeit, one armed with a large knife, but a boy nonetheless. Regardless of his intentions, he was no match for an adult with a gun, even one as rattled as she was.

She heard a young male voice call out and instantly picked up the pace. It hadn't sounded at all like her son, but her maternal instincts had kicked into overdrive. Thoughts swirled like soapsuds in a drain: why hadn't they locked the—*pah, like doors mattered.* Her husband was right: real protection requires twenty-four hour vigilance. It was why he was so clueless about his family: he was too busy keeping them safe so they could work out their problems on their own. Anyway, if the voice she'd heard did belong to her son, the three of them might have enough power to level the ship.

Her internal sonar told her the cry had come from around the corner ahead. In a few seconds she would find out just how good her remaining senses were. Regardless, she decided they were sound enough to risk setting the bullet to fire first time—where it would kill, if necessary—and picked up her stride.

She reached the corner and saw the faint image of her husband seated at the bottom of the stairs. The shotgun lay by his side and a large knife was pointed at his chest. It looked exactly like the one she'd seen through the kitchen window.

She held the gun with two hands and searched for a target in the dark. Frustration mounting, she asked, "Ken, who's with you?"

"It's a boy, honey. I thought he was Kenny, but he's not."

"He's got a knife pointed at your chest, baby." The words dripped from her lips like water from a crazy straw.

"Yeah, I know. But I can't shoot."

Barbara pulled back the hammer of the gun and heard it click into place. "Step away, or I will," she said, each word charged with deadly intent.

But she couldn't shoot, either.

⛤⛤⛤⛤

Marcus Mayberry dried his palms on the football helmet on his sweatshirt and tried in vain to keep from grinning. He just bagged two witches, both armed, with nothing but a machete. They had heard the Lord in his voice, no doubt, and it brought them to their knees—or in this case, their butts. Joshua, Zabdiel and Nehemiah were finally going to have to recognize that he deserved a special name, too. No more calling him Blueberry. If respect were skee-ball tickets, he'd earned enough for a top-of-the-line super soaker and was ready to cash in. He'd looked straight down the barrel of a gun twice—no, three times—and didn't flinch once. There had to be a character in the Bible who had done something like that, someone who had stared death in the face and doubled up laughing. If there were, Lt. Odekirk would know him. Yep, he was bound for glory—finally.

The lady witch had run to her warlock husband and cried evil tears on his shoulder.It looked as if she'd lost the strength to hold her gun, but she was still able to take the bullets out and throw them away like the fat one did. They didn't go very far, although it was too dark in that part of the house to see, which was exactly why he'd picked it. He had come in through an open basement window, and not once had he felt scared. In fact, once these two were squared away, he might come back for that ammo. Then he'd really be the man.

He heard footsteps running down the stairway and shouted the code, "Skin to win!"

"Alrighty, Almighty!" answered two voices, and seconds later two boys came into view. The Ackermann twins were exactly the same, but different. Which is to say they looked alike, but Richard had gotten into a fight that left him with a milky eye and Carl was missing the thumb and first two fingers of his right hand. He had gotten a short fuse on some cheap fireworks and the stupid things had gone off before he could throw them out the school bus window. "Spare Parts" is what Odekirk called them. They were both fifteen, with white-blond peach fuzz that barely covered all the scars on their scalps.

"Where the heck you been?" asked Marcus, trying to sound bossy.

Carl said, "We couldn't find a way in so we had to climb a tree to one of the upstairs windows." Then he pointed to the people on the bottom stair with the remaining two fingers of his hand. "They're almost naked!"

"I know," said Marcus. It wasn't a big deal.

"I thought you said you only got one?"

"She came in later, so I got her, too."

"Hella, Blueberry, that's awesome!" said Richard, leaping over the two prisoners. He turned his head like a toucan and focused his good eye on the catch.

"I know it's awesome," said Marcus. "And quit calling me Blueberry."

"What should we call you?" asked Carl.

"How 'bout my name, asshole? Until I get a better one, anyway."

"Easy, Marcus," said Carl. "We got names, too."

"Boys, listen to me," the woman said, "where are your parents? You don't think they want you doing this, do you?"

Marcus pointed his knife at her and said, "Shut up or I'll cut out your tongue."

"Yeah, shut up, witch," echoed Carl, still behind her.

"Watch your mouth, boy," said the man.

Carl leaped a high arc over the couple and slid to a stop. He pulled a pair of nunchucks from his waistband and zipped through a five second routine that became a whizzing blur in the low light. He finished in a threatening stance and thrust out his knobby jaw.

The man let out a big sigh and said, "Why don't you put those down, son, before you hurt someone?"

Carl dropped the nunchucks and held out his hands like the talons of a slightly crippled eagle. "Each finger's named after one of the seven sins, mister. And unless you and the harpy here want to know what they are first hand, don't you ever call me 'son' again."

Kenny crouched behind the central support beam and observed his parents being led into the room. They were seated at the table where he worked on the man, and it felt like days had passed since he'd fixed his broken face. There he was, sitting opposite his family like he was ready to deal them a hand of cards.

He was thankful his parents and sister were still alive, but wondered why they hadn't used the guns. Whatever the reason, the kids had them now. All that was left was the pickaxe in the den, and the Swiss Army knife he'd taken off the dead guy in the closet. Not exactly a formidable defense.

It might have had something to do with the fact that he was practically invisible, but he wasn't the least bit scared. His family was, though. Their posture was slumped and defeated, recoiling when the tall man spoke. And the way that creep had abused Amanda—yanking her around by the hair and shoving her to the ground—succeeded in upsetting her but only managed to piss him off. It took a lot of effort not to jump down and stab him until he apologized.

The group introduced themselves, and Kenny was happy to learn the train was "too much trouble to disconnect". That meant it was unlikely they would bother looking up again. This allowed him to work out how many of them there were, and what each of them was carrying. He could also plot a course to a space on a far wall that looked connected to the ceiling rafters of an adjacent room. If he could make it there without being seen, he might be able to help. A few common household items could be used to fashion a simple weapon like a wrist rocket or a dart gun. Still, the odds of winning a one-man assault with anything less than an Uzi were stacked higher than the furniture.

Just how he and his family had been overtaken again was a mystery. He figured someone must have switched on the generator, which he might be able to switch off if he could get to it. However, he couldn't see it granting them much of an advantage. Things went off by accident in the dark all the time, and he was already invisible, so there was little to be gained by adding any more confusion to the situation. Besides, there was nothing stopping them from switching it back on unless he destroyed it, itself more work than it was worth. They were also equipped with flashlights, so the only side that would be at a disadvantage from a destroyed generator would be the wrong side.

As far as he could tell, there were only two other options he could try. One of them was to get into the attic and see if there was anything there—laughing gas, a golem, maybe an army of zombie squirrels—that could get them out of this mess. The other was equally hopeless, but he might have no other choice.

One thing was for certain: he didn't have time to sit on his perch and wonder why he and his family were once again being put to the test. As he watched the tall man scream in his mother's face while the others held machetes to her throat, all Kenny could afford to think about was how to regain the power they once had. The answers may be waiting behind the door that wouldn't budge, or they may lie in one other place. As quickly as he needed them, he would also have to take his time. One mistake, and any possibility of putting his family back together could be lost.

Carefully coordinating his arms and legs, he spidered from beam to beam, working hard to stay silent. As difficult as it was to choose such a dangerous mission, and despite being one tiny slip from doom, he was grateful he had the choice. He had learned that tonight. He could choose whatever he wanted, and if he wanted it badly enough, he could have it be so. Right now, what he wanted more than anything was to make it safely across a central, lateral beam that passed against a tower that was once an old bedroom set. It was a straight shot, requiring approximately twenty feet of amateur acrobatics. If he could do it without being seen, he saw another straightforward path to the opening.

He waited for the tall man to resume yelling, and hugged his way around an intersecting upright. Minding the several layers of dust that coated the beam, he began crawling, keeping his center of gravity as low as possible. The idea not to spill any dust would have been a great one if it had been possible. Every time a hand or a foot set down, a clump of the stuff went hailing onto the scene below. When one of them nearly landed on a kid with a messed up eye, he knew he couldn't stop. It was hand over hand and foot over foot, dust trailing below in a curtain of acid rain. Halfway there, he so wanted to stop to see if anyone was watching, but he knew he had to keep moving at all costs.

He couldn't help himself. He held his breath and looked down to see the boy with the messed-up eye looking back. His mouth hung open in bemused wonder as if waiting for him to fall.

That was it; he was caught.

Just as he was about to scramble madly the rest of the way, the boy gazed off into the distance and Kenny instantly realized what was happening. He hadn't been spotted at all. Something else was mesmerizing the boy with its steady chugging and puffs of smoke. It was then that Kenny took notice of a three-inch wide groove in a layer of inch-deep dust that extended the length of the beam.

He was in the path of the train. Now he would have to move quickly before it drew attention to him, or worse, knocked him off, announcing his presence to the entire room with a devastating and humiliating final touch.

He reviewed his movements briefly—*hand over hand, foot over foot*—and got busy. The buzzing of the train grew louder as it cornered behind him and closed in fast. The bedroom set tower was still a good dozen feet away, but he couldn't afford to take them slowly. Hoping the sound of the train would mask his efforts he scurried to the spot, ducked behind a bed-sheeted chair and waited anxiously for shouts of his discovery. The train whizzed past and on to the next stop, but there followed no shouts. Afraid to even blink, he reminded himself that it was his choice to set the moment.

And there, in ghostly secret, he chanted in whispers and willed his moment to come.

The tall man with the stupid hat halted his sermon and looked up behind him to where the boys were staring. He followed as the train coughed a black cloud and turned sharply out of sight. Just as the caboose disappeared, he got two surprise eyefuls of filth.

"Son-of-a-bitch!" he said, scratching at his eyes. "Would you forget the damned train and pay attention?" The boys returned their faces forward, but Barbara could tell they were fighting an insistent urge to laugh. It looked to her like the tall man might put a heel into one of them, but seeing as the boys had calmed quickly, he returned his attention to her.

"I'll ask you again, you foul slut of Satan, where are you hiding the male spawn?" He pushed his hooked nose right into Barbara's face as if the closer he got, the closer he would be to getting an answer.

"I don't know to whom you're referring, sir," she said, letting an air of disrespect linger for a moment or two.

"The name's Odekirk, missy. Lieutenant Louis P. Odekirk, thank you so very frigging much. And that's not what the man with the holes in his face told me."

Ken Sr. spoke up: "I already said I was the one who did that."

Odekirk nodded to the boy with the missing fingers, who then struck Barbara's husband in the hairline with one of his sticks. He bared his rotted teeth as he watched a purple lump rise instantly to the surface.

"Is that how you opened him up before you stuffed his skull full of putty?"

"I'd say I did it with far more skill," said Ken Sr., and got another hit for his trouble, this time in the ribs.

"You do realize that Phineas there will probably lose half his face to infection?"

"I'll what?" asked Phineas.

"It's the least he deserves," said Amanda. Zabdiel had hold of her and squeezed her arm. "Ow!" she snarled. "Watch it, dick."

"That's enough out of all of you," said Odekirk. "Time for me and the boys to convene and decide how to proceed with the trial. We'll need silence so our prayers can escape this den of denigration, and I swear sure as Jesus wore sandals—one peep out of anyone, and judgment will be swift and weighted to excess."

"Judge me all you want," said Barbara, "but you will not touch my children."

"Oh, won't I?" asked Odekirk, leaning in again.

"You have no right," she said, and fought an urge to bite off his beak and spit it back in his eye.

"Oh, you're wrong there, missy," he said. "*Dead* wrong," Barbara saw him look her up and down, and thought he might have hesitated at her bra. *Pig.*

"My right is divine," he continued, "bestowed in me by Him—in *His* name. You'll rot to pieces, if I say. All of you! And trust me, we'll find your boy. His little ass'll be first."

"What about me?" whined Phineas. "What about my face?"

The one called Zabdiel cleared his throat, leaned towards Odekirk, and whispered something behind his hand. Odekirk stabbed him with a look and turned it towards Phineas.

"You need to stay where you are and await further orders," he told him. "We've got a few questions for you, as well."

⛤⛤⛤⛤

The tall man took a long step back, removed his hat, and

ordered the others to join him in prayer. They huddled in a circle, pushing their shaved heads together like a feeding flock of vultures. What struck Kenny the most was how unconcerned they were about those at the table. None of them were tied up, and Kenny wanted so badly to call for them to reassemble and will back control. But it was obvious they hadn't an ounce of strength to move. Even if they had, he knew they wouldn't have gotten far. Those whisker-headed freaks would wrestle them down before they set a single foot outside the room.

There was one above them, however, who felt in complete control. Stepping onto the rafter that would lead him into the next room, he knew he would return and make the shaved ones pay. Inch by inch, he crossed over their prayer huddle knowing in the next few minutes he would be free. He just hoped that one of his father's often repeated adages would hold true, and by the time he decided on a plan of action, the debt he returned to collect preceded any future debts they managed to accrue.

CHAPTER 12
SWINGERS

Kenny peered through a crack in a stained glass window and surveyed the room below. The opening he had crawled through back in the train room hadn't extended into the open air of another room, but instead put him in the hollow of one of the house's wide, sheltering eaves. The light leaking up from a second story window was just enough for him to make his way across the sagging, rotting supports until he found himself in an interior enclosure of a completely different sort.

It was a cramped, circular space hovering over a fancy chandelier in what must have been the formal dining room. The room's design had allowed for a dome of sorts to be suspended above the central dining area two stories below, and various light fixtures had been installed every few feet to shine through the colorful and elaborate shapes. Judging from the direction of the shadows, nothing was plugged in on the ground floor yet most of the bulbs shone brightly from above, leaving the room bathed in a vivid shower of color that splashed across everything like spilled sunset juice.

Pressing his eyelids against the crack, he tried to take in as much of the room as he could. Several massive serving stations surrounded a long, ornately designed wooden table that remained set for the company that never came. Were it not for the obvious signs of age and entropy that covered everything in view, he could easily picture a family and friends gliding in to share a meal. He realized if he wanted to share another meal with his family, the first order of business was to get to the ground.

He used the Swiss Army knife's screwdriver attachment to remove the window, which presented him with a horizontal footlocker's worth of space to squeeze through. The challenge, once he was hanging from the other side, was transferring to the chandelier without falling the twenty-odd feet to the hardwood floor. If he could manage that, he could take the more reasonable drop to the table. Unfortunately, the window's being flush with the low angle of the dome's perimeter meant covering the distance would require a strong push off the wall, as he wouldn't have the height to buy a comfortable amount of hang time. Then there was the problem of the chandelier holding. At the very least, a few seconds of suspension would probably ease his fall even if its long chain did eventually snap. And if it did, he should have a minute or so to hide if the racket alerted one of the baldies. *Piece of cake.*

He stuck his head into the opening, stretched an arm through, and stopped. This was stupid. If he went through headfirst he would end up upside down. He pulled his head back out and hiked his foot through the gap as if he were mounting a small horse. With a few more contortions he squeezed his entire body through and was now hanging above the ground, flush with the wall, his back to the chandelier.

Now he had a new problem: his back to his target meant pushing off and turning en route if he wanted to land on the giant fixture facing the right direction. He had never considered himself an athlete, although to be fair he couldn't say either way. Gym class was easily avoidable, and trying out for school sports never interested him, so there had never been enough opportunity to determine an official amount of athletic prowess. Hanging twenty feet above the ground wouldn't have been his first choice to decide the matter, but his arms were starting to tire and it was now or never.

He worked his feet flat to the wall and took a deep breath. Letting it out slowly he thought of his family suffering at the hands of that horrible, tall man and his disgusting minions. With an angry tense of his thighs, he pushed and let go of the ledge. The twist proved easy, but the relief was short-lived when he saw the chandelier rushing towards him, itself a nest of sharp, decorative barbs that he could not have seen before the jump. The real scare, however, came when he realized he had pushed too hard and was now in danger of clearing the ludicrous light entirely. He needed to stop himself, and fast.

He stuck out his left leg and hooked the chain with his foot. The effect was a sudden arrest of trajectory, sending his upper body swinging down towards the barbs. Instinctively, he reached out, grabbed two handfuls of hooks and held on, keeping his arms straight as possible. The barbs dug into his palms as the chandelier swung to and fro, his foot still hooked around the chain. The pain burned into his hands and urged him to let go, but he refused. So there he swung, a poor man's

Spiderman, feet pointed at the ceiling and head aimed at the table below.

He took a moment to catch his breath then unhooked his foot. The introduction of gravity reversed his position with increasing speed, driving the barbs in deeper. Afraid they would penetrate completely and leave him hanging there forever, he let go. After a short drop, his coccyx bone landed squarely in the center of the spread. The dishes flipped into the air, along with every glass tipping, rolling and shattering on the floor. *And now for my next trick…*

He gritted his teeth as an initial numbing gave way to an incredible pain. It was as if a thousand, hot needles were being pushed into his spine at once, and jiggled around for good measure. He wanted so badly to scream, but instead puffed out his cheeks and swallowed his anguish whole. The last thing he needed was for all his effort to be undone with a girly wail. Luckily, the next few seconds saw the pain disappear and his confidence return. The lack of commotion in the air made him think his lame circus act might have gone unnoticed. Either that, or they were still praying. If they were, he hoped whatever god would be stupid enough to listen was back in his celestial warehouse fucking up the order.

He laid back and lifted his sore butt in the air until further contact with the wood was possible. He would have stayed that way for an hour but he didn't have an hour. In fact, it might already be too late. *Fuck that,* he thought, *time to see if the legs still work.*

He rolled off the table and onto his feet. The needles gave one last stick until one by one they were mercifully withdrawn. Once they were gone, he stood up straight and saw the light from above fall across his body. The lively, colorful patterns filled him with hope, so he followed them with his eyes to the floor, and onward to a tall door in the corner. He didn't even have to open it to know it would put him right where he needed to be.

⛤⛤⛤⛤

Barbara, her husband, their daughter, and the man who had violated her sat scrunched together on an old porch swing. The "Skins", as they referred to themselves, had pried the dusty old thing from a crowd of cluttered furniture and hung it from an overhead beam having decided it would make an ideal "witness stand". It allowed the lieutenant to swing it when he felt he wasn't getting the kind of cooperation he wanted, but the effect, as far as Barbara was concerned, was more comical than intimidating. What she didn't find funny was being pressed up against the man they were calling Phineas. She took solace in knowing it wasn't her daughter being forced to inhale his breath as his broken face sold them up the river. What's worse, whenever she was able to get the three of them to start a low chant, he took it upon himself to alert their captors. It was all the Skins needed to rev them up again.

Once the lieutenant grew tired of pushing them around, he ordered two of his Skins—twins from the looks of their filthy faces—to steady the swing while the others looked on from various perches in the room.

"Mother witch," he said, "tell us again why you're here. What is your evil mission?"

Barbara blew a strand of hair from her eyes and said, "I won't answer any of your ridiculous questions until you call me by *my* name."

"Alright," he said, "tell my Skins what you call yourself. They could use the education. I reckon it's a normal sounding name that makes it easier to blend in with the God-fearing population, so let me guess...Michelle? No, too vibrant and youthful. Dorothy? Nah, she was an innocent one who knew not to stray from the path. Maybe you go by Wendy? That starts with a "W" like "witch". I bet you think that's clever, don't you?"

"Not at all."

"Okay then, why don't you show us just how clever you are. What *is* your name, witch?"

"Barbara Streisand Szubanski Ducharme—or Mrs. Kenneth Ducharme, if you like. And you and your brainless brood will show me respect and refer to me as such or every single one of you will be sorry. Is that clever enough for you?"

"Oooh...hear that, boys?" he sneered. "The witch is adopting a threatening tone. What a surprise. Reminds me of another woman who was fond of doing that. Ms. Phlegming, I think she called herself—an old hag with a Tasmanian temper like yours. Ring any bells, Mrs. Kenneth Ducharme?"

Barbara stared two hot pokers into his eyes. The strand of hair she'd blown away fell back again, inflicting a cursive wound across her gaze.

"That 'old hag' had a name, too," she said. "Ivetta Phlegming was my grandmother. She owned this house, and before her, her father—my great grandfather—owned the land all the way down to the road. And now this house and the hill it can legally claim belongs to me. So it's my feeling you weren't any more welcome here then, than you are now. Therefore, on any occasion she adopted a threatening tone with you, I'm certain it was more than justified. Just as my tone is now, you rude and deluded old cuckold."

Odekirk leapt back and shook his head in disbelief. Then he began pacing in front of the swing like a flabbergasted preacher.

"You want to talk about justice, Mrs. Ducharme? Fine, let's talk about justice. Justice is what *He* decides is righteous and fair. Driving your grandmother out of this home—as you call it—and out where He could judge her is the only justice this evil lair has ever seen." He stopped his pacing and turned to address the choir: "And all it will ever see! Isn't that right, boys?"

"Alrighty, Almighty!" they shouted together.

"Alrighty, Almighty, is right." He returned his attention to the swing. "And unless I hear some contrition—some humble and *proper* contrition—we may have to take more drastic measures until justice is served." He sauntered a few steps away and faced the direction of the surrounding woods. "You do realize Lake Wallenpaupack is but a few miles from here as the crow flies, don't you Mrs. Ducharme?"

"No."

"Well, if I were in your position I'd start confessing as to what you and your hellish seedlings are really doing here or you're not only going to find out exactly *where* it is, but how *cold* and *deep* it is. Now is *that* clever enough for you?"

"Just for the record," said Phineas, "I don't know how to swim."

"Shut your hole," shouted Odekirk, insulted by the interruption. "You are a disgusting sexual deviant and will not speak unless given permission."

"But I— "

"I said *shut* it!"

On the third word he pushed hard on the swing and straight into the face of one of the twins. The boy's head snapped back and wobbled before he crumpled to the floor. A bright river of red poured unfettered from his slack, and now partially toothless, mouth.

His fellow Skins came running, not so much to help, it seemed, but more out of morbid fascination. As they spread out to look for missing teeth, Odekirk cursed the developments and counted their naked heads aloud.

He came up one short; one called Zabdiel.

⛤⛤⛤⛤

Kenny found what he was looking for, and as he suspected, needed only to step outside the room to do it. Straight ahead, catching the faint remnants of stained light escaping through the doorway behind him, stood the closet where his father had killed the tattooed man.

He worked his way through the clutter and unwound the wire hanger used to bind the handles. Knife gripped firmly in hand, he pulled on the doors and shone his penlight towards the floor. There, as expected, were the mostly headless remains of the man who had carried him from the upstairs bathroom against his will. Next to him, serving her sentence out quietly, was the girl with the mask.

⛤⛤⛤⛤

Zabdiel watched Odekirk give the witches holy hell and thought about his position in the group. He hadn't become alpha Skin of the Lake Wallenpaupack Bible Skins through impressive physical stature, rugged good looks or a Bible-geek's knowledge of scripture. The truth was he could never rely on anything but street smarts, sheer nerve, and dumb luck to get a leg up in life. Zabdiel's mother was a meth-addicted prostitute who tried to drown him in the kitchen sink when he was two. His father, also a meth addict, had saved him by rushing in at the last minute and hitting her over the head with a waffle iron. Unfortunately, he had forgotten to unplug it, so Zabdiel—known to all at that time as Jonathan Liddel III—ended up taking 110 volts to the neck for approximately ten seconds before his father realized what was happening. The medical team that arrived with the ambulance pronounced the young boy dead and placed him in a tiny body bag, only to get the shock of their lives when little Johnny started to cry. The brain damage, they said, would see him require living assistance for the remainder of his days.

No one was ever able to prove if the accident had stunted young Jonathan's growth, or if it was responsible for his bad temper, violent mood swings, and incomprehensible ability to endure pain, but he always felt like he was a real-life super-villain and not one of those costumed fruits kids booed in the funny papers. His secret identity was only reinforced when others his age began growing past him, thinking past him, and developing socially beyond his wildest dreams. Being raised by a foster family had taken a further toll on his self-esteem, especially since his new parents only took him in to rid themselves of the pain caused by losing their biological son. He never lived up to the dead boy's promise or any adjusted expectations thereafter, but that wasn't what tore at him most. That he never became the supernatural evildoer the young

Johnny thought he would was what really rotted his gut. Three failed suicide attempts only made him feel worse.

Lieutenant Odekirk changed all that. He had busted him smoking a joint one blistering summer afternoon, and gave him a long talk about Jesus and God and how he, too, had been a victim of evil. He had lost his wife to the seduction of sin—the same variety that had robbed Jonathan of his family. Drugs, he told him, were how the Devil found his way into the hearts of good people. But there were other ways, too—new ones every day—and the Devil was always looking for more. Odekirk said if he wanted, he could be the first to help him fight evil up close.

Jonathan accepted immediately, more for the word "fight" than any of the other words he'd said. He didn't give two shits about God; he just wanted to hurt things. It hardly mattered what side he was on, he knew he would be good at it. That an officer of the law supported this desire only made him feel stronger. It was settled over a glass of lemonade: Jonathan would take the weird name that began with a Z, move his mouth at prayer time, and help Odekirk find more lost souls to aid them in their struggles. In return, Odekirk would reward him with power.

Each new recruit had their own story to tell, but none were as bad as Zabdiel's. Consequently, none of them were as angry or as tough. That's why he remained Odekirk's number one. Occasionally, one of the boys would test him with a prank or call him a name and Zabdiel would snap. It was on such a day that one of the boys used a magic marker to draw a mustache on his sleeping face. Once discovered, Zabdiel blinded him in the eye with the very same magic marker. In his defense, he was half-asleep and hadn't remembered doing it. Nonetheless,

Odekirk beat him senseless before sitting him down and telling him he had a special gift and needed to protect it. Using it for selfish reasons was the easiest way to put it in the hands of the Devil. If he wanted to keep it, he would have to take his beating and ask God for forgiveness.

Zabdiel saw things differently. In his first declaration of belief in something other than the existence of pain, he felt he would have to give something in exchange for that boy's sight—something he could spare. He needed both his eyes to fight, and both his ears for balance; he was of little use to the group if he couldn't be their greatest weapon. So one night he disappeared with an empty jar, and returned with a smile on his face. He handed the jar to the boy, the boy accepted, and it was done.

Zabdiel, sworn to abstinence, hoped not to stay that way forever—not even for the Lord. His sacrifice would change nothing, but he took consolation in the fact that he could still produce a son with what remained; a son he would never, ever electrocute in a sink full of meth water.

He heard a crash, and it snapped him back to the present. At first he thought it was the wind, or possibly the result of an overactive imagination. Several smaller crashes followed, and without thinking to tell anyone he set off to investigate. The trial was boring the shit out of him, anyway. He was a hunter, one that could flush out evil from the darkest furrows in the blackest earth, not a member of some jerk-off jury. There was talk of a boy still loose in the house and the parents had denied it up and down. But of all the lies spilled from the half-breed with the fucked up face, his insistence that one family member remained at large rang true.

Zabdiel worked his way through a dark and winding hall.

Now and then he would kick something that had fallen onto the floor—at first by accident, later on purpose. Nothing sounded like the crashing he had heard. What he'd heard sounded like glass.

He continued on, alternately running and walking, and came upon a room with a fireplace, and in it, a dying fire. He saw a cake—or what was left of one—and recognized a Devil Star in the frosting. The people Odekirk were grilling back at command were definitely witches, no doubt about it. Everything out of their mouths would be lies, but not because witches were real-life servants of the Devil or any of that paranoid nonsense. They were just evil. As far as he was concerned, God and the Devil were invented because evil was as real as pain, and it lived in those people who sought to cause it. These evil folks were shit-scared, which meant his instincts were probably right: there was someone else in this house—a boy—and they were doing whatever they could to protect him.

He looked down and noticed blood puddling around his feet. He hadn't seen it when he came in, probably because he had been focused on the fire. There was a lot of it, but not so much that whoever had lost it had died in the process. He had seen that amount before, and it shocked him how little of the stuff people actually needed. The truth was, human beings were like cockroaches but worse: they were hard to kill like roaches, but roaches didn't kill their babies.

He studied the blood more closely and saw that it led into a nearby hall and on to fuck knows where. Like a good hound—or ferret, a nickname he embraced—he pointed his nose to the floor and started on the trail.

"Why you wearing a mask in here?" asked Kenny for the third time, and for the third time the girl didn't answer. He could see her eyes blinking, so he knew she was alive and conscious. "What's the point?"

"I'm used to it," she said.

"Don't try anything, by the way. I've got your knife and I know I'm stronger than you." She sighed loudly like she was fed up, so he thought he'd try being nice: "How's your neck?"

"It's not bleeding anymore, if that's what you mean."

Kenny could tell by her lackluster tone that she would rather die than meet him halfway, but something was making her respond. She must have realized she was well and truly beaten. He knew the feeling. Sometimes you played along just to see if you were still sane.

"Good," he said. "We just wanted to teach you a lesson, really—for screwing with us and stuff. We didn't think killing you was cool since we were okay and all the other threats weren't, like, threats anymore."

"So you're saying the stupid cake thing wasn't sharp enough."

"You don't have to be like that, you know."

"Look—can I help you or something?"

"Actually, yeah, you can. There's a bunch of skinheads in the other room and I think they want to finish the job you and your asshole friends started." He figured he'd get tough and play the guilt card, even though he was pretty convinced he was pushing his luck.

Delilah leaned her head against the back of the wardrobe and let her body go limp. "Yeah?" she asked. "Well you killed my fucking friend and probably my other fucking friend, so you can kind of get fucked."

Kenny wasn't about to relinquish the upper hand. "Think of all the stuff they'll do to you when they find you." He paused to let the statement sink in. "If you're *lucky*, they'll shave your head and ask you to join."

"Jesus, you little brat, will you fuck *off* already? I can't stand your voice."

"What's wrong with my voice?" he asked, realizing it would work her nerves. He also kind of wanted to know.

"Arrgh…you're all pubescent and gross—and you've got a bubble in your throat."

Kenny felt his first pang of insult since arriving at the house and didn't much like it. "Don't you care that you're stuck in here with some dead guy's brains all over the place?" he asked.

"Fuck you."

"Okay…that's cool. Sorry to bother you. I bet it'll smell real nice in here come morning." He closed the door in front of the tattooed man and pushed on the other.

She stuck out her foot, stopping it.

⛤⛤⛤⛤

She said her name was Delilah, and plopped down in a chair at one end of the dining room table with Kenny at the other. A fractured rainbow dappled the distance between them like a peace offering from above. After a minute of the world's most awkward silence, she looked around and asked, "What the hell are we doing in here?"

"I thought it was safer since I found it by accident. One way in, one way out. And it's got a lock."

"Ooh, sounds a *lot* safer. Good thinking, Baywatch."

"Look—you gonna help me or not?" He was growing

tired of her attitude and the last thing he needed was another headache.

She faced him straight on and said, "I don't know, maybe I should go and help *them*."

"Go ahead. They'll think you're just as evil as we are."

"Well, what the fuck do you want me to do? You're the killers here, not me. I didn't kill anyone. Go kill, I'll wait." She pushed her chair away from the table and slouched. Technically, she was right. She hadn't killed anyone—not that he knew for sure. Nonetheless, he couldn't let her have her moment for long.

"We had to kill that guy and you know it. He had a freakin' *knife* in his hand."

"It was a nail file and *you* know it."

"No I don't. I mean, we didn't know that."

"Please. He was probably exactly how I left him…carving for comfort and completely out of his mind."

"He was holding it like a knife."

"Just forget it. There's no use talking to you. I can't change your pathetic little peanut and frankly, I don't want to. It's just boring now…I want it all to be over with."

Kenny started to think getting her out was a mistake. Freeing her from a rotting corpse wasn't turning out to be quite the bargaining chip he had hoped, and if he wound up losing the gamble he'd be stuck with someone else to worry about. He would have to try everything.

"What?" he asked.

"What, *what*?"

"What do you want?"

"For what?"

"To help me and my family get out of this shittin' mess."

Delilah laughed so hard she almost choked. Once she had her coughing under control, she said, "Are you kidding? I don't even care what happens to *me,* so why would I help *you*? I mean—are you stupid, or something?"

Kenny thought for a second and said, "Your other friend's alive, you know."

"Bullshit," said Delilah, suddenly serious. "Where?"

"In there with them. They think he's a witch, too."

"Is that what you fucking people are, witches?"

"I don't know...maybe."

There was a sound, unmistakable in the present context. Someone was fiddling with the doorknob.

Kenny lowered his voice: "Well?"

⛤⛤⛤⛤

Zabdiel was certain he had heard people talking. Like his abilities to see in low light and smell the faintest trace of fear in a storm, his heightened auditory senses had picked up a pattern of stuttering vibrations that "resembled" language. The blood trail had taken him to an open closet-like thing and from there he followed the frequency emissions to a large door. Unfortunately, it was locked, and his turning the knob had scared the emissions away. There was no choice but to break it down if he wanted to retain any advantage.

He ran back a few steps and jumped in the air to raise his heart rate. After a rapid succession of breaths to tweak his brain, he took a bursting stride towards the door and immediately slid to a stop. The door had opened on its own.

⛤⛤⛤⛤

Odekirk shouted for "quiet" and got it. The only sounds were the whizzing train above and the slow creak from the swaying swing. The boy who had taken it to the teeth—Richard, the one-eyed half of the twins—had regained consciousness and was resting with his hand cupped over his maw, blood dripping through his fingers and down his chin. Odekirk put his thoughts of Zabdiel on hold and approached him.

"Richard, I'm very sorry," he said, placing his hand on the boy's head. "If you pull it together, I promise to give you a special name when we're through with the trial. Alrighty?"

Richard slowly removed his hand from his mouth. "Awrigh-ee, Awmigh-ee," he said, and clamped his hand back over the gushing wound.

"Why does he get a name?" asked Mayberry.

"He was injured in the line of duty," said Odekirk. "More than once, in fact. Don't worry, your day will come."

"When?"

Odekirk snapped: "When you close your fat mouth and do as I say!"

Mayberry slumped into his paunch, a plump lower lip protruding from his face.

"Bless you," said Odekirk, and returned his face to a solemn scowl. "Joshua, take our brother Richard here to get cleaned up. I've observed the accused looking in the general direction of that archway, so I assume they've nested somewhere in that vicinity."

"Think I saw a kitchen over there, sir."

"Good boy. Hurry, now."

Joshua separated from the group and went to Richard. Before he could take him away, Odekirk caught him by the shoulder and spoke so only they could hear, "Keep an eye out for Zabdiel. He's gone off and you know how he can be. If he's found someone, I want them returned to me unharmed, understand?"

"Yes, sir," said Joshua. He put his arm around Richard and led him out of the room.

"Very well," said Odekirk, "while they're getting cleaned up, I want you boys to take the condemned, and—"

"Condemned?" griped Phineas, his voice pitched to a fearful height. "We were 'the accused' just a minute ago! Was there a trial? I didn't see a trial. If there was a trial, I must've missed it."

Odekirk took a billy club from his waistband and poked Phineas in the face, causing him to cry out in agony. "The Lord tried you on his own, stupid. He just didn't tell anyone but me."

"That's not fair!" complained Phineas, holding his face. "I thought God was supposed to be fair?"

"Correction…the Lord is *merciful*. But He's through taking chances with the Devil. He's asked me to take you to the lake with the others and cleanse these woods. If you were lying with this young witch, you're surely contaminated with evil."

Phineas shook his head in disbelief. "How can I be contaminated with evil?"

"Evil germs. You've probably got them. Lots of them, and God knows where."

"With all due respect, officer, this is fucking bullshit. We ain't never even did it! Tell him, Amanda. Tell him how you were just fixin' to cut my pecker off."

"I really don't think the Lord gives a shit," Amanda hissed.

"What did you say?" asked Odekirk, his boys closing in behind him.

"I said fuck you, fuck your God, fuck these little pieces of bald-headed shit, and fuck that fucking douche bag over there. He kissed me when I was passed out. For all I know, he raped me, too. You ask me, he's as sick and fucked up as you are."

Odekirk opened one of his huge hands and slapped Amanda across the face. The thunderclap had barely dissipated before Ken Sr. leaned from his seat and swung at Odekirk's head. His sudden movement foiled his intentions, sending the swing backward and pitching his bodyweight to the floor. Being fairly high off the ground, his bicycling feet never quite found terra firma and he landed flat on his face.

Odekirk lit up with delight. "Ha! Look at you! Like an overfed fool in a carnival dunk tank. Get him, boys."

The Skins descended, savaging him with their fists and legs, dozens of blows landing at once. His vision became clouded with concussive sparks as he struggled vainly to defend himself.

Barbara had seen enough. She timed her leap on an upswing and propelled herself towards Odekirk with a scream, using her nails to claw for his face. Before she could reach it, he halted her advance with a clutch of her throat and squeezed. Amanda lunged for his outstretched arm, but was dispatched with a backhand so sharp it spun her a full 360 degrees before she went down.

"Enough!" he bellowed. Everyone froze, including the boys. Only the swing's screeching laugh could be heard as it untwisted itself.

Odekirk pulled Barbara's lips perilously close to his own. She tried to object, but his grip closed tighter, forcing her to choke on her words.

"What's that?" he asked. "I'm sorry, I can't hear you. All I hear is the Lord, and you know what he says?"

With a mighty push he threw her straight into the swing, collapsing her into a heap underneath. Only lack of air kept her from moaning into the floor as the swing jerked wildly above her like a giant, wagging finger.

"He says *guilty*."

Joshua knew all about Zabdiel. He knew he was bad on the inside, and that he didn't really believe in the Lord. He also knew he was crazy. Odekirk felt he needed Zabdiel to keep the rest of them in line, but Joshua felt it was *he* who had become their rightful leader. It was *he* who took care of the kids when they got hurt, *he* who led the prayers, *he* who scoped out fresh territory and put himself at first risk—*he* who truly believed. And for a long time now it was *he* who waited for an opportunity to expose Zabdiel for what he truly was and show the rest of them that *he,* Joshua—named for the man who had led the children of Israel into the Promised Land—was God's greatest warrior. So what if he was young? He was smarter than most and knew deep in his heart that he could take Zabdiel one-on-one if it came to that.

He dropped Richard off at the kitchen and told him to get cleaned up. The water wasn't the best, but it was cold enough to numb his busted chops and clear out all that spurting gunk. Once his charge was situated, Joshua snuck into the den and had a look. The first thing he saw was the blood—more blood than had come out of Richard's face, for sure. He figured Zabdiel had seen it, too. That boy had a wicked blood lust. In fact, the very sight of blood seemed to bring him alive. Every kid likes a little action, but Zabdiel was always charged up and itching for trouble—always moving a knee, looking around, and sniffing the air. He made Joshua nervous, truth be told, and he expected more of the same once he followed the blood to wherever it led. Wherever that was didn't matter—he'd be ready. He, his machete, and his God would be more than ready.

⛤⛤⛤⛤

Zabdiel tiptoed to the open door and peeked an eye out beyond the frame. He was careful not to expose too much of his body in case whoever was waiting was armed, and he altered his elevation to make a confusing target. It was strange to be the one in for the surprise, and when he followed the length of table that greeted him to its center, a surprise was exactly what he received.

Standing there was a girl, about his height, maybe a little taller. She wore a darkly stained, unbuttoned button-down dress shirt, revealing the savory contrast of a tanned torso against a pair of smallish, light-skinned breasts. B-cups, he guessed, shaped like acorn tops. Perfect nipples, too: red poker chips he'd kill to cash in. She wore a mask that looked like a doll's face—some weirdness he could have done without—but it hardly mattered as she gyrated to a song only she could hear, using the edge of her short skirt to wink a hint of panty when it moved her. The light dripping in from the colored glass above covered her body in a splash of rainbow petals, from the tips of her finely boned fingers to her sock-sheathed, slender ankles, touching every curve along the way with the promise of a wet dream.

Zabdiel walked to the center of her command, his eyes glazed with a viscous coating of lust. He pulled absently at his crotch and jammed his tongue into the hollow of his cheek. This room—this chamber of earthly delights—felt more like a church than any he had ever visited. An angst that had preoccupied his existence was now replaced by an urge so hot and dizzying he nearly lost his balance. Every drop of fluid inside his body wanted out, and in seeking one opening or another would succeed if something weren't done, and soon. He needed this girl. He needed to clean her, devour her, vomit her up and consume her all over again. Violence and sexual desire, lashed together by the unbreakable chains of his past, now became a single thing—a monstrous, glandular, slithering thing. He could feel legions of jagged hormones pushing through the walls of his veins as he transformed into the creature he knew lived within. This creature had nothing to do with God or God's plan. When he pictured it he saw a forked tongue and tail, horns breaking the skin of a protruding forehead. No wonder he always listened to Odekirk's stories of evil with a whetted appetite. It wasn't evil he wanted to destroy—from the time he was a small boy, it was evil he wanted to be.

He opened his mouth and speared out his tongue, curving it down and curling the tip. With eyes wide, he reared his head back and screamed an eruption of carnal rage that consumed the air and sealed the room.

The time had finally come for him to feast.

Kenny waited until the rat-looking boy was completely lost in Delilah's dance before crawling out from under the table. When the boy let out an inhuman yell, he saw his one and only chance and thrust the knife into his neck, leaving the weapon to sag from a bulging vein. An instinct to leap back proved wise when the boy swung his arm out like an angry blade, slashing it violently through the air.

The next beat would prove his guile to be a fluke. Instead of continuing his retreat, he was overtaken by a powerful combination of fear and curiosity and stood his ground. Before he could regret his decision, the boy launched like a tripped spring and caught Ken Jr. with a head butt to the chest, sending him straight to his back. In the next second, he was being hit in every exposed part of his body, with every punch finding its mark. All muscle control disappeared with the first hit—a strike to the chest that emptied his lungs—allowing the punches that followed to rattle his rib cage and skull with a repulsive freedom. As a contest, it was over. As a matter of life or death, the verdict hung in the balance. Either way, he'd have to wait to learn it; he would be comatose in a few seconds.

Delilah hadn't moved since the attack. She simply watched the brutality unfold like a ring card girl idling between rounds. It wasn't that she was interested in savage brutality as a spectacle, or that interfering could provoke the little monster to turn on her for an unspeakable encore, she just hadn't felt like participating. She had promised to help, but that wasn't why she eventually jumped down from the table and yanked the knife from the crazy boy's neck.

It was the wound. She wanted to see it. It bubbled and spit, and she put her hand to her own neck, feeling it again for the first time in hours. She had nearly lost it tonight, and recalled how resigned she had been to the prospect.

You don't know what you've got 'til it's gone.

She reversed her grip so the knife was pointing down, and stabbed a new hole in the boy's neck. Encouraged with how easily the flesh gave way, she pulled it out and repeated the move—once, twice, three times, leaving the knife in with each turn before returning to retrieve it. She could tell he was getting weaker as his punches began to soften, and her stomach spasmed at the realization of her power. She would have stabbed him all night had the knife not spun from her grasp when the boy faced her and threw his hand up her skirt. He did it with such force, her feet left the floor and she flew back onto the table, fingers grasping for the front edge to keep from toppling off the other side. She managed to stay on, slack jawed and staring, as the maniac pumped her like a bloody machine. The knife rose and fell in his neck, dark plasma jettisoning from yawning hyphens like a sprinkler on Dracula's lawn. She took hold of the knife again, slid it out, and raised it triumphantly in the air. The metal steamed as hot juices wept down her arm, sending her into a convulsive stream of orgasms that racked her in palpitating bursts. A moan filled the domed cavern above that she barely recognized as her own voice.

When she heard someone enter the room several minutes later, the last of her orgasms had only just stolen away. She couldn't tell if she had experienced a high number of them or simply one long, savage ordeal from which she hoped never to recover. She giggled at the thought of someone stumbling upon a sight unlike any seen before: there she was, spread-eagled on the table, mask flung to the furthest reaches of the room, knife wedged in hand like a ceremonial mace. Her mind had gone from skittering with endorphins to drifting in a profound contentment where it now remained, hovering and sampling from her memories like a naughty hummingbird.

⛤⛤⛤⛤

The girl on the table looked as if her face had been melted with whatever had erupted into Joshua's throat. He would have thought she was in agony if it weren't for her grotesque, lipless smile, and the indecent way she rubbed her legs together. It was best not to risk any presumptions, so he turned to Zabdiel who lay flat on his back in a puddle of the blackest blood he had ever seen.

He knelt down and lifted his head. "What the heck happened here?" he asked, and lowered his ear to listen. Zabdiel gargled something incomprehensible before clearing the blood from his mouth with a hacking rasp.

"She tried…to kill me."

Joshua laid him down gently and thought hard. He wouldn't have put it past Zabdiel to assault her, but how could he have mutilated her like that? And what was she doing here in the first place? Had she come with the dark-skinned man with the funny mustache and been captured and tortured in some kind of a depraved, Satanic sex ritual before somehow managing to escape?

"Hey, sport," whispered a sweet-sounding voice behind him, "gotta minute?"

A cold snake wrapped around Joshua's spine. This was not the voice of someone in anguish; it was the voice of some-*thing* in bliss, and somehow that made it worse. Fearing regret, he left Zabdiel's side and faced her. It was only then he noticed the knife in her hand, and chastised himself for turning his back. He must have gone stupid after seeing her face, which was no excuse for a true warrior of God.

He held out his machete and said, "You're a witch—or a demon of some kind, aren't you?"

She let out a high-pitched, monkey laugh that bounced off the walls like a ball of crazy. He knew instantly that he needed to stop her. What if she was putting a spell on him? What if she had fooled Zabdiel into having sex with her, and now he lay dying, too weak-willed and unrepentant to fight her off with prayer? He lifted the machete above his head and took a step in her direction.

"No, wait," she said, "please..."

Her voice sounded sweet again—like it didn't belong with the rest of her. He braced himself for a spillage of lies, and watched as she held out her knife, dangling it from two bloody fingers.

"Use this," she said. "It's okay."

Joshua had always been taught to behave in an opposite manner when advised by someone under the influence of darkness. But a few miles of gooseflesh wasn't exactly proof that she was a bona fide minion of Satan. Maybe he had caught her mid-conversion? Or maybe she really was the victim of some horrible, black ceremony and had simply lost her mind?

He reached out slowly and took the knife, reciting The Lord's Prayer in his head for protection. Unfortunately, he kept getting the words wrong—itself, a bad sign. Despite an imminent threat, his concentration was again compromised as he watched the girl stroke her left breast with a shiny red finger and rest it somewhere near the center of her chest.

"Here," she said, the word escaping from her hole of a mouth like a dry leaf. "Please."

Driven by an impulse he barely understood, Joshua took the knife and placed it on her chosen spot. Prayer now spilled from his tongue—phrases borrowed from dozens of sources jumbled together to form a single work of pious apprehension—causing her to press her finger against his lips. With mortal conflict raging in his soul, he held his breath, shut his eyes and pushed.

Delilah felt the blade enter her heart, and lost all voluntary control of her body. As she listened to this new boy pray to a god whose existence for her had never been proved—in truth, quite the opposite—she shuddered with another climax, this one as small and sacred as a wish. And there, beneath the colored lights, she declared quiet victory as the room fell away, further and further into a shrinking void, until only the chilling peace of blackness remained.

Joshua looked away. He couldn't risk dwelling on his actions for fear of losing perspective. He had done as she wished out of mercy—and something else. It was the "something else" he couldn't afford to consider. The Devil could use it to play tricks on his mind, and it was his allegiance to God that mattered.

He returned to the floor, and pressed hard on Zabdiel's wounds. "Pray with me, Zabdiel," he said. "Ask God for forgiveness."

"Fuck that," said Zabdiel, blood escaping with each word, "I'm going to…live."

"No," said Joshua, "you're wrong."

Joshua placed both hands on Zabdiel's throat and squeezed. Zabdiel tried to pry them away, but his palms were too slick for a firm grip. They were also on the small side, which made it difficult to encircle Joshua's large wrists with enough leverage to count. When he did manage to get something of a hold, his vigorous pulling only served to relinquish it, each attempt losing him cupfuls of gore. Just when Joshua thought he might give up, Zabdiel grabbed his shirt and swung him down. The move slammed his shoulder against the hardwood floor, and pain shot deep into the muscle. But no matter how much it hurt, or how hard Zabdiel twisted or pushed with his feet, Joshua refused to break his deadly lock.

"Pray," commanded Joshua. "Pray before it's too late, damn you!"

Zabdiel let go of Joshua's shirt and pushed his thumbs into Joshua's eyes, but Joshua simply leaned away from Zabdiel's shorter reach and answered with a tighter squeeze. Finally, the blood loss and lack of oxygen began to tell. Zabdiel's arms dropped, and he pressed his hands together on his chest as if to pray. If he had meant to do it, the Lord would probably have to settle for the gesture as his hands quickly fell apart and splashed at his sides.

Joshua counted to five and released his chokehold. Then he stood up and leaned on the table, waiting to catch his breath. Looking around at the carnage, he struggled to fathom what had just happened. As best as he could tell, he'd been to the bowels of hell and made it out alive. What's more, he had fended off spells and defeated a powerful evil in the fallen Zabdiel. The fact that his faith had been tested and held fast proved God had given him the strength to prevail. He'd always known God loved him—God loves everyone who accepts Him into their hearts. But today was different. Today, Joshua had made Him proud.

He straddled Zabdiel's body, took hold of his wrists, and with a long grunt pulled him into a seated position. With a quick jerk, he threw his arms into the air and hooked the crooks of his elbows under the boy's armpits. Clasping his hands behind Zabdiel's back, he let out another grunt and stood him up. Before the dead weight became too great, he bent at the waist and grunted one last time, lifting the boy over his shoulder.

As he worked his way towards the door, he wondered if the former alpha Skin had been able to ask God's forgiveness before he passed. If he hadn't, Joshua—leader of children and successor of thrones—had him covered.

Joshua the warrior, on the other hand, relished his victory.

CHAPTER 13
Branching Out

Joshua carried Zabdiel over his shoulder, spilling the last drops of his blood over everything within a five-foot radius. He felt like a fearless hunter returning to his tribe with the carcass of a wild boar and in relative terms he wasn't far off. He would have to explain the girl, or better yet, get the man with the broken face and stupid mustache to do it. In any event, Odekirk would send back one of the others—Nehemiah probably—to confirm his story. It would look as if he was too late to save his brother in arms, but had possessed the skill and bravery to destroy his killer. There would be no doubt he had defeated a powerful witch, she who had taken down such a formidable force as Zabdiel. The real truth—one more righteous and glorious than anything he could make up—he would keep between himself and God. And if the euphoric feeling in his bones was anything to go by, the Big Guy was cool with that.

He followed along the same blood trail that had taken him to the room and stopped to have a look in the kitchen. Richard was gone. The entire place held an eerie quiet that opened a trap door in his stomach. This sudden sense of vulnerability so soon after experiencing an invincible sense of inner strength had a humbling effect that weakened his knees. The full weight of Zabdiel's body pressed down on him now, and he realized his hands were too full to defend himself. Eager to fix the problem, he entered the den and flopped Zabdiel's lifeless body onto the couch.

Free and agile, he slid out the machete from under his belt, hugged the wall, and crept cautiously towards the main room. The sound of the overhead train provided small comfort, but it, too, was fleeting as he heard a steady, insistent creaking of the big swing. Its rate was constant; a haunting reminder of time, so precious during raids, being lost to a black hole. When he finally reached the clearing, he saw the room was empty except for Richard who lay flat on his back on the hanging bench, kicking a leg to keep it rocking. A rag was stuffed in his mouth and his eyes were locked on the circling train.

"Where is everybody?" asked Joshua.

Richard sat up and removed the rag. "They wenth thoo the lake," he tried to say. "They thold me thoo waith for you an—"

"Right," said Joshua, "I get it." He slid the machete back under his belt and said, "Let's go."

Richard slid off the swing and looked at Joshua. Then he looked past him. Then he looked behind himself.

"Whereth Thabdeel?"

Joshua approached with his head bowed and placed a

hand on Richard's shoulder. "Witch got 'em, Richie. But I got her back, so it's cool."

Richard lowered his head to the ground. "Man...thath horrible. He gave me one of hith thethicles and everything."

"Come on...let's go make them pay."

⛤⛤⛤⛤

Kenny rolled out from under the dining room table clutching his ribcage. Unable to contain the horror in his lungs for another second, he let go a plaintive howl that trailed into a sob. It was extremely hard to breathe, and every time he tried, stars banged off the inside of his skull like bees in a burning hive. He had forced himself to lie still until the coast was clear, but it had been very difficult. He was covered in fist-sized welts, and he could tell parts of him were swelling by the way his clothes felt against his body. He assumed the remaining skinheads would be on the warpath after what had just gone down, and the prospect made him nauseous. If they were to arrive now, he could only hope vengeance would be quick.

To think it was something he had started but was in no shape to finish brought the "fail" on hard. Depression flooding into his bones, he concentrated on the lights above and tried to will the hunk of useless flesh that was his body to its feet.

Useless; he was too weak. Minutes vanished, ripping chunks of hope as they fled. Then, as if the evening couldn't get any stranger, the lights that earlier had been a source of optimism began dripping onto his face. He thought he was hallucinating until he wiped a finger on his cheek and held it to his eye. It was blood—warm and sticky—and he could see it now dribbling from the table.

The girl. In his anguish she had slipped from his mind. She was history—had to be. You didn't have to be a medical student to sense the presence of death in the room. Imagining the sight brought an invigorating disgust that roused his limbs and made getting to his feet finally possible. That didn't stop it from being a slow, pathetic process much like the gradual unfolding of a crumpled and discarded piece of paper, and he paid for every inch in the currency of agony.

Fully upright, he cleared tears of pain from his eyes and beheld the lifeless body of Delilah. He'd been in and out of consciousness since his beating, but remembered enough to know this tragic creature had saved his life. Whether she had intended to or not mattered very little. He was alive, and couldn't help but feel a small debt of gratitude.

His head pounded as he recalled furious flashes of fists accompanied with the dreadful notion they would persist until he was dead. Delilah was supposed to finish off their guest after the first stick, but she waited for reasons he would never know. And now she lay there with a knife inserted neatly next to her boob. He thought to pull it out in a begrudging show of respect, but there was too much wrong with the idea—even for a budding, sex-obsessed surgeon such as himself. Retrieving her mask would have to do.

He lifted it from the floor where it lay face down. Turning it over, he saw a few specks of blood dotting the forehead and awaited the series of insults that was certain to flow from its fixed, complacent lips. No doubt she would have cut his poor performance to the bone. Nonetheless, he placed the mask over the wreckage of her face and tidied up her arms and legs. If he were her he would have wanted it that way. Judging by her fossilized grin, he was right.

⛤⛤⛤⛤

Kenny limped through a hushed house. Only the sick smack of his shoes against a wet floor disturbed the silence. He didn't need to look down to know what he was stepping in, nor did he need to look down to see it. Blood was everywhere: on the lamps, across the furniture—he even thought he saw a few drops threatening to fall from the ceiling. He followed them like a ghastly trail of breadcrumbs and braced himself for where they may lead. He knew what he would find as much as he knew his family name; as much as that name would be the only thing left of them.

He thought about the clock he'd been studying back when his father surprised him. He'd been wishing so hard for his old man to recognize something good in him that he'd almost willed him to show.

He had almost willed him to show.

The thought pumped life into his heavy legs. There was something he needed to find and he thought he had last seen it in the den. When he arrived, he ransacked the room but the item was nowhere to be found. Then his eye caught a glimpse of a familiar texture folded under the half-eaten cake. He lifted it and there it was: the needlepoint map. He opened it and inspected it closely. His head throbbed, as did a sizable lump on the side of his nose, but his enthusiasm overrode the distraction. He began repeating the "family mantra", the words conjuring a subtle trace of the strength they had shared; the strength that had set the world on its side. At the time they'd believed they were in control, truly and together, the four of them locked in perfect synchronization. It was as if the fatted universe had rolled over and opened its coat, exposing its secret treasures. And it had all started with the map.

He continued to examine its every detail. There were so many walls and doors and windows, and whereas before they'd offered only puzzles within puzzles, each now promised an opening to a new possibility. He traced his finger along the path from the den to the attic and focused on the circle over the door. So much had happened since they'd summoned the wind—before the storm of light and sound chased it back into the shadows. So much pain had been caused, so much blood spilled. Did this violence not hold power? And if it did, could he not use it somehow?

His chanting became more forceful. He barely knew what he was saying, but it hardly seemed to matter. The more the words came out of his mouth, the more they made a larger sense beyond his imagination.

He thought of the terror he and his family had endured. He thought of the murders he had witnessed and the raging sea of misery engulfing his body. Then he imagined the horrors still to come if he didn't act correctly and quickly. He thought about praying, but instantly dismissed the idea. He would not beg anymore. What sense did it make to wish for some desired outcome if one could never be sure of fully understanding the situation? Surely, it's better to take matters into one's own hands based on will and observation. Yes—he would make things go as he wanted them to go and he would do it now.

A sound entered the room. It was as if the puddles of blood at his feet had begun to sizzle on a skillet. Looking down, he saw it was nearly true. He continued chanting as the dark red bubbles chased each other around the floorboards before vanishing in a most peculiar way. Looking closer confirmed his suspicions: the blood wasn't evaporating but instead being sucked into the cracks of the floor. Despite that concept making no sense whatsoever, he reviewed his observations in his head: *the house is absorbing the blood.*

Spellbound, he watched as a pattern became apparent: the puddles were vanishing in a path that led out of the room. He kept his mouth moving and soon the blood was gone from sight. Anticipating a correlation, he looked back to the map and there on the stitching of the door glowed a circle. It wasn't as bright as before, but it was definitely there and most certainly active. His instincts had been right; the connection was complete. And the lack of any moving marks across the map's surface meant he was alone.

Or was he? Returning his attention to the circle, he noticed something new: every few seconds it appeared to stop and change direction, and when it did there appeared a tiny star symbol much like the one Amanda and his mother had drawn on the cake. It lasted for just a brief moment before it resumed spinning, silently and obscured, fixed yet suspended above the cloth. Then it slowed again, its details growing more defined. When it came to a stop, the image of the star had been replaced by a very convincing blue eye.

The eye blinked. Or was it a wink?

⛤ ⛤ ⛤ ⛤

The attic door sighed an inch, and a warm current of air availed itself of the breach.

⛤⛤⛤⛤

The only sound in the mountain woods was a shimmering duet between the katydids and the rustling leaves. The procession of doom led by Odekirk along a winding, downhill trail was similarly subdued, and it irked him. There were no heated protests or attempts at reverse psychology from his demonic detainees, and while it wasn't exactly cause for alarm, he was forced to rely on a theory he'd been formulating that had yet to produce any solid evidence.

He believed their power was derived from the evil trapped in the house, and now that they had been pulled from it, they were nothing more than disloyal subjects of His righteous kingdom. It was the main reason he'd dealt with them as quickly as possible before herding them outside. The issue of a boy still loose in the lair troubled him some, but a young witch left to his own devices was hardly a foe of great measure. There was even the likelihood that, if the boy did exist, loneliness and fear could see him repent and join the ranks. If his Skins were to grow into a force of reckoning, they would have to add to their number sooner or later.

Now, it was time to focus on ridding the world of the others. He had considered tying them down and setting fire to the house, but Satan and his minions reveled in flames. It was exactly that punishment—burning at the stake—which past warriors had employed to no avail. Had it been successful, evil would no longer exist. Having studied trial by water, Odekirk concluded that somewhere along the line the whole mess had gotten turned around. It wasn't the innocent that sank, but the guilty. Therefore, rescuing them (when possible) released evil back into the world while true innocents were destroyed, thus leveling the playing field. As a result, evil enjoyed an ascendance throughout the Middle Ages that in turn created today's cancerous world. Had they been drowning them instead, Jesus would have probably returned by now and restored heaven on earth.

Despite the method being both simple and effective, something else ate at his resolve: the absence of two of his most prized officers. He didn't care to empower the witches with accusations of conspiracy, or by vocalizing his concerns over a weakened and malleable squad, but it did change his mind about how to spend the remaining minutes marching to their destination.

"Nothing to say," he offered to whomever, "now that you've been flushed from your grotto?"

"Guess they gave up," said Nehemiah, nudging the father witch down the mountain with his machete.

"Oh, no, Nehemiah. Evil is an ancient, clever scourge. It remembers a time when silence got you killed."

"It did? How?"

Odekirk wracked his brain and said, "Stumbling unannounced upon a herd of tigers, for instance. Tigers don't like to be surprised."

"They don't?" asked Nehemiah.

"Not the sabre-toothed variety, for the love of God. No, sir—silence among the wicked is never a good sign."

Phineas made a break for it. He'd been planning one for the last mile or so and was waiting for a soft spot in the brush. When he saw one, he broke right and darted away like a two-legged buck, dodging trees and hopping logs.

The boys screamed and started in behind him, hacking at

the brush with their machetes. He hoped only a few would actually commit, and when he looked back he saw a single flashlight in his wake. *Small mercies.*

He could feel the cold, night air penetrate the wound in his face and waited for a surge of adrenaline to numb the horrible soreness there. Unfortunately, the surge wasn't coming. He must have drained all the precious juice during surgery. All he had was the spastic mechanism of twitch muscle reacting to fear and desperation.

An opening gap between he and his pursuer meant his plan was working. Jasper had given him the name "Lucky", and other than the hazy recollection of a few loose women back in the day, he never thought it would amount to anything more than an ironic gag. But for sure he felt lighter as his legs picked up speed, and he got to thinking that maybe old Jasper knew a thing or two about a thing or two after all.

When the steel toe of his left boot drove into that rotted stump hidden under a drift of leaves, he heard his shinbone snap before he felt it. The whole of him flew headlong into a mess of nettles, and by the time he came to rest, he was looking up at his leg looking down. To add even more insult to the situation, his entire body was on fire from hundreds of bush teeth biting through his clothes and into his flesh. He figured the only thing worse than his present condition would probably be his future one. "Lucky my ass," he grumbled.

When he was found, he had long stopped giving a shit. But he wanted a chance to say what was on his mind before the inevitable came upon him in the horrific manner he was expecting. So when the boy who had stuck with the chase got close, Phineas hocked a loogie to back him off. *Boys will forever fear hockers,* he thought to himself with a laugh, and that absurd fact bought him just enough time to give the world's shortest speech.

"You're going to hell, boy," said Phineas. "The devil just told me himself. He said he'd be waiting."

"Bullshit," said the fat boy through rasping, shallow breaths.

"Oh no, it's true," said Phineas. "And let me tell you something else. That sweatshirt makes you look like ten pounds of dog shit stuffed inside a five-pound bag. That didn't come from the man downstairs, by the way, that came from me. True all the same."

The boy crinkled his runny nose and raised his machete.

"Now hold on for a second," said Phineas, "I got something else for you." He grabbed a handful of leaves, threw them in the air and watched as they fluttered back down. "You see that? That's life. One minute you're up, flying high, light as a feather, and the next you're crashing back down to the cold, wet earth."

"Maybe you are, not me."

"Not you, huh?" Phineas laughed until a throb from his shin shut him up. "Listen, son…before you kill me, I want you to think about how you're wasting your youth with all this skinhead hooey. That man back there—the one you call your leader—he ain't taking you nowhere but to a sad and pathetic demise. Hell, he ain't no better than me and in a lot of ways he's probably worse. I know I don't seem like much now but believe it or not I used to be something to look at. Had a pot to piss in, too. But I got lost in some bad business just like you're doing now, and what I'm trying to say is—think about how much time you got ahead of you. Don't fuck it up now just 'cause you ain't figured it all out yet by yourself."

The boy lowered his machete and began fidgeting. He shot a few looks back to a half-dozen beams crisscrossing through the dense cover of trees and tapped the dull edge of the machete on his leg.

"This is witch talk," the fat boy said, "I'm not listening to you."

"Aw, shit…" Phineas combed his hand through his hair and rolled his eyes back to meet the boy's pudgy face. "Maybe you're just too stupid for good advice."

The boy crinkled his nose again and raised the machete high in the air.

"Wait!" said Phineas, his voice dry from wasting his breath. "Please, son…just one more thing." He smiled and felt handsome for the last time. "You really do need to stop wearing clothes that don't fit your fat ass. You ain't never gonna get laid looking like a warmed-over burrito, and you sure as hell can't rely on your personality."

He laughed a bird from a tree as a flashlight found the machete coming down.

⛤⛤⛤⛤

Odekirk waited for Marcus to return with news of his success. He would accept no other possibility. The boy was too infused with the Lord for anything other than pure deliverance. When he saw his round, blue frame crashing through the underbrush, he looked to the sky and winked.

Marcus walked straight to Nehemiah, his rounded belly spotted with blood and heaving with exertion. "I'm gonna get a name, 'Miah. Just like you, Zab and Josh."

Nehemiah studied Marcus and said, "Okay…so where's your machete?"

"Back there. I used it…I—"

Odekirk could see Marcus shaking, most likely from shock. Before his reaction to whatever barbarous act he'd performed could distract the others, he placed a hand on the stunned boy's shoulder and said, "And it came to pass, when the evil spirit from God was upon Saul, that David took a harp and played with his hand. Saul was refreshed and was well, and the evil spirit departed from him." Odekirk squeezed, adding, "That's from Samuel 16:23, son, and it speaks of God's gift to those who would do things for Him that may seem—well, harsh and ugly. But all is well because He understands and loves you even more for what you've done. So what do you say we call you Saul from now on?"

Marcus' eyes went huge. "Yes, sir!" he said. "I'd like that, sir!"

"Very well," said Odekirk and clapped him on the back. "Everyone is to refer to Marcus as Saul from now on, got it?"

"Like *chain*-saw?" asked Carl.

"Shut it, Parts," said Odekirk. "Now, let's move these witches out!"

⛤⛤⛤⛤

Moving again in formation, Odekirk left his position in the back of the line and walked alongside Barbara.

"Guess I was right, wasn't I? Always plotting, aren't you?"

Barbara was too busy listening to a tiny voice that had

entered her mind a mile or so back—a tiny voice replicated hundreds and hundreds of times. There had been a lull in the wind when they were waiting for the chubby boy, and there, in the song of the katydids, she heard her son chanting.

Normally, she would have blamed the peculiarity on her overly taxed nervous system, but the event had the reverse effect: it relaxed her. She knew her son and how he talked, and other than his sounding more assured than she was used to, there wasn't a doubt in her waters that it was him. He wasn't there among them, that much was obvious. She heard him via a connection—free forest WiFi, she joked to herself—and she knew what he was saying by his choice of messenger.

Sing with them, he said, *and soon they would be in the trees.*

Soon, they would be everywhere.

Soon, they would be free.

CHAPTER 14
SLIPPERY SLOPES

Kenny hoped what he saw in his mind accurately reflected what was happening on the trail. His family was still alive, and they appeared to be listening—and more importantly, understanding. He tried not to think too far ahead to a time when they would be together again, but it was impossible not to indulge at least one fantasy of sharing what had just happened to him. Thinking about it now was like searching one's mind for the details of a favorite dream, but he only needed to look into the center of the circle in front of him to refresh his reality.

He had followed the blood as it was sucked into the warping floorboards of the house. Each step sent a reverberating ache through his bones, but this time the excitement of what he might find kept him going. His father had always warned that, *to move the earth, one must pay a heavy price.* In other words, when something is perfectly happy being where it is, and has been for a long time, a great deal of persuasion is required to get it to go elsewhere. Persuasion of that magnitude can only come from tremendous sacrifice.

What he didn't tell him—and what Kenny now understood—was that the very idea of moving the earth was nothing short of a magical triumph. It's just that to most of us, that sort of magic is so commonplace we no longer see it as magic at all. So we call it "reality", and if it suits us, our will is satiated and it becomes all the magic we allow ourselves to know. It's when something doesn't suit us—or when something out of our control needs changing—that we either deny our ability to change it, or far more rarely, seek a way to make it so.

Kenny had learned that way, and replayed it over in his mind.

His mother had started it. When she led them in chant in the den, they were all under severe duress. He recalled escaping from reality bit by bit, as if his brain simply couldn't accept what his eyes and ears were telling it. If his parents and sister were anywhere near his mental state, they were half-mad and well on their way to a full diagnosis. That was their sacrifice. Then, when they chanted together, they combined wills. Simply entering into this type of unspoken contract is hardly a big deal. People do it all the time. He thought of all the times he cheered on his father's softball team or sung to one of his favorite songs along with thousands of other people; all were exercises in simple group participation. But when those participating are genuinely connected and honestly believe they can change reality, real magic—the unfamiliar kind—is possible.

But belief, he learned, was a slippery slope. The instant you stopped doing it, you lost ground. Of those who do stop believing, very few are able to get back up the hill. The majority lingers just below half-belief, as if it costs them something to go the rest of the way; something vital to their tenuous grip on reality they can't afford to lose.

Kenny had always been afraid to look silly. It was the influence of others that made him feel that way. He remembered that, as a little kid, life seemed far more magical. It made more sense. Pleasure felt "good", "permissible" and "safe", and it felt that way because that's the way it was. He had permitted himself to see things as they were without applying any enforced order to them. Most children do. Therefore, as children we make magic all the time because we don't know better.

And contrary to what those awkward, ugly sweater, side-part hairstyle, family portraits imply, children embrace darkness right up until they're taught to fear it. Scientists talk of inherited survival traits dating back to early man—fear of the unknown among them—but they're easily overcome if not repeatedly nurtured in the first place. Sadly, practical necessity eventually steps in and slaps out our fearlessness, but most people can recall a moment before they "grew up" when the universe seemed to bend to their will. The change may have been negligibly small, which is usually the most one little person can manage. But soon, the moment is pulled from deep in their pockets and mixed with the rest of the collected flotsam of the day until it's lost in the multitude of experiences that follow. Also lost is the idea that magic is possible, and that much of it comes from the dark. Over time we forget it's an integral part of who we are, and that because it is, we're all a part of the greater universe—a universe comprised almost entirely of dark matter.

The good news is there's help if you know where to look. Among us are a precious few who remain on the upper slope, reaching back for our hands so we might one day touch the beckoning shadows. If we're lucky, we may actually meet one of these people in our lifetime and recognize them for who they are. The truth is most of us will dismiss them, afraid of the discord their new ideas create. No matter what they do, or how convincingly they proclaim the truth, we simply refuse to accept their wisdom. We would much rather see a movie or a show, or listen to a piece of music that sets our soul alight, allowing ourselves a modest amount of time to taste what could be, or what so briefly was. Then, as soon as we're aware of our connection to influence—the moment we realize our ability to alter reality lies tantalizingly at our fingertips—we yank our hands away like naughty pupils. In other words, fear takes over. A learned aversion perfected over time to keep us from harm becomes the very thing that anchors our souls to emptiness and rivets us to danger. Fear is what shrinks our eyes, our minds, and our hearts. It is the very thing that dissolves us in the end, because what we begin to believe exists at the top of that slope is something that will hurt us. So steadfast are we in those beliefs, we add evidence for them as we go.

All this she told to him without speaking. She had been waiting to tell one of them—hoping against hope—but she wasn't sure she would get the opportunity. Circumstances would have to play out; sacrifices would have to be made. In the past she may have been able to guide them, but her soul had only so much energy to lend, and so powerful was their resistance to learn. Even if they had felt it once—believed it once—once was hardly enough. The power of sacrifice, while potent, is finite; it is directly proportional unto itself. The more you lose, the more you gain. It really is that simple. This elfin axiom pervades every aspect of our respective cultures, but again, we would rather taste—disregarding all assurances lying in wait within—than swallow.

Kenny had swallowed until he was full, and in his stomach swelled a truth that his system absorbed in much the same way the house had absorbed the blood. When at last the power of his transformation reached the locked room, a wealth of energy was returned, releasing the door like a thorny, forbidden fruit ready to share its seeds.

And share, it did. When Kenny came to the end of the blood trail and reached the attic stairway, he didn't think he would make it to the top. When he saw the door ajar, he hauled himself to the summit. He didn't know what he would find, but believed it would be there even before he knew what "it" was. He didn't seek an answer; he didn't know the question. Yet, as he shuffled through the door, he was reminded of a younger boy who used to anticipate all that he knew would delight him. As children, we know. Closer to a child than the rest, he remembered.

He pushed the door open, and entered a room saturated with warmth, yet cool to the skin. It held its own light, yet no sources were apparent. A soft glow generated by a phalanx of long mirrors positioned evenly on the walls, all focused inward, created a core of concentrated energy in what felt like infinite space. Once he'd reached the center, what he saw made him forget all about his pain.

There, on the floor, was a perfect circle carved into the wood. Inside was a star symbol like the one he'd seen on the cake, and later, the map. He counted the points—five in all—

each crisscrossing in the middle. Staring into the intersection, he became aware of a new shape–this one obscuring his view of all but the outermost points.

It was the body of an old woman. She was dressed in a black robe and lay flat on her back. Her eyes were shut but her mouth was moving. Closer now, he could see she was forming words. Closer yet, and he could hear them: they were the same words coming out of his mouth—the same words he had been saying since finding the map in the den.

The woman sat up as if attached to invisible strings. When she opened her large, expressive eyes and faced him, Kenny felt the chill of a hundred window fans close over his body, but he refused to look away.

The woman smiled, then winked.

⛤ ⛤ ⛤ ⛤

Lake Wallenpaupack came into view as a giant, hungry mouth in the black earth. According to Google Images, the lake was a mildly impressive body of water, trimmed with scrubby clumps of pine, tangled brush, and the occasional stretch of fairway grass. By a dull and cloudy moon, it mutated into a shape-shifting reservoir of terrors to come.

An insistent, malevolent ripple lapped at Barbara's feet while she and her family shivered on shore. She traded glances with them, each understanding they had been in this sort of position before. She could also tell they had been concentrating just as she had been—like Kenny had asked them to.

However, another signal penetrated her anxiety, one she couldn't quite place. She had first felt it at the kitchen table with the map. It was a profound awareness of being connected to something, or perhaps someone; an extrasensory perception not unlike the feeling one gets when being secretly watched. Only, this connection was benevolent—more like an overseeing—and it had instructed her in so many ways to gather her family in front of the attic door. Not long after, her inkling had proved false—or so she thought. Perhaps she had read the map incorrectly? She would give anything to try again.

"I think it's about time you three got wet," said Odekirk, standing behind them flanked by his minions. "Go on, now—jump in. I'm sure the water's fine."

The Ducharmes huddled close and inched as far forward as they could without suffering the water's liquid bite. Barbara could already feel the bone-snapping cold emanating from the surface, but did her best not to let it disturb her focus on the night's song. What did frighten her a little was how the katydids seemed to be singing louder, as if they knew time was running out.

The fat one—Marcus—stepped away from the group and jabbed a round fist into the small of Barbara's back. "Do it now!" he said, affecting an authoritative tone. The boy had just been promoted, so his audacity was just the signal the other boys needed to participate in this, his finest hour.

"Yeah…you, too," said one of them to Amanda. Barbara thought his name might have been Nehemiah, but by this point they were all mindless monsters.

"Means you too, mister," said a twin, placing his crippled hand on the sticks in his waistband. "You can go in like that, or with a couple of black eyes." The others chuckled at his joke, and he puffed out his bony chest.

Barbara joined hands with Ken Sr. and Amanda,

and together they stepped into the lake. The boys' cheers disappeared under the water, and she would happily have stayed there longer if the frigid temperature hadn't collapsed her lungs. She'd also lost contact with her husband and daughter the moment they went down, but figured, like her, they needed their hands to swim to the surface.

Once her head cleared the water, she saw them. Her relief, however, was short-lived. "Drown, witch, drown," the boys repeated, their voices nearly covering the song of resistance in the surrounding wood. It was a battle of sound, just as it had been in the house. The only advantage her side had —a definitive one, she hoped—was that their persecutors had no idea they were in a battle at all. Despite the terror she now felt for herself and her family, she clung to the notion that somewhere in the ether was an upper hand yet to be played.

⛤⛤⛤⛤

Richard walked side by side with Joshua, who wisely informed him that the lake was still a mile or so away. His hero was still buzzing from killing the witch, and his enthusiasm made Richard forget all about Zabdiel.

"Then she come at me with her nails out like this," said Joshua, holding up his hands to demonstrate, "and I was like, 'Whoah, bitch, you better chill'."

Richard laughed and felt drool extend from lip to lip. "Whath thee do then?" he asked.

"She must not have heard me 'cause she kept coming. So I pulled out my knife and I was like, 'Okay—I only warn witches once'."

"Ha! I onwy warn withes oneth," said Richard, working

extra hard to form the words. He was delighted to be the first to hear Joshua's story, and ate it up like a handful of gummy worms.

Then a sudden heat arose on the back of his neck. It was mild but noticeable, as if he'd somehow received a small case of sunburn. When he reached back it felt wet and slippery like oil. It might've been blood from his injury, which could have made sense if it hadn't happened so long ago. Could it be some kind of post-trauma disorder? He'd heard about how a person's nerves could do all sorts of crazy things.

Then it felt as if someone had doused him with hot coffee—a punishment Odekirk handed out from time to time—causing him to yelp and lurch forward. If he was getting it on the neck he must have screwed up double bad.

He turned, expecting to see Odekirk standing there with an evil eye. What he saw was a rushing, golden mist that enveloped him like a giant splash of bacon grease. It dug into his eyes and worked a scream, sending a searing heat into his throat that turned cries into chokes. He stumbled backward, taking the fiery fog everywhere that wasn't covered: on his lips, up his nose, even in his ears. His thoughts blanked white from the pain. All he could do was drop to his knees and push his face into the cold ground.

It was no use. He was burning alive.

When Joshua felt the heat hit his back he broke into a sprint—something that came naturally. Luckily, the trail was on a downward slope, so it was easier to escape the chasing, oven-like temperatures. To match them, he moved at a blistering pace, careful to stay on his feet. The buggy sounds around him grew deafening, filling his head with an extra helping of madness, but it only made his legs move faster. He hadn't a clue as to what was happening behind him or why. All he knew was that Richard had screamed and hit the dirt. *Some kids have no luck at all.*

He rounded a bend and saw a large clearing where he knew the lake to be. He was still a few hundred yards away, which was nothing for a young athlete like himself. If he could stay upright, he'd be there in less than a minute. Trees flew past, their branches reaching out to grab him, but they would be unsuccessful. He was Joshua, leader of men, vanquisher of Zabdiel, and from this day forward, Odekirk's right-hand man. If anyone had a problem with that, he wouldn't think twice about throwing down. It was all about *him*, now. In fact, the idea to yell a warning at the first sight of a Skin was one of self-interest: it would allow him to gauge the seriousness of his situation by their expressions. If they gaped in horror, his only hope was the water. Whether or not it would protect him from a spell was another question, but at least he'd be the first to find out.

His flashlight bobbed wildly with each step, creating a state of panic in the fog. He concentrated on plotting a course by placing the beam as far into the trail as possible, and so far it was working. He had ducked some low branches that could have taken his head off, and there were a few times a tricky ditch had forced him to alter his tack on the terrain.

When he saw a pair of glowing eyes heading in his direction, he thought they belonged to a large deer that had lost an antler. Drawing closer, he recognized the dark-skinned, witch-fornicator with the moustache. He was hobbling badly, and it looked as if something was sticking out of his forehead. He was heading straight up the hill, arms out and flailing as if trying to grab hold of anything that might pull him from his nightmare.

Then Joshua saw a sight that made him gag: a machete was stuck in the man's forehead. It must have severed an artery, as blood jettisoned freely into the air, hitting every leaf lit inside the beam. Realizing he was closing in too quickly, Joshua leaned back and stiffened his legs—a combination that sent him straight to the ground and sliding forward on his ass. He scrambled to his feet, snatched the dropped flashlight from the swirling dust, and stumbled back up the hill. Again, what he saw made him slam on the brakes. The burning mist churned towards him at a predator's pace. He had no choice but to about-face and juke past the injured straggler.

He was too late—the hobbling servant of Satan was upon him.

Joshua pulled the machete from the demon-lover's head with a reverse slurping stroke and hacked away blindly, striking the man over and over and sending him to the ground. The deviant refused to quit, grabbing at him from every direction and pulling at his clothes. Joshua felt trapped inside a box of body parts and hacked away at every conceivable angle. Finally, the grabbing stopped. A few parting swings and he was up and barreling down the hill, working to catch his breath. Between puffs he prayed for free passage, as the hellish haze closed in on his heels.

The next hundred yards went by in seconds disguised as years. Now and then he would let out a savage yell and slash at the air so that anyone hiding would think twice about getting in his way. When he finally reached the clearing, he saw the Skins gathered at the lake's edge shouting at the family in the water. This section of lake was believed to have a steep drop-off only a few feet from shore—Odekirk had selected it based on Joshua's recommendation. Joshua never thought he'd have to find out for himself.

He slowed a little and checked his fellow Skins' faces. All at once their eyes went wide and their jaws dropped, telling him everything he needed to know. Without letting go of the machete, he ran straight past them and dove head first into the icy, black hole.

The impact of the cold shut down every muscle in his body, and he imagined a fossil frozen inside an arctic glacier. Once the shock subsided, he dropped his weapon and remembered that he'd been taught to swim. Completely blind at this point, he was unsure as to which way was up. He felt for the bubbles coming from his face and used his arms to propel himself in their direction. Although confident he could stay afloat, he worried about cramp—something he'd experienced before in a similar lake that had nearly cost him his twelfth birthday—but his limbs held out, and it wasn't long before he was filling his lungs with air.

He opened his eyes and saw the backs of the water-treading witches. He must have swum directly beneath them without realizing it. About ten yards past them he could see the Skins on shore waving him in. Since there was no yellow death mist surrounding them, he swam around the family and climbed onto the muddy bank. As the others used the corners of their shirts to dry him, he heard their voices for the first time.

"What happened?" they shouted. "Where's Joshua? Where's Zabdiel?"

"Whath are you thalking abouth?" answered Richard, although theirs were better questions. Like being awakened from a bad dream, his head cleared and his memory returned.

The last thing he remembered was laughing at Joshua's story, in awe of his bravery as always. Then he recalled running down the hill convinced he was Joshua. Then there was the horror that awaited him—

"The withh-fucker—he athacked me!" Panic set in with lightning speed. "And there was thith fog! Id burned!" He knew he had felt it, just as he knew the long-haired man was real. So what had happened to his hero?

Joshua emerged from the trail, his body covered in deep cuts and bloody biology. He opened his mouth to speak but the words failed to form, dissolving instead into a sickening death rattle. He fell forward, his mutilated form hitting the ground with a meaty thud. At that horrific moment, Richard realized a few of the hands that held him on the trail had probably been helping ones.

Thanks to a night course in pediatric first aid, Barbara knew they had a minute—two, at the most—before they succumbed to hypothermia. Swimming for the bank was still too dangerous—they'd be cut to pieces before they climbed onshore. Desperate or not, she wouldn't let her family die at the feet of those scum.

Then something disturbed their ranks. She couldn't see exactly what it was, but everyone began running and yelling and it made her more determined to withstand the torture her body was experiencing. If their captors were losing control, it meant that help was on its way. There was nothing left to do but concentrate on the song and stay above the surface. But as simple as the plan sounded in her head, it was getting harder and harder to execute. Muscles she didn't know she had were striking in numbers all over her body.

As if on cue, the lieutenant yelled something and pointed in Barbara's direction. He looked to be ordering the boys into the water. The boys looked confused, cold and less than willing, causing their "fearless" leader to push one of them to the ground. It was the chubby one that had held them hostage at the rear stairs of the house. He rocked himself back to his feet, pulled off his sweatshirt, and stood at the edge of the bank. She could make out his flabby pectorals shivering like teeny jellyfish. With machete in one hand and nose in the other, he jumped and disappeared.

The others waited for him to surface before following him in like hairless, over-sized lemmings. Immediately they began slapping at the chop and treading water with great difficulty. Barbara could see one of the stronger boys dog-paddling in her direction, but his flaccid attack was the least of her worries. He may have been better than the others at staying above—wisely opting to hold his machete between his teeth—but he was no better at swimming, and made far more noise than progress.

Barbara saw her daughter turning blue. "Amanda...grab my hand, baby."

"I c-can't keep my h-head up," said Amanda through rattling teeth.

"Yes, you can!" scolded Barbara. "Just a little while longer—you can do it." She could see Amanda losing hope, her eyes bulging and searching wildly.

"I'm s-s-sorry, mom," she said, "I c-can't." With horrifying ease she went under, the water swallowing the final floating strands of her hair until only a few bubbles remained.

"*Ken...*" Barbara said her husband's name like she had never said it before and hoped never to say it again. In such a short word she managed to fit all the urgency, terror, and helplessness the world had ever shown her. She had even caught the attention of the boys, who watched on through flurries of droplets like helpless puppies.

Ken Sr. could only assume his wife had called his name. He'd been watching his daughter desperately hanging on, and when she went down he wasted no time kicking his feet to the sky. Before he half knew what he was doing, he was sinking like a hairy old warship into a void as lonely and cold as deep space—or like he always imagined it to be. Refusing his body's desire to retreat, he willed himself forward until at last he made contact with his daughter's arm trying feebly to gain upward purchase.

He squeezed her forearm and accompanied her descent, straining to see through the murk with eyes so cold they felt as if they might shatter at any moment. Amanda's movements protested the grim inevitable, and he nearly called out to her. He knew his decision to follow her down wasn't helping her peace of mind, but his hamstrings had cramped almost to the point of rigor, and expecting to reverse his momentum and swim her back to the surface was entirely unrealistic. Only one option remained, and to do it he would require every bit of mobility he had left.

The further down he went, the heavier the water grew around him, constricting his breathing and punishing his eardrums. With no idea how deep the lake actually was, he knew his only chance—something that went against every aching bone in his middle-aged body—was to surrender to the unknown and ride it to the very bottom. At least the consequences of the risk were as simple as they were bleak: if they didn't find the ground soon, both of them would drown.

Amanda's arm stopped moving. He didn't know if she was unconscious or had finally accepted her fate. Either conclusion was unthinkable, but the fire in his lungs started him wondering if he wouldn't have to make the same, horrible choice very soon.

When his toes hit the silted vegetation of the lake floor, he let his body fall one more beat to load his legs and extended them with a mighty, garbled scream. Amazingly, Amanda must have understood his plan as she pushed up with him in perfect synchronization. In tandem they rose towards the lightless surface and with a sweep of their arms broke through its soft barrier.

Ken Sr. roared for air and scooped the water from his eyes. Vision now clear, he saw Barbara almost on top of them with a hand around each of their wrists. He'd been too numb to feel her pulling him the last few feet. One look at Amanda told him she hadn't known it, either.

"Come on," said Barbara, determination steaming from a head of matted hair, "we're going in."

"Good idea," said Ken Sr.

They rafted their limbs and worked their way to shore, bypassing the school of teens that continued to thrash the lake into a pointless froth. In fact, the boys were so busy creating a curtain of disturbance, they missed the Ducharmes paddling in sync, coordinating all working appendages. By the time they took notice, all three were safely on shore, huddling their bodies for warmth.

Barbara feared the worse when Odekirk pushed up from a dead-looking boy on the ground, and rumpled his face into a mask of pure hatred. "By God and the baby Jesus, it ends now!

He balled his fists and barely got a step before his head jerked forward as if overcome by a silent sneeze, sending his hat over his eyes and his face to the ground. Behind the long, motionless heap stood Kenny, hammer at his side. He looked as if he'd been thrown into a cement mixer with some red paint and a half-dozen bowling balls, yet his eyes kept smiling through the prodigious swelling around his face.

"Hammer-nail interface," he said with a demented grin and gave Odekirk a little kick. "By the way—Grandma Phlegming said you all should have brought sweaters."

Barbara laughed with relief and held out her arms. She needed to hug her son and kiss his bruised, lumpy cheeks. Only then, would she quiz him about his conversation with Grandma Phlegming. Because, sweaters or not, there was little need for warmth once Lake Wallenpaupack started to roil and steam.

CHAPTER 15
THE OLD GUARD

The Ducharmes stood on the bank of Lake Wallenpaupack watching the Skins slap the water. Their thin, pubescent screams grew indecipherable and elicited catcalls from deep in the woods—as if birds of every feather were growing annoyed at this butchering of their language. They may have been cheering Barbara and her family, and she preferred to think of it that way—as a welcome of sorts—but the idea of them heckling the boys' pathetic display cheered her up immensely.

She could see heat rising from the lake's surface, wavy distortions like fleeing spirits heading skyward in search of home. In them, she saw the image of an old woman's face. Fine details were few, but the woman appeared to behold her family with great affection. Barbara was soothed by her look of contentment—the kind seen in Renaissance oil paintings, or if you looked close enough, aged wood. But there was more, too: a familial connection. It must have been why the warmth she was feeling not only came from the simmering lake, but from a deep well of hope within her soul.

Barbara summed up the evening in her head. Much had been done to them against their will. Essentially, all manner of volition had been stripped without mercy. But instead of giving into an appalling logical conclusion, she'd led them into believing all could be undone by the pure repossession of choice. Through her guidance they had been truly convinced that as a collective power they were the ones in control. The rest was a simple application of meditation and focus.

As it was, she and her family were together again, and for the most part, all in one piece. With this treasured confirmation came the idea that these were young boys—violent, certainly, but also misguided and completely senseless. At the very least, only one had been taught to swim, so neglect had played a starring role in their lives, and unquestionably, in their actions that evening. As she observed them floundering, she searched for any measure of value that could be applied to their pathetic lives, knowing a decision would have to be made, and soon.

She pulled her children close—causing her son to wince with pain—and said, "So, my darlings, what do we do now?"

"I don't know about you guys," said Kenny, "but I want to watch."

"I don't think that's what your mother's asking, son."

Kenny said, "Sorry," and gave his dad a wink.

"Is there anything we *can* do?" asked Amanda. "If we *wanted* to save them, I'm saying. They're seriously spazzing and I'm not going in no matter how warm it looks."

Barbara watched her husband summarize the predicament. The boys were rapidly running out of strength, and the bits of skin she could make out with her flashlight looked pinker than Pepto.

Ken Sr. sighed loudly and began removing his pants. "Go find a long branch, Kenny," he said. "And don't lose that hammer."

⛤⛤⛤⛤

Barbara thought it funny how quickly big, scary boys became timid, little boys when they were cold, wet and tired. Of course, once the toothless boy explained how another of their group had met his end back at the house, she had to consider that they were scared for their lives most of all—and as well they should have been. Right up to when the last boy was dragged to shore, she had considered letting one of them drown in repayment for nearly losing her daughter. It had taken every ounce of mercy left in her heart to hold their losses at two.

Her husband donned his engineering cap and figured a way not only to get everyone back to the house, but also to relieve himself and his family of any heavy lifting. Lieutenant Odekirk was rendered immobile with a few pairs of shoelaces and muted with a couple of wet socks. To get him up the hill, Ken retained the services of the stronger boys, who were more than obliging after a trinity of conditions were set: the granting of their lives, the assurance of a warm fire, and the promise of cake if they kept their mouths shut. To tidy up proceedings, Kenny walked beside them with the blood-covered hammer in plain view. His reputation as the one who had bested their master assured their best behavior, with the added benefit of frightening them out of their wits.

Back at the house, Ken Sr. gave Amanda the responsibility of taking the van into town and returning with the authorities. She accepted without fuss, which he took as a sign she might be rejoining the family not just in body, but in spirit. Whether he would be allowed to resume his rightful throne in front of the television remained in question, but it was the first time in a long time he had been able to say anything to her and have her take his words as intended.

She turned to leave and an impulse overtook him. He put a hand on her shoulder and said, "Amanda—"

She spun and threw her arms around his neck with such force they nearly tumbled backwards. Balance regained, he lifted her up and buried his nose in her hair. As a father he had been exceedingly proficient in some ways, and just as deficient in others. Holding her like that—tightly and without reservation—helped him understand how truly agonizing it can be to lose the luxury of an honest hug from your first-born. He never wanted to be reminded of it again.

The sun crested slowly over the tree line, signaling the official start of a new day, but the boys had been afforded very little time to rest. The chubby one who had accosted Barbara and Ken Sr. on the stairs refused to rest at all, opting to repeat until exhaustion how he was definitely going to hell. Barbara listened with a reserve of compassion that wouldn't have registered on a polygraph, but was definitely there. Her maternal instincts were strong—something she'd learned in those last few horrible hours—but they were not without their limits. She had done her part as a woman and human being, and still considered herself unevenly rewarded for her efforts. Now, she was just flat-out spent.

"Close your mouth!" she told the boy, and he did. "Hell is too good for you with the way you've acted. If there is a point to your life, I hope in due time you find it because I certainly don't see one."

She moved to the center of the den and spun slowly, firing uncompromising glares at the vanquished Skins who listened in silence, their heads hung low, faces hidden in trembling hands. As for their lieutenant, he lay in front of the fire, bound and gagged at the feet of the boy who had felled him.

"You've all been misled," she told them, "but that doesn't excuse what you've done. If we decide you're worthy to be on this earth—*if* we decide it—it'll be because we see an advantage to it for our purposes, not yours. "

She crossed the room to Odekirk, who beseeched her with cow eyes.

"But you," she said, kneeling by his head, flames drying the tears in her eyes, "you, we see no reason to spare. My family and I thought it over on the way back from the place you tried to drown us, and we decided that you, Lieutenant Odekirk, offer nothing to this world but hate. And as much of a disgrace to all creatures great and small as you are, I still afford you the respect of knowing what we're going to do with you. You see, when it comes to disposing of hazardous material such as yourself, my family do things a little differently. We don't waste our time setting it on an old porch swing and spitting in its face. No, sir, we prefer our judgment swift and weighted to the side of excess." She leaned in closer and lowered her voice to a whisper. "No trial, no clemency—no opening statements, no closing arguments—no greater good, no vengeful God. Just a sentence, simple and plain—'fuck you, low-rent John Wayne.'"

Barbara got to her feet and held her hand out to her son. He looked nervous as he handed her the bloody hammer, as did her husband who had only just arrived on the scene. In fact, the only sounds in the room were the crackling of the fire and the moans of the lieutenant, who shook his head and begged for his life. He screamed from the back of his throat as if to rally his charges but not one dared move save the one with the missing fingers, who rubbed his nubs and looked to Ken Sr. as if pleading for intervention.

"You see this?" said Barbara, reflecting the flame-lit hammer into Odekirk's pupils. "My grandfather used this to build this house." She snatched Odekirk's hat off the floor and said, "You see this?" She tossed the hat into the fire, producing a billowing flourish that lit up the room. "If, when you expire, you find yourself in a place built by someone with their own bare hands—have the decency to remove your fucking hat."

She raised the hammer high in the air, held it there for a terrible moment, and brought it down beside Odekirk's head with a scream that shocked him unconscious and reclaimed the Phlegming mountain all the way to hell.

⛤⛤⛤⛤

Once they arrived, the police pieced together what had happened fairly quickly, and apologized profusely for the danger that had befallen the Ducharme family in what they assured them was a normally hospitable mining/resort community. To be enjoying a family weekend in the country one minute, and trying to survive a Biblical clash between good and evil the next, didn't seem like their idea of a vacation either, or so they claimed. They were right, thought Barbara—mostly.

After they left, Kenny led them all to the attic room. When they got there, Barbara saw the mirrors and the large pentagram in the floor, but found it otherwise empty. Her son had been adamant about who he had seen, and while no one celebrated his "vision", no one felt much like contesting it. She didn't know exactly with whom he had spoken any more than she knew who had visited them at the lake—that is to say, she didn't know how those things could have happened—but who had made them happen, and the fact they very much did happen would never enter into dispute.

Barbara toured the attic awhile and looked at the map with fresh eyes. She ran her fingers over the fine brown thread that comprised much of the stitching. The color and texture reminded her of Amanda's hair when she was very young. Of course, they couldn't have been one and the same. Amanda had never even met her great grandmother.

Then a scene flashed into her mind: Barbara had met her grandmother as a young child—the single time the old woman had ventured out of her cloistered existence to pay her daughter, Barbara's mother, a visit. Barbara was told this version of the story every so often over the years, and throughout her youth she had assumed it was true. When as an adult she asked better questions, the lack of convincing answers caused her to suspect that her grandmother's criminal negligence had been fabricated by her mother to solidify their estrangement. Shortly before Grandma Phlegming's death, Barbara's mother had confessed to elaborating, saying she had allowed her mother to see Barbara one time and one time only. She'd even allowed her to give her a bath. In those days—blocks of time since relegated to a forgotten drawer—Barbara had the most beautiful, long hair. She knew this from pictures.

Now, she could see for herself.

Barbara gathered her family into the pentagram on the floor and threw her arms around them.

"Mom?" asked Kenny.

"Yes, baby?"

"You believe me, don't you? About Grandma and that I saw her and stuff, right?"

"Of course I do." And she did. After all that had happened, what couldn't she believe?

The answer could have been that her husband would begin a chant on his own. It was a low thing, devoid of any language known in or outside that circle, but it rolled along in a lively manner and was easy to remember. The others joined in and pulled closer, their heads bowed to the floor. Every once in a while, one of them would look up and into the mirrors, which meant looking back at them all.

Their chanting became more deliberate and assured, their voices blending into perfect unison until they were a single voice comprised of four distinct colors. Soon after, a comforting presence closed in around them like a warm pair of arms. More chanting bled the colors, spinning them like a tide pool into the deep blue of twilight sky or early dawn. Then, while the sun's rays awakened all creatures great and small, a delicate line of white entered the cerulean swirl and brought with it the windy, weathered tone of another.

At once, the Ducharmes raised their heads and looked into the mirrors. Everywhere, from every angle, stood Grandma Phlegming, dressed in a dark, flowing robe. Her face was just as it had been at the lake: tender, doting, and fulfilled. Barbara studied her family and understood that in their minds they all heard the same thing. In a voice both bright as the moon and dark as wet, forest earth, Grandma Phlegming said, "Welcome home."

Barbara knew she didn't mean the house or the woods around it. Where we are on this planet rarely matters at all. The home Ivetta Phlegming referred to had nothing to do with walls or trees, or the mountains that towered above freezing cold lakes. The home she spoke of was the slice of chaotic universe that they, in blood, shared together.

By midday the mountain air had found its place in the solstice, being chilly and damp as late fall weather tends to be. The Ducharmes loaded up the Outback with everything they had brought, plus a few items to which they had become curiously attached. Once the front door was locked, it was time to lean against the car and have a long last look at the sagging eaves, boarded-up windows, intruding vegetation and mottled wood siding that was the old Phlegming—now Ducharme—estate.

"Well…what do we think?" asked Barbara, brushing a lock of hair from her eyes and tucking it under a black barrette. She had done a nice job of covering any bruises she'd received the night before with a generous application of foundation, and was surprised to find she liked the slightly unreal way it made her look. "Should we put it on the market?"

"I dunno," said Ken Sr. "She's got a lot of potential."

"If we keep it, we should pay someone to fix it up," said Amanda. "I'm not scrubbing those ugly floors again."

Barbara chuckled and asked, "What about you, Kenny—should we sell, or no?"

Her son didn't hear her. He was busy staring at a high window where the attic most likely would be. Barbara hadn't remembered seeing a window when she was in there, but that didn't mean there wasn't one behind a mirror somewhere.

Amanda shifted impatiently and said, "Well? You want to come back or what?"

"Sure, why not?" said Kenny, finally back to earth. Then he shot her a naughty look: "It might be funny to see what else shows up in the bathroom cabinet."

Amanda pushed away from the car and smacked her little brother on the head—much to his delight.

Barbara and Ken Sr. looked at each other and shrugged.

Then they all climbed into the car and pulled on their seat belts. Ken Sr. gunned the engine to life, backed carefully out of the drive, and with a neat K-turn, pointed them down the mountain and back towards civilization—such as it was.

CHAPTER 16
WANNA COOKIE?

Barbara Ducharme pulled open the oven door just enough to stick her nose in. The smell of ginger invigorated her spirit, and she was pleased to learn that each perfectly round cookie was plumping nicely. In a few minutes she would pull them out, let them cool on the center-island butcher block and get to work decorating them. She had already decided which design she would use, and thought each point painted in white icing would be a nice way of remembering her grandmother. She knew her birthday fell somewhere around this time of year—although the exact date had always been in question—so she chose December 23rd as the perfect day to celebrate it. The little exchange of gifts she and her family had arranged was a nice touch. Everyone else in their development would be doing it soon, and while that sentiment and its accompanying customs barely registered among their ranks these days, there was nothing wrong with "doing as the Romans" when it suited you.

She closed the oven door and wiped her hands on her apron, careful not to get any flour on the new, black bandanna dress with the tiny red skull print that she wore underneath. It had been her family's group gift to her, and the instant she put it on she felt ten years younger. The red heels that propped up her posterior and lent a sculpted look to her calves were her gift to herself.

Slap!

Ken Sr. had crept sock-footed into the kitchen wearing a t-shirt that read "Particle physics gives me a hadron," and given Barbara's rump a sharp hello. It was something he did at least once a day, and it filled him with the same amount of depraved mirth every time.

"Don't threaten me with a good time," said Barbara. "Wanna cookie?"

"Why not?" He wrapped his arms around her from behind and buried his stubble into the nape of her neck. "They smell delicious."

"Well, you'll have to wait—they're not ready."

"That's how I like them."

"You're awful." She turned and faced him. "You know… we never discussed what you said to me back at Grandma's."

Her husband scowled and said, "I have no idea what you're talking about." He migrated his hands mischievously around her new frock, demonstrating a strong inclination to move on to other subjects.

"Yes, you do," she said. "You just don't want to admit you made a mistake."

"The only mistake I ever made," he said, leaning in nose to nose, "was letting you out of bed this morning before I could show you how much I loved you."

"You mean show me again."

"Yep, *again*."

They kissed just as a vehicle pulled up outside the house. Barbara broke from her husband and leaned into the window above the sink to have a look. It was a van. Not just any van, but a news van. Her eyes narrowed and she began untying her apron.

"That's it. This time I'm telling them to go away or I'll blow up the station."

Ken Sr. grabbed her by the waist as she passed on her way to war. "Barbara, let me handle it. I'll make them go away—promise."

She relaxed in his arms. "Okay. But make sure you tell them what I said." She threw her arms in the air: "Boom!"

He gave her gently jutting derrière a light tap and headed out of the kitchen.

Ken Sr. walked down the central hall towards the slate foyer. He had been focused on the front door, but something made him look into the living room, where the house's large front bay window stood like a lens into the outer world. When they were making plans for the renovation, his wife had wanted one that was "three-dimensional, creating a dramatic look that added style to the exterior as it expanded the interior space", or so she had explained in fluent ad copy. All he wanted was bullet-proof glass. They compromised over a bottle of wine and everyone ended up happy.

Especially his daughter, who was now rushing to the window with her girlfriend, Amy. Both had just come back from a salon in Philadelphia and were extremely proud of their new "mod" haircuts. The straight-across-bangs look had taken a little getting used to, just like the nose ring had a few weeks earlier, but he liked the new color right away. The "so black it's blue" hue reminded him of the night sky, and the color of power they all shared. Even his son liked the color, and said as much. The look on his face when Amy pinched his cheek and said, "If only I liked boys", was priceless.

His son's face still fresh in his mind, the boy charged down the stairs just as Ken Sr. was passing the bottom step. As usual, he had his pet rat, Zeke, on his shoulder. How Zeke managed to stay there was beyond human comprehension, but he did so, it appeared, quite happily. Kenny had not decided to change his hair, but his wardrobe had been given a major overhaul. Long gone were the wrinkled khaki pants and ill-fitting, button-down white shirts. In their place were an assortment of denim jeans and black, rock band t-shirts. At first, Ken Sr. was chagrined to learn that his son wanted to look like every other kid in school, but when he saw the selection of bands he had chosen—Led Zeppelin, Jimi Hendrix, Frank Zappa, The Who—he was reminded of his own rambunctious youth. They had swapped so much music in the last month that at times it felt as if they had grown up together. Only, every time Kenny had to explain to him how to download an MP3, the truth was again harshly revealed.

Ken Sr. hadn't changed anything about his own appearance except the addition of a salt and pepper goatee at his wife's insistence. And ever since he had stopped the late-night eating and picked up a late-night activity of a different sort, he had lost a little weight. This allowed him to get into an array of interesting costumes his wife had begun insisting he wear. Lately, however, they had done without extras of any kind—except for her shoes. He had adopted his wife's love for shoes, and longed all day to see her naked and wearing them. He even dreamed of them: the old ones, the new ones, the black and the blue ones. He even thought of designing a pair for her birthday. As long as they didn't come out looking like small, well-heeled fortresses, he figured he just might go through with it.

His son cut him off at the doormat and asked, "Can I get it this time?"

"Your mother's on the warpath, Kenny. If we want her back to normal, I need to end it now."

"Hammer-nail interface," he said, toothily.

Ken Sr. turned the newly installed, brushed-steel, triple-lock doorknob and opened the heavy, steel-reinforced, oak wood door just as a reporter was about to knock. The man had a face carved out of honeydew melon and hair that might have passed a wind tunnel test. Behind him was a man with a video camera wearing a red baseball cap swung around backwards.

"Well, hello there, Mr. Ducharme," said the reporter. "My name's Timothy Keys and I'm—"

"You're with Channel 10," said Ken Sr., relieved to cut short the fawning sales pitch that came with every "man on the scene".

"So you watch Channel 10, do you, sir?"

"Actually, no. It's on the van." He gestured with his chin to a white vehicle parked along the front curb with a large number "10" painted on the side.

Keys gave a rehearsed, self-conscious snicker. "Heh, I've been doing this so long I hardly even notice the van anymore."

Ken Sr. leaned against the doorjamb and folded his arms. "Yeah? Well, we do. We notice it all the time. In fact, we can't miss it. You and all the other stations have been cruising up and down the street here for the past six weeks and I can't figure out why. We gave our statement to the police, and if I remember correctly, asked nicely to be left alone."

"But you have to agree it's a very interesting story, don't you Mr. Ducharme?"

"I don't have to agree with anything, Mr. Keys. Listen... my family and I are just trying to live our lives and my wife—" Ken Sr. waved Keys closer so that he could whisper, "—my wife's getting a little skittish. And when she's skittish, she can't relax. And when she can't relax, *I* can't relax. For a man like me who works hard like I do, I need to relax. You know what I mean?"

"Sure," said Keys with a wink, "I absolutely *do* know what you mean."

"Do you?"

Keys' expression became sincere. "I believe I do, sir, yes."

"Then what can I say to make you folks happy, huh? You want the gory details? You want to know how a little family like ours managed to survive a bloody battle between hardened criminals and a gang of Jesus freaks, is that it?"

Keys glanced back to his cameraman and held his microphone up to Ken Sr.'s face. "Yes, Mr. Ducharme—how *did* your family do it? How *did* you survive?"

The remaining Ducharmes gathered tightly behind Ken Sr. and bore steady gazes into the anxious reporter.

"We stuck together and did what we had to do," said Ken Sr. "We didn't wait for anyone to help us because we knew no one could. But we didn't start feeling sorry for ourselves, and we sure as hell didn't give up. Shit happens and you deal with it, Mr. Keys, end of discussion. We're just happy we're safe and dry back home and not floating around somewhere in the bottom of a lake.

"They tried to drown you, isn't that right?"

"For the hundredth time, yes. If you want to know why, you're going to have to ask them. If they don't know, maybe you need to ask yourselves. People drown people every day, don't they? You don't always need a body of water to do it." Ken Sr. waited a long second and asked, "Now, is that good enough? Will that make you go away?"

Keys ignited a veneer-capped smile and adjusted his head so the camera could catch his profile. "That'll do just fine, Mr. Ducharme. I think our viewers will be happy to hear that, while the world can still be a mean and scary place, good fortune shines down on good people every once in a while." He faced the camera and said, "For Channel 10 News, I'm Timothy Keys." After a few seconds, he said, "We're done."

His expression dropped and he directed his attention back to Ken Sr. "Thank you, sir. You and your family have a nice day."

Keys started back to the van, stopped and turned back. "Oh, Mr. Ducharme—you don't mind if my camera guy here takes a little B-roll around the property, do you?"

Ken Sr. straightened his back and shoved his hands in his pockets. "On one condition—when you go back to your studio and edit your segment together I want you to add something."

"Oh?" asked Keys. "What's that?"

"You tell them luck had nothing to do with why we're here today. You make your own luck, Mr. Keys. You tell them that."

Keys nodded his conciliation and gestured for his guy to start shooting.

Ken Sr. gave his head a shake, stepped backward into the house, and closed the door with an airtight seal.

The camera guy got his orders and surveyed the immediate surroundings with a professional disinterest. The house had been built to look like all the others in the development, but lacked a certain polish that would have popped on screen. It was at times like these when he wished a fire would break out—or at least a fight. A real hair-puller would have been awesome for his reel.

Something at the end of the driveway caught his attention. It was set off dramatically by the too-long grass and looked straight at him as if waiting its turn. Content to oblige, he got down on one knee and framed a close-up.

"Wait'll they see this shit," he said, letting the camera roll for a few. Satisfied, he stood up and headed towards the van. He didn't ask his subject to identify itself, or explain how it had survived, or what it had planned for the future. He just logged what it was and returned to the van.

But when he got back to the station and did his research, he would find his log incorrect. That wasn't just a lawn jockey; that was Jocko Graves, forever holding his position, eternally marking the shore.

sWitch

About the Author

Scott Norton lives and writes at the New Jersey Shore where they roll up the sidewalks in winter. He also performs with his band Surrounded by Idiots, and as a solo acoustic guitarist. Other hobbies include surfing, staying fit and battling a dermestid beetle infestation which serves as the basis for a new horror novel in progress.

www.scottstories.com

Looking for more domestic darkness?
Check out the official sWitch blog:
www.blog-de-suck.com

www.ingramcontent.com/pod-product-compliance
Lightning Source LLC
Chambersburg PA
CBHW020911200626
46814CB00001BA/283
9780982836408